The Lost Girls

A VAMPIRE REVENGE STORY

Sonia Hartl

PAGE STREET
PUBLISHING CO.

PAGE STREET
PUBLISHING CO.

Copyright © 2021 Sonia Hartl

First published in 2021 by
Page Street Publishing Co.
27 Congress Street, Suite 105
Salem, MA 01970
www.pagestreetpublishing.com

Distributed by Macmillan, sales in Canada by The Canadian Manda Group.

25   24   23   22   21   1   2   3   4   5

ISBN-13: 978-1-64567-314-9
ISBN-10: 1-64567-314-6

Library of Congress Control Number: 2021932097

Cover and book design by Kylie Alexander for Page Street Publishing Co.
Cover illustration by Mercedes deBellard, Folio Art

Printed and bound in the United States

Dedication

For every girl who has ever been punished for wanting to be loved.
I hope you know you deserve the world.

Chapter One

"Welcome to Taco Bell. Order when ready." As I punched in the number of soft and hard tacos the drive-up wanted for their Grande Meal, I cursed every movie that made the life of a vampire look glamorous.

No one told me immortality was going to be like this. I should've been given a warning. Someone should've pulled me aside and let me know that trying to find a decent job that pays a living wage when you're forever sixteen is a trip to hell in a brown paper sack filled with hot and mild sauce.

I finished ringing up the total and handed my headset to the night shift manager, Jimmy, so I could take a smoke break. I didn't even smoke. I just liked taking breaks.

Outside, the last hint of a summer breeze mixed with the crisp air of fall. I flexed my long, pale fingers and tried to appreciate the few minutes I had to myself, but I couldn't stay calm. My heart beat in skips. Thump, silence, thump. The telltale sign that I needed sustenance.

It had been four days since my last kill, and I wasn't used to going so long without feeling the flood of warm blood beneath my teeth. The satisfying metallic scent filling my nostrils. My vision blurred, and I clenched my fist. There were only a few hours left in my shift, but if I stayed, I'd end up dining on Jimmy.

Things got complicated the last time I drank one of my coworkers.

I pushed open the metal door we used to haul out trash and went back inside, where I tapped Jimmy on his bony shoulder. "I'm going home. Cramps."

He wiped his sweaty forehead, tucking a greasy lock of hair back into his hat. "Weren't you having cramps last week?"

"They come and go." It had been my birthday, and the idea of spending it with Jimmy on the night shift at Taco Bell depressed me. So instead, I checked out a few books from the library and spent it alone. As a special treat, I fed on a guy who smelled like birthday cake, but I'd been fooled by his vape. He tasted like protein bars. Happy birthday to me.

Once Jimmy gave me permission to leave, with a heavy dose of stink eye, I tossed my hat onto a back counter and scooped my crimped hair into a messy bun. The crimping had been a poorly thought-out but fashionable choice—in 1987. The last time I'd been able to make changes, before I became frozen, both mentally and physically, for all time. Along with my questionable hairstyle, the spot I missed on my knee the last time I shaved would also haunt me for eternity.

The buses stopped running an hour ago, and I had to walk back to my motel after every shift. Most nights, I didn't mind. My route took me downtown and up the street that catered to the local college scene. The perfect feeding ground. I passed a mix of start-up breweries and clubs, where people spilled onto the sidewalk. A girl who smelled like jasmine and honey bumped into me as she teetered on her ice-pick heels. She turned with a smile frozen on her bright face, the apology already forming on her lips, but she faltered and backed away at the sight of me. I had that effect on the living.

When I reached a darkened alley between a macaron shop and a sushi bar, I sized up the space. The dumpster that catered to the apartment units above the shops would provide good cover. Music poured out of the piano bar across the street, a badly sung rendition of "Sweet Caroline" (bum, bum, bum), and I took a step into the shadows to wait.

A group of college guys walked past, fist-bumping and shoving one another. One stumbled into my alley. The burned-out streetlamp above my head cloaked me in darkness, allowing me to observe my dinner for a moment. He wore a U of M shirt that looked like it had been freshly pressed by his mom that morning, the sleeves just short enough to reveal his generic tribal armband. If I had to guess, I'd say it was baby's first tattoo.

I took a step forward. A slice of moonlight danced across my pale skin. When he caught sight of me, he wiped his mouth with the back of his hand. He had the air of someone who'd always slept on clean sheets and ate three square meals a day since birth.

"Hey there, girly." He leaned closer to me. His friends were already half a block down the street and didn't seem like they'd be coming back for him. "What are you doing out here all by yourself in the dark?"

His lips peeled back in a feral grin, and he had a slight flair to his nostrils. I'd become familiar with his type. Over the years, I acquired a taste for the pampered frat boys, bored with a life of endlessly being told yes. The kind of guys who thought they deserved more than all they'd been given. This one had been drinking; not enough to be drunk, but that's the excuse he'd want to use the next morning when he looked in the mirror with bloodshot eyes and tried to convince himself he was still a good person.

"You have two seconds to leave," I said. I always gave them a chance to run.

Elton used to laugh at these games I played with my dinner. He never understood why I bothered to pick and choose. In the early days, preying on the guys who'd corner a young girl in an alley assuaged the guilt of having to be so casual in my kills, but it had become a code I continued to follow. A routine that kept my own humanity within reach. I made a promise to always adhere to the rules I created and stay accountable to the only person I could count on: myself.

College Boy leaned in too close by then. He crowded my space, towering over me, and he knew it. "I'm not going to hurt you. I just want to be friends. Don't you want to be my friend?" His breath reeked of cheap beer and, oddly, some kind of ointment. He trailed a finger down my arm and shivered from the cold he found there. Still, he didn't run.

He really should've run.

"What's your name?" he asked.

I didn't answer.

"You're just going to ignore me?" When I still didn't answer, he pushed me against the cinderblock wall. Rotting garbage spilled out of the dumpster, blocking us from view. He grabbed my face, digging his fingers into my cheeks. "That's not very friendly. You're lucky I'm even looking at a girl like you. Did you know you smell like tacos?"

Honestly, I could've killed him for that alone. I flashed my fangs, and the first hint of fear crept into his eyes. He tried to run then, but it was too late. With the quick reflexes gifted to the undead, I wrapped my hand around his throat and brought my teeth down on his neck. He didn't even have time to scream before I crushed his windpipe.

As soon as I felt the sweet whisper of death shudder through him, I pulled back and pressed my lips against his ear. "My name is Holly."

I wanted my name to be the last thing he'd hear before life left his body. As his heartbeat slowed and stopped, mine returned to a normal thump, thump, thump. He tasted like jelly beans and beef jerky. Not entirely unpleasant on their own, but wholly gross mixed together.

After checking his cargo shorts—finding nothing more than a wallet with a ten-dollar bill, license, debit card, student ID, and a plastic baggie filled with pills—I flung him into the trash and covered him with bags that stunk of old Band-Aids and Hamburger Helper. The ten dollars wouldn't do much for me. It wouldn't even cover half a night in my crappy motel room. Nobody carried cash anymore. I missed the '90s. Everyone carried cash in the '90s.

Footsteps, two sets, sounded at the entrance of the alley, then stopped short. They smelled like black cherries and clean cotton. Not typical scents of the living. From the harsh rasp of a voice, it sounded like an argument, though I couldn't make out the words. I wouldn't need to feed again for a few days, so I pressed my back against the wall, hoping they'd go away. Then I could make a quick exit.

"Holly, you can come out. We know you're here."

"You can't just say it like that. You're going to scare her."

Now they had my attention. Their voices weren't familiar, and as far as I knew, Elton was the only one aware of my presence in this city.

Maybe he'd had a change of heart and sent these two to retrieve me. I could only hope that I'd finally get the opportunity to tell him to go to hell. I was doing fine on my own. Admittedly, not great. But fine. I didn't need Elton. I'd learned to stop depending on him the moment he stranded me at that Quick Stop in Tulsa.

I stepped out from behind the dumpster. "If Elton sent you—"

"He didn't." A girl who looked to be about my age—the age I appeared, anyway, not my actual age—held her palms out as she approached. She was a good six inches shorter than me, with storm-gray eyes and swinging mink-brown hair cut into a bell-like bob that curved along the line of her heart-shaped face and didn't quite conceal the pimple on her chin. Her fangs glistened in the moonlight.

I gasped and took a step back. "Who are you?"

"We're like you," the other girl said. She looked maybe a year older than me, eighteen at most. Her dark hair hung just past her shoulders, styled with finger waves. She had a sharp chin and deep-brown eyes a century older than her physical age suggested. She also had fangs. "I'm Ida Radley. This is Rose Mackay." She nodded to the petite girl beside her. "We were also made by Elton."

"That's not possible." Elton told me there hadn't been anyone else. I'd been the first. The only. According to him, we were fated. A once-in-a-lifetime match.

"I assure you, it's true." The one introduced as Rose bowed her head.

There had been others? A fresh and sharp pain stabbed me in the chest. He ditched me after more than thirty years together, yet still found ways to make me feel like a fool. "He said he was alone for a hundred years before he met me, he said I'm . . ." I swallowed the hurt that still lingered, even after everything Elton had done. "I'm the one who made him believe in love."

Ida snorted. "And you bought that? Did he also tell you that you weren't like the other girls? I bet you were a sensitive loner who read poetry for fun and snacked on hand-rolled granola."

"Ida, stop." Rose smacked her arm before taking my hands. The clean-cotton scent enveloped me, and I was too dumbstruck to do anything other than stare at her. "What Ida is trying to say—though she could stand to be less bitchy about it—is that Elton lied to you. He lied to us, too, and we want to help you."

I snatched my hands back. "I don't need anyone's help. I don't know you, and you don't know me. For all I know, he sent you both here."

"You've got to be kidding me." A muscle in Ida's jaw ticked as she turned from me and addressed Rose. "I told you it was too soon. She's still in love with him."

"No, I'm not." I was hurt and angry, feeling endlessly betrayed and a million other emotions, but I wasn't in love with Elton Irving. Not anymore.

Maybe once upon a time, when I'd been a living girl who believed in soul mates and true love. He made me feel special when I'd only ever been invisible, he told me he'd walked this earth for a hundred years before he found me, and we'd be forever. I knew better now.

"Listen." Rose put a hand on both of our shoulders. "We need one another."

Ida stiffened, but she gave a short nod of confirmation.

"We came to you, Holly, because we know how difficult it is to be on your own when you'll never age past sixteen," Rose said. "I'm sure you're surviving, but is that all you want to do with your eternity? Survive?"

"We've both been there," Ida said. "We hated it."

"What do you want from me?" Nothing came for free in life. Not in death, either. There was always a cost in dealing with vampires. I'd learned that the hard way.

Rose and Ida glanced at each other, and a darkness passed between them. Rose turned back to me. "We can't discuss it out here in the open. Words carry on the wind. But if you come back to our apartment, I promise we'll explain what we can."

An apartment that probably had white walls, a clean bathroom, and chairs that weren't made out of razor blades. I would've given anything to have just a few hours in a place that didn't make my skin crawl. While I was hesitant to show my hand right away, I really didn't want to go back to the motel that took my weekly rent in cash with no questions in exchange for me not complaining about the roaches and stained mattresses.

And I was so tired of being alone all the time.

"I guess I could hear you out," I said.

We rounded the corner of the alley, and just as we stepped back onto the busy sidewalk, I caught sight of someone familiar in the crowd outside the piano bar, her bloodred scarf flapping in the wind.

Stacey. I hadn't seen her in thirty-four years, but I knew the face of my old best friend as well as my own. The fresh blood in my veins rushed, as if the part of me I'd exposed and given up so long ago still remembered, but I blinked and she was gone, leaving me breathless and barely standing as round two of "Sweet Caroline" echoed through the night.

Bum, bum, bum.

Chapter Two

Rose and Ida lived in an apartment above a meat market. Other than the vague scent of raw beef lingering in the walls, it was charming. Nothing like my dark and dusty lair, otherwise known as the Gas-and-Go Economy Lodge. Hand-sewn curtains with a cheery sunflower print covered the windows, which matched the tablecloth of a round dining table that had two wicker chairs. A squishy couch with a light-blue cover, nearly the same shade as my eyes, and a chair in the same fabric sat in the living room.

The apartment had two bedrooms, a small open kitchen, and a bathroom with a claw-foot tub. It was the nicest room I'd stood in since I fed on a traveling insurance salesman in his Marriott suite two months ago. I nearly cried at the sight of clean towels on the linen rack.

"You're welcome to stay with us for now," Rose said. "We can go with you to get your things from the motel tomorrow. Once Elton finds out you're with us, it'll probably be best if we all stick together, anyway."

"How do you know where I'm staying?" The amount of information they knew unnerved me. Especially because I'd never seen them before, and if Elton really had made them, they would've been somewhere in the various cities where we'd resided. They would've had no choice but to be around if they had the same draw to him that I had.

I couldn't entirely explain it. I hadn't even discovered it existed until Tulsa. It started a few hours after he drove away, a pounding inside my head, an overwhelming need to follow him, stronger than any hunger I'd faced. It wasn't love, or missing him, or attached to any emotion I could recognize. It felt like dying all over again, but worse. Permanent.

So I hitchhiked, then fed on the person who picked me up and drove their car until it ran out of gas, and then started the process over again until I crossed the state line into Michigan. Once I made it to Glen River, the city I'd called home while I'd been living, the clawing need subsided. I settled into my new routine of working at Taco Bell, hiding out during the day in my cheap motel room, and barely getting by while I waited for Elton to move on to someplace warmer.

Ida sunk into the couch and clunked her feet onto the coffee table, mud flaking off her heavy boots. "We've been following you for a while now."

"Why?" What could the two of them possibly want from me? "If you're planning on selling my organs on the dark web, joke is on you. They'll just grow back."

"We know." Ida flashed her fangs. "We'd just keep you on ice and do it again. How else do you think we can afford this nice apartment?"

My muscles tensed, but before I could run for the door, Rose patted my shoulder. "Ida is messing with you. She's old, and being an asshole is the only thing that brings her joy."

Ida mimicked shaking a cane at me. "Get off my lawn."

Annoyed but curious, I slowly lowered myself to the edge of the chair, nearest to the balcony in case I needed to get out of there quickly. I had so many questions, but I didn't know where to begin. How long ago had they been with Elton? When did they find each other? Why did they want to help me? Rose peeked in her room, then shut the door again and took a seat on the couch and crossed her legs at the ankles. Her 1950s polka-dot dress and proper-lady manners made me feel like I'd just crawled out of the swamp.

"I'd offer you some of the guy I have in my room, but seeing as you just ate, I'm assuming you're not hungry at the moment," Rose said.

My jaw dropped. "You bring your kills home?"

So gross. Elton went through a phase about a decade ago where he brought kills home. We nearly split up over it. He kept leaving them in the foyer, like he expected me to clean up after him, and he had the nerve to be pissed when I let the bodies pile up until he took care of them.

"For the record, I think it's a disgusting habit," Ida said. "If she forgets to take them out, they start bloating, and then we have a hell of a mess on our hands."

Rose's brows pinched together as she frowned at Ida. "One time. That was one time I forgot to take out the body."

"One time is too many," Ida muttered.

Rose fixed a polite smile on her face when she turned back to me. "I occasionally enjoy a little snack at three in the morning, and fresh kills are harder to find at that hour."

"That's really not a good enough excuse," I said.

"Thank you." Ida threw her hands in the air. "Finally, someone else who gets it."

"Anyway." Rose's fixed smile faltered for a moment. "Since Elton never bothered to fill you in on his past, I'm sure you have questions about us. We also have blank spots with you, since Ida and I didn't meet up until after you'd been turned and moved down to Louisiana."

"I'd like to hear from you first." I wouldn't give them a thing until they explained exactly who they'd been, what it had to do with me, and what this all meant.

Ida and Rose exchanged a look, as if they could communicate that way. Ida nodded, and Rose turned back to me. "I was the second. Elton turned me in 1954. He also fed me that line about how he'd been alone for half a century, and he didn't believe in love until he met me, and blah, blah, blah. Ida came before you and me, but I didn't know about her until she found me in New Orleans in 1989."

I'd also been in New Orleans with Elton at that time. Which confirmed we all had the same clawing need to be near him, binding us for all of eternity. Just when I thought working at Taco Bell was the worst part about immortality . . .

"Why do we have to follow him everywhere?" I asked.

"We have theories, but we don't know for sure," Ida said. "We think it's because he made us. His blood runs in our veins, so we're a part of him. Where he goes, we have no choice but to follow."

"And he follows no one? How is that fair?" I crossed my arms. Elton told me none of this before he turned me, but I'd been so in love, had trusted him so completely, I wasn't sure; nor did I want to examine if that would've made a difference.

"His maker is dead," Rose said. "He goes where he pleases."

My breath whooshed out of me. "What?"

"We don't fully understand how he did it," Ida said.

As far as I knew, we were nearly impossible to kill since we were already dead. Most of the modern-day myths about vampires were wrong, even if they had the smallest basis in truth. We could go out in sunlight, but since we didn't require sleep, we were also active at night. I imagined most vampires preferred to stay indoors during the day because of the amount of people around. We didn't enjoy the company of the living any more than we'd felt the need to strike up a conversation with a cow or chicken before we'd become undead.

Stakes in the heart didn't kill us; they just hurt like hell for a few hours while we healed. Garlic and crosses didn't do a thing, but I could see a vampire acting like those things repelled them if they were in the mood to play with their food. We had reflections, and we didn't require an invitation to enter a home, but we still waited for one because that was the polite thing to do.

When I'd confessed to Elton that I was becoming accustomed

to immortality, he went ahead and ruined it by telling me about how we could be starved. It wouldn't kill us, but we'd go mad with bloodlust, our bones would become brittle, and our skin would shrivel to paper-thin scraps clinging to our aging bodies. Yet we would live in that form until we could feed again. A cruel fate I wouldn't wish on anyone. Just the thought of it made me shudder.

I'd once heard holy water could kill us, but it had to be the purest form, blessed by a priest without sin. So, good luck finding one of those.

"What's your story?" I asked Ida. "How are you so sure you were the first?" If he lied to Rose and me, there was a good chance there were more like us out there, somewhere around this city where we'd all been drawn.

Ida shook back her hair. "Because I was engaged to Elton when we'd been living."

I sat up straighter. Elton never talked about his life, nothing about who he'd been or where he lived before he'd been turned, and I'd asked him several times. A million questions burst through my mind. "What happened? Who made him? Did you know his family?"

"Slow down. I'll answer all your questions, but we'll go tit for tat." Ida tucked her hands behind her head and leaned back. "So far we've done all the talking, and we need some answers from you too."

"Okay." That seemed only fair. And since they'd already had plenty of time to contact Elton or harvest my organs, I had to believe they hadn't brought me up here for either reason. "What do you want to know?"

"Where did you live when he turned you?" Ida asked.

"About ten miles away from here, in this city." So much had changed in thirty-four years, but the feeling didn't. It coated my skin like the soothing balm of home mixed with the aftertaste of remorse for who I could've been if only I'd stayed.

"Interesting." Ida exchanged another look with Rose, as if I'd confirmed something she already suspected. "I'm also from here. So is Rose. So is Elton. I was born in 1903 and died in 1921, just a month after my eighteenth birthday. Elton and I fell into a wild kind of love, but our families didn't get along. They owned rival general stores, and the rivalry became more intense when I developed a knack for building vacuums in 1919. They forbid us from being together, which only made us want to be together more. How did you meet Elton?"

"He said he was a transfer student at my high school," I said. "He saw me sitting alone under an oak tree behind the football field, engrossed in *Jane Eyre*, and he sat beside me."

I'd never forget it. It had been a quiet winter with an early spring. Sweater weather. I'd taken my British Literature assignment out to the oak tree when my mom had forgotten to pick me up from school again. I had strawberries left over from lunch, and I'd just taken a bite of one when he approached me. Juice dribbled down my chin as I looked up at him. Instead of laughing, he swiped it away and licked it off his finger. It was annoying and sexy, and I didn't know what to do with either of those feelings.

To this day, I can't smell strawberries without thinking of Elton.

"*Jane Eyre*, huh?" Ida's dark eyes sparked with amusement. "I knew it was either Austen, Brontë, or poetry. Elton certainly has a type."

"Ida, quit being so judgmental," Rose said. "I think more teens today would benefit from pleasure reading some of the classics."

"It wasn't for pleasure," I said. "I had to write a paper on it, and he didn't know I usually kept a Sweet Valley High book tucked into the pages during lit class."

Ida let out a barking laugh. "Point for you, young one. Elton's father had set him up with a girl named Amelia. Publicly, Amelia and Elton were to be married, but we made plans to run away. Amelia was reluctant to let him go. I don't know the full story of how she'd been turned, but she made Elton shortly after, hoping to keep him with her."

"Seriously? How many girls has he kept on a string? And what the hell is wrong with all of us that we fell for it? He's not that special." I could say that now, after we'd spent over three decades together, and I'd begun to see how selfish and careless he could be. We always had to move where he wanted, and we had to live with his coven. I got no say in who stayed with us. If we got in a fight, he would leave for a week to pout and try to guilt me into apologizing when he returned, without any concern for my feelings. It was always The Elton Show, and I was just his pretty little accessory. But when we'd met, he'd been incredibly charming, good-looking, and had a way about him. He knew exactly what to say to get what he wanted.

"I don't think he kept Amelia on a string," Ida said. "She was a spoiled girl who wanted him solely because he didn't want her. He didn't lead her on, and after he'd been turned, he came to me and told me what happened. I chose to be with him. I chose to become this."

Rose laid a hand over Ida's. "We all chose."

Not knowing if it was my place, and not really caring, I stood and laid my hand over both of theirs. I was part of this too. "We all chose."

Rose looked over at me, and her smile was equal parts sweet and terrifying. "Now it's just a matter of what we're going to do about it."

"What can we do?" I asked. As far as I knew, we had no way out. We were at the mercy of Elton's whims, stuck trailing behind him for all eternity. But it turned out there were a great many things I hadn't known before tonight.

"He's going to do this to someone else," Rose said. "It's why he's dragged us all back here. It's the only reason he ever comes back to Glen River."

"Like Pennywise rising out of the sewers every thirty-some years," Ida said.

My heart raced, and not just because I'd recently fed. I didn't care for the living in general, not much, anyway, but the thought of another girl going through that made my blood boil. The promises, the future, the endless days of loving and being loved were all pretty lies sold in attractive packaging. Eventually she'd find herself alone, so painfully alone.

If present-me could go back in time and stop past-me from ever making that choice, I'd do it without hesitation. Even if that meant I'd be fifty now, and I'd have a handful of decades left, at best, before I died.

"We can stop him." Rose squeezed my hand. "The three of us can stop him, save the girl, and free ourselves."

"How?" My throat had gone dry. I knew. Deep down, I already knew.

Ida raised her dark gaze to mine. "We have to kill Elton."

Chapter Three

"No." I took a full step back. "I can't."

I had a lot of resentment toward Elton. I hated what he'd done to me without giving me all the facts, I hated who he'd been the last few years we were together, and I hated the way he'd left me, but that didn't mean I wanted to kill him. We'd been in love at one point. That had to matter on some level.

"There isn't another way," Rose said. "If we don't kill him, we'll never be free from this binding; our deaths will forever be entwined. Not to mention the girls whose lives will be cut short before they know what they're really getting into."

"We cut lives short regularly." Even as the words tumbled out of my mouth, I knew it wouldn't be the same. Once he turned the next girl, she'd inevitably be on her own without a clue. The quick deaths we offered our meals were a kindness in comparison.

"If he turns the next girl, we'd have to wait decades to attempt this again, and if she doesn't—" Ida stopped, took a deep breath. "Every time he turns someone new, it limits our chances. We could end up being bound forever."

"Why?" I asked.

"We don't want to get into that until we're sure, but we're working on it," Rose said. "But we do know that everyone he's turned has to be involved."

"Can't we set up an arrangement with him? Like, share custody of our time?" If someone came to me and presented the option of either living in a less-than-desirable city for six months out of the year or certain death, I'm fairly sure I'd make any location work.

"It's not just about where we live." She stood and paced the length of the living room. "You're still young enough that you're thinking short-term. I've seen a full century pass, and I'll see another one soon enough. What do you think will happen when there are twenty of us? Fifty? All living within the same city limits?"

I couldn't fathom next week, let alone centuries from now. If there were fifty of us in a city, even twenty, we'd be in over our heads. Too many bodies would begin to disappear. Vampires weren't made for large packs. Occasionally we had small covens, but that was more for companionship than anything else.

"What Elton is doing is unnatural for our kind," Rose said. "Vampires rarely turn more than one, if that. There's so much risk in having that many vampires tied to one maker, and he's not taking it seriously. It concerns us."

A chill crept over my already cold skin. Memories of Stacey bleeding out on the concrete beneath the Dairy Queen sign flooded my mind. The night I made my best friend into a demon, and she never forgave me. It had been a painful process, like tearing the very fiber that stitched me together to give her a piece of myself. I wiped my damp palms on my pants. I had no desire to repeat the process ever again, and I had no idea how Elton had done it three times over.

"If he's come to enjoy the pain of ripping one's self apart to give life to another, we're worried he'll increase the frequency of his turnover, so to speak," Ida said.

"I understand what you're saying." I really did. I still couldn't wrap my mind around killing Elton. Maybe I was being sentimental for who he used to be, or maybe because I'd been frozen in time at sixteen, I'd always carry those old feelings with me, but there had to be another way. "Have either of you tried to talk to him recently?"

"We talked to him last week," Ida said.

"We asked him what happened to you," Rose said. "He said you were probably living in a sewer, since you had never learned how to take care of yourself."

That pissed me off. Here I was trying to convince these girls not to kill his sorry ass, and he didn't even care if I had a proper roof over my head. And so what if I didn't really know how to take care of myself? I wasn't supposed to know how to fill out a job application or balance a checkbook at sixteen. I was supposed to test-drive adulthood in college.

But Elton had made me into a toy, created specifically for his amusement and to feed his ego, until he grew bored and tossed me away without a second thought. Leaving me alone with the consequences of immortality.

"I'll think about it." It was the best I could offer.

"That's better than no." Rose gave me a gentle pat on the arm. "Ida and I have to run some errands, but we'll be back in the morning. If you get hungry, that guy is still tied up in my room. If he wakes up and starts making noise, there's some chloroform and a fresh towelette on the nightstand for you to subdue him again. You've already had to process a lot of information tonight. We'll let this settle for now."

"We don't have time to—" Ida said, but Rose cut her off and ushered her out the door.

With the two of them gone, I had time to gather my thoughts and poke around the apartment. They didn't have dishes in the kitchen, but the glass-front cabinets displayed mid-century styled ceramic figures. Blue cats with pink paws, birds with chipped wings, and butterflies made of sea glass. The guy in Rose's bed, still tied up and asleep, wore nothing but boxer briefs. He had a tattoo of Foghorn Leghorn peeing on Tweety Bird on his right thigh. I'd never be able to unsee that.

Back in the living room, I found a photo album with painted

sunflowers on the light-blue cover. I settled into the squishy cushions that seemed to swallow me up and looked through the pictures. They were all black-and-white, of Rose and her life before she met Elton. Her short mink hair was teased into the bouffant style of the early 1950s. There were pictures of her with her parents, with what must've been siblings, with a small kitten she held to her cheek. More pictures of her in a hamburger joint, laughing with a group of girls by the jukebox, sitting shotgun in an old Plymouth with a boy who looked at her like she hung the moon.

The longer I looked through her album, the more my heart broke for who she'd been and the reason why she'd given it up. My heart broke for all of us. The lost girls who could've been so much more, if only we'd been given the chance to grow.

I'd been staying with Ida and Rose for nearly a week when they came back just after sunrise with the battered rolling suitcase that held all of my worldly possessions. My clothes smelled like Taco Bell, thanks to one of my uniforms tucked inside. It couldn't have taken them more than fifteen minutes to clear out my motel room, but they'd been gone for nearly six hours.

"Oh, good. You took a bath," Rose said. "You can borrow some clothes from us until we get a chance to wash yours. We're going out on a mission."

"What mission?" I jumped up from the couch, where I'd settled in to read Alyssa Cole's latest romance while I waited for the girls to return. "I don't want to mission."

"We're at war now. Get your shit together." Ida dumped my suitcase at my feet.

"War?" I tucked my fists under my chin. I couldn't war. Other than my biweekly ritual of drinking the life out of a body and discarding it in the nearest dumpster, I was a pacifist. "What the hell happened while you were gone?"

A new guy in Rose's room woke up and started screaming. I rubbed my temples. This one had woken up twice in the middle of the night, and the second time, I nearly drank him dry myself for interrupting my bath. While Rose went to deal with her breakfast, Ida began pacing the length of the living room, the scent of black cherries wafting behind her.

"This is why I can't stand it when she brings her kills home," Ida said. "Here's what happened last night: Rose thought we should go talk to Elton, so we could prove to you that we'd taken all alternative measures."

I lifted my chin. No way was she going to pin whatever went down on me. "I didn't ask you to do that. I already told you I'd think about it."

"I know, but Rose has a soft heart, and she wanted to ease any lingering guilt you might have about Elton. Anyway, long story short, he now knows you're with us, and he said if we interfered in his relationship with Parker Kerr, he'd make us pay. Since we intend to do exactly that, I guess we'll be paying or whatever."

I couldn't wrap my head around this hard and heartless version of Elton she described. He'd been no peach to live with those last few years, but he hadn't been cruel. Though he had been known to throw some epic tantrums when he didn't get his way. Like that time he locked me out of our rental cabin after I'd led his coven into revolting against a move to Alaska. His blood always ran colder than most.

"Who's Parker Kerr?" I asked.

"His new lady love." Ida batted her lashes.

It hadn't even been three months since he ditched me in Tulsa, and he already had a new girl he wanted to turn. Of course that's why we'd all been brought back to Michigan, but I thought he'd wait until the end of the school year at least. I dug deep within myself to find some reason, any reason, why I'd want to spare the life of the guy I'd given away my mortality for, only to come up empty. And that was the saddest feeling of all.

"I'm sorry it's come down to this," I said.

"I'm not." Ida shrugged. "We'd be headed that way sooner rather than later. He's got Gwen and Frankie with him."

"That's not a surprise." Gwen was vicious. She must've killed her maker too, though it had never occurred to me to ask. She didn't talk about her past, either. I only knew she'd been with Elton since she turned Frankie sometime in the early '70s. "Does it matter?"

"It's just an extra layer of protection for him. They're strong." Ida tapped her chin. "Rose doesn't want me to say anything until we got a firm yes from you, but I think you deserve to go into this with eyes wide open. She thinks we'll have to give up something important to get this done. She doesn't know what yet, but Rose's instincts are usually correct."

"I don't have anything important."

Ida tilted her head in consideration, but before she could say anything, Rose opened her door and dabbed her bloody lips with a dainty little handkerchief. "I'm set to go, if you are."

"What did you do with the body?" Ida asked. "I'm not cleaning another bloated mess."

Rose waved her off. "I took him down the fire escape and finished him in the alley. You really need to get over that one time; it's been six years. And why isn't Holly dressed yet?"

"Where are we going?" I asked.

"Glen River West High School." Ida took my arm. "Rose will help you put on something pretty, though her dresses might be too short. We introduced ourselves to Parker yesterday, and we think you need to meet her as well."

Ugh. The living. No, thanks. "Is that necessary?"

"We think it'll help you understand what's at stake here," Ida said.

"You'll need to blend in." Rose rubbed her chin with her thumb and index finger. "We'll have to do something about your hair."

Self-consciously, I pulled it to the side and twisted it hard enough to disguise the crimping. "I don't like talking about my hair."

Rose took me into her room, which was now guy-less. She thrust a plain black dress with capped sleeves into my arms. It smelled like line-dried linen, the scent coming more from Rose than the fabric, and it had a swinging A-line skirt. It ended up being a little on the short side, but Rose assured me that was probably for the best. After she ruthlessly tamed my hair into a fishtail braid that hung over my shoulder, she declared me high-school passible, and we all headed down to the bus stop.

The bus driver shuddered as Rose dropped her coins into the toll. She looked at him and dipped her head, gazing up through her lashes. He fumbled with the change ticket that would get us home again and licked his lips when he gave it to her. She touched his hand as she took the passes, and he recoiled.

Morning commuters huddled together, holding their collective breaths as we passed, exhaling when we didn't sit near them. Yet they still leaned forward in their seats, as if they didn't know how to keep their eyes off of us. And this was why vampires preferred to stay indoors during the day. It wasn't just our pale skin or unearthly stillness that got their attention. The living were attracted to death in ways that horrified them, and we were walking death personified. We threw off their equilibriums.

An old lady with deep wrinkles and five bags of yarn looked Ida up and down. Her lip peeled back, revealing five teeth and black gums. "Shouldn't you girls be in school?"

Ida sneered. "Shouldn't you be rotting in a box, six feet under?"

"Please don't." Rose laid a hand on Ida's arm. "We don't have time for this."

"You're right." Ida stared out the window. "I hate the bus."

Half an hour and four stops later, we pulled up across the street from Glen River West High. Nostalgia tugged on me as I viewed the woods where Stacey and I had split our first and last cigarette. The bleachers where I'd let Bobby Becker touch my boobs, also for the first and last time. The school I'd attended for three years while I'd been living. Where I'd first met Elton. The girl I used to be rose up and smacked me in the face with such force, I bent forward, putting my head between my knees. Times long gone and forgotten squeezed at my chest.

How could Elton bring me back here? How could he do this to any of us?

The old oak tree behind the football field still touched the skyline. I wondered if Parker spent time sitting beneath that tree. Dreaming of the people she'd meet when she graduated, making plans for all the places she wanted to see, the career where she'd make her mark. Or if she was already so enthralled by Elton, all she could see anymore was him.

Rose rubbed my back until I got my breathing under control, murmuring encouraging words. She'd been here too. She knew what it felt like. When I finally lifted my head, she linked her arm through mine. "Ready or not."

Ida linked arms with me on the other side. "Here we come."

Chapter Four

I wrapped my hand around the front-door handle, my fingers tingling against the grooves in the metal like a half-remembered dream. "I can't do this."

"You can." Rose straightened my shoulders and pushed against my lower back, jutting my chest out. "Act like you belong here, and no one will question it." She pulled open the other door and passed through with her head held high.

Ida followed her inside, and I brought up the rear. The halls of Glen River West still smelled like Lysol and pencil shavings, but the metal detectors were new. I eyed them as a sickness rolled through my stomach. The same school, but in a lot of ways, not the same.

Rose's heels clicked against the cement floors. Ida dragged her nails along the lockers. They'd been mud brown in my day but had since been painted red, the color dry and faded. A whole generation had come and gone since I'd last been here. The remnants of whom we'd been lingered in the old brick walls and dusty trophy cases.

Second period was still in session, but Ida and Rose had been doing recon all week and timed our arrival perfectly. The bell rang the moment we hit the senior hall. Even in the chaos of students rushing to their next classes, they gave us wide berth. As if the three of us were rocks in a rapid river, splitting the flow of the tide.

This place fit wrong, like an itchy wool sweater a size too small. I scratched at my neck, rolling my shoulders to shake off a feeling that didn't really exist.

Ida leaned in closer to me and pointed to a pretty girl with shoulder-length auburn hair and a splash of freckles across her nose. "There's Parker. Follow her to her next class."

"What are you going to be doing?" I asked.

"Dealing with Frankie." She jerked her chin toward a bulky guy I'd recognize anywhere. He had terrible bangs and dark hair that curled just past his collar, a popular style in the decade he'd been turned. His thick eyebrows hung low over his eyes. The nostrils of his wide, flat nose flared as he caught sight of Ida.

I spun around before his slow gaze could move toward me. If Frankie roamed these halls, Elton couldn't be far behind. I wasn't ready to deal with Elton yet. I said I'd give killing him some thought, but that didn't mean I wanted to see him, talk to him, or think about him in a concrete sense.

With my orders given, and no idea where else to go, I followed Parker to her next class. She wore a thin sweater with red, navy, and gray stripes, and I counted the colors down the curve of her spine. Four navy, four gray, five red.

I'd gotten so caught up in the ridiculous game to distract myself, I ran into her back when she stopped in front of a door. "I'm so sorry."

She turned her head, the side of her cheek resting against the contour of her shoulder peeking out from the wide neckline of her sweater. She responded with something I couldn't hear because her smile, full and without reservation, had knocked me back a step. Bee-stung lips turned up at the corner gave her the look of being mid laugh. She had a straight row of teeth, minus a slight overlap on her bottom front tooth, and the imperfection made it all the more perfect. If we'd met in these same halls a generation earlier, I would've done everything in my power to sit at her lunch table. She had a certain kind of magnetism.

It surprised me that Elton went for her. If she went missing, people would notice, the way they'd notice if the sun blinked out.

He didn't bother with the bright girls, the ones who had their own gravitational orbit. Far easier to turn the girls no one would miss.

Girls like me.

I shook off the morose feelings. I'd been missed by exactly two people, more than some ever got in a lifetime. Unfortunately, one would never forgive me for what that cost her, and the other would soon die with no memory of me at all. But once upon a time, over three decades ago, I'd been loved by two people. And I could hold the memory of that forever.

Parker took a seat at the back of the class, near the row of windows. I assumed she'd be surrounded by friends within minutes, so I hung back, waiting to find a desk I could slip into without drawing attention to myself. Why Elton chose to go back to high school, of all places, was beyond me. Couldn't he just as easily troll for girls at the mall or at Starbucks? I hadn't enjoyed this phase of my life while it had been mandatory; I couldn't be paid enough to relive it on a voluntary basis. And I said that as someone who worked at Taco Bell.

The blackboard that used to be at the front of the class had been replaced by a whiteboard with dry-erase markers. The ancient teacher's desk had probably been there since Rose had been a student. Someone had put some poppies along the windowsill in an attempt to spruce up the place, then forgot to water them, so they hung over their stems like they'd given up.

A group of girls came in, chattering loudly and flipping their hair. If I had to guess, I'd say they were the rest of Parker's crew. They paused their conversation as they passed, unconsciously trying not to get too close to me, the sparkle in their eyes fading until they'd gotten a few feet of distance between us. Parker sat up a little straighter, then slumped when the larger group of girls took the group of desks on the opposite side of the class.

Interesting.

I slid into the desk next to Parker's. She'd been staring out the window with her chin resting on her hand, and she startled when the metal legs of my chair scraped along the floor. "Is anyone sitting here?" I asked.

She blinked once, her long lashes fanning her cheek for the briefest of moments. She glanced at the group of girls on the other side of the room. "No. No one sits there."

Her simple statement, more honest and vulnerable than I knew what to do with, tapped on that jaded, empty place in my heart. After living with Elton for so long, I'd forgotten what sincerity looked like. "I guess I sit here now."

Her lips turned up, revealing that brilliant smile again. "Are you new here?"

I resisted the urge to slouch down in my seat. "In a manner of speaking."

New enough. Though that itchy feeling on the back of my neck reminded me that I'd been here once before and had no place here now.

Being back at this school, sitting in one of these classrooms, wasn't something I could look back on fondly. All I had left were my "should've, could've, would've" feelings. The regrets I couldn't let go because I still lived with them every day.

"I'm new too." There was a sigh on the end of her words, like she was tired of saying it but resigned to accepting it anyway. "Senior year might be the worst time to move, but leave it to my mom to not give a shit when she found a new boyfriend who really needed to start his auto repair shop on the other side of the state this year." She sucked in a breath. Her eyes widening, like she realized she said all that out loud. "I'm sorry I just dumped all that on you before I even told you my name. I'm Parker, by the way."

"Holly Liddell." I pointed at myself like a complete weirdo. "No need to apologize for the dumping. I know how it goes." My mom had her share of boyfriend problems, but at least she never shipped me all over the globe. I got to stay right here and face the kids she had hurt in order to salve her own ego.

"At least some people are nice here." Parker trailed off in a wistful way. I had a feeling I knew just whom she was thinking of. An eternally beautiful boy who knew how to coax and charm the lonely girls no one else noticed.

The teacher came into the room, snapping the door shut to get everyone's attention. I froze as his eyes roamed the room. The only teacher who'd ever been immune to Elton's charisma, Mr. Stockard. He'd been so young when he started, he quickly gained the rep of being the cool teacher. The one we could talk to about real stuff. Now, his black hair had gone a peppery gray, and his sad-puppy eyes drooped, exposing red rims. His once prominent nose was now spiderwebbed with capillary veins.

He took roll, pausing after he called out "Parker Kerr," and I held my breath. Did he remember? "I didn't get a note about a new student. What's your name?"

"H-Harriet." I cringed. That name was too old even for my day, but I'd been caught off guard. Who knew there would still be teachers around from thirty-four years ago? I was surprised Elton didn't kill him on sight. Unless Mr. Stockard didn't remember him, either. Though Elton would be hard to forget.

Parker whipped her head in my direction but kept her lips pressed together.

"Harriet." Mr. Stockard drew the name out, crunching down on the "et" as if it were a displeasing bit of food that required swallowing. He narrowed his eyes. "This is British Lit. Are you sure you're in the right class?"

"Yep," I squeaked. "This is where they told me to go."

"Hmm. Open to page fifty of *1984*, stop when you get to page eighty." He dropped a crossbody bag by his desk and turned toward the whiteboard. "Goddamn ghosts wandering these halls," he muttered under his breath, but loud enough for the class to titter nervously.

"Don't mind him," Parker whispered. "He's kind of a dick."

"He is?" When had that happened?

I glanced at Mr. Stockard, at the harsh florescent lights reflecting off his bald spot. The teacher I remembered would get so worked up about symbolism and theme, he'd jump on his desk and throw Jolly Ranchers at us in rapid fire if we kept the conversation flowing. He gave me my first copy of Sweet Valley High, never once putting down what others considered unimportant fluff. His classroom became a place to unburden the things that troubled us. In turn, he gave us books, made us readers, and opened the world. To this day, books were the only things that saved me from drowning.

"I heard he was really cool, like he made literature fun," I said.

Parker snorted. "Either you misunderstood, or someone was messing with you because you're new. This is called Sleep Period for a reason."

"Sleep . . . ?" I looked around, and she wasn't joking. People had their chins in hands, heads propped up by backpacks, and the guy two rows over already had an impressive puddle of drool forming on his desk. "I see what you mean."

Parker turned toward me, her soft brown eyes bouncing between mine, her full eyebrows scrunching slightly. "Holly is an unusual nickname for Harriet."

"Can I tell you a secret?" I asked.

Parker nodded, leaning forward in her desk, a little on the eager side, like it had been too long since she'd had anyone who wanted to share secrets with her. It made my chest ache in a way it hadn't for the living in a very long time. Once again, I couldn't help but see snippets of the girl I used to be. We didn't wear our hair the same, or dress the same, and we probably didn't want the same things out of life. But underneath all that, I recognized the hungry desperation for someone, anyone, to care. It unsettled me.

I shifted in my seat. "Never mind. It's nothing."

"Come on." She gave my arm a playful poke. "You can't open with that and drop it."

Her smile was infectious. Like a light that only glowed for me. It was so easy to let myself believe I was a normal sixteen year old, and this was a normal class, and I was making friends with a girl who didn't yet know she should fear me.

I leaned toward her and lowered my voice so I wouldn't draw attention. "My name isn't Harriet, and I'm not supposed to be in this class."

"Ooh, are you, like, an undercover narc?"

"What? No. I—" I broke off when I caught her lip twitching at the right corner. She was totally messing with me. "Very funny."

"If you're not a narc, what are you doing here?"

"I'm friends with Rose and Ida."

"Oh." She frowned as she faced forward in her desk, her back straight. "I guess that explains why you were being so friendly. You want something from me."

"I don't." Ida had pushed me into this situation without any indication of how I was supposed to proceed, so I figured honesty was the best way. As honest as I could be, anyway. "I want to warn you."

"About Elton?" She let out a short laugh. "I didn't realize he had so many stalkers."

"We're not—" I pulled back, drew in a deep breath. I was going about this all wrong. Getting into our history with Elton wouldn't win us any points with Parker. "This isn't about us, this is about you. He's dangerous."

"How so?" She pursed her lips, her expression more skeptical than mine the night Elton told me vampires were real.

I didn't know quite how to proceed. While I had no doubt Elton would reveal himself eventually, we didn't necessarily go around waving a neon flag that screamed "vampire" to the living. That was an excellent way to either end up in a government lab or have people begging for immortality like lemmings off a cliff. People had no idea how hard it was to be sixteen every second of every day until the end of time.

No matter what I said, she was fully prepared to not believe me. The best way to go about it would be to explain what he would do without explaining what he would do, which would require some delicate wording. "He'll try to change you."

Wow. That was so vague and not at all helpful, I almost impressed myself.

"Good thing I could use a change." The bell rang, and she yanked her backpack over her shoulder, leaving me behind without a backward glance.

So that went well.

Not that I could blame her. My best friend had tried to warn me about Elton, and I hadn't listened. No way would I have listened to a stranger, especially not another girl. I'd been trained at way too early an age to view girls as competition and boys as the prize to be won.

It took thirty-plus years of living with a perpetual boy to understand they weren't that much of a prize to begin with.

The rest of the class filed out before I'd found my bearings again. I had no backpack, making it even more obvious I wasn't a student here. But Rose told me to act like I belonged, and they'd believe it. Any other alternative was too ridiculous to entertain.

As I moved past Mr. Stockard's desk, I could feel his eyes on me. My shoulders scrunched with each passing step. "Harriet, a moment if you please," he said.

My nerves hummed as I turned, my expression utterly still as I kept my gaze at my toes, fearing that a flicker of recognition I couldn't control would give me away. He reached into his desk and pulled out a copy of *Sweet Valley High #3: Playing with Fire.* The exact same book he gave me over thirty-four years ago. He slid it across his desk with an encouraging nod.

My fingers shook as I pushed it back at him. "That book is a little old, don't you think?"

"Some books are timeless." He sat back in his chair with his fingers steepled over his stomach. "Don't you think?"

I shrugged. "I suppose. But that one doesn't seem like my style."

When he didn't say anything, just stared at me as if patiently waiting for an answer to a question, like this was still 1987, and I was still his student, I turned around. I didn't need to stay here. Maybe I could find Parker and try to talk some sense into her again.

Mr. Stockard's ancient and unoiled chair squeaked as he stood. "Holly."

On instinct, I spun around at my name and swore under my breath.

"Did you really think I wouldn't remember? Christ, I'm not that old." He gestured for me to take a seat at the desk directly in front of his. When I shifted toward the door, he let out a long-winded sigh. "I'm not going to hurt you, or even tell anyone who you really are, least of all because it would likely have me committed. I just want to talk."

"Okay." I slowly lowered to the seat in front of him. "Just so you know, if you're still pushing Sweet Valley on the kids, I think you're way past due to update your reading list."

He let out a humorless laugh. "I pulled that one out of the attic when I saw Elton's face in the halls at the start of the year. I figured it was only a matter of time before you'd be along, eventually, when

I saw another girl who didn't look like she belonged in this century, and who made me extremely uncomfortable when I got near her. The same feeling I got from Elton all those years ago. The same feeling I now get from you, a girl I taught thirty-four years ago, but who somehow still looks like she's sixteen."

"Is that what you want to talk about? To gloat about how you'd been right?" I frowned as I ran my finger over a divot in the desk. "You must know we're not together anymore."

"I want you to be careful." The sincerity in his expression took me aback. A shadow of the teacher he'd been showed through, before life and monotony had beat him into whatever he was now. "You were one of the brightest students I had the pleasure of teaching in those early days. Back when I believed that anything I did would make a difference." He hung his head. "Anyway, those days are over, I understand that. But I mourned you when you died the first time. Please don't do so again anytime soon."

I gave him a strained smile. "Don't worry about me. I don't die easily."

As I left his classroom and roamed the now empty halls, I let my mind wander back to classes with Mr. Stockard in his prime, the counsel he'd given me on more than one occasion, and the warnings he'd tried to issue about Elton. I wrapped a fist around the memories and held them to my heart. I could now count three people who had cared.

Three times more than I thought I'd had when I'd gone.

Chapter Five

It had been decades since I'd wandered these halls, yet I could still find my way to the lunchroom. Parker and Elton probably took their lunches outside or off campus, but it was a place to start. I turned a corner in the hall and a door shot open. Someone grabbed my arm, pulling me inside. Before I could scream, they clamped a hand over my mouth.

"It's me," Rose said. She stood inside a darkened and empty classroom that held only a scarred wooden desk, a whiteboard, and gray walls. "Where have you been?"

"Ida told me to follow Parker to class."

"And?" Rose leaned toward me a bit, anticipation vibrating off her skin.

"I'm in."

After what Elton had said about me, and the way I'd been able to evaluate our relationship outside his influence, I likely would've eventually agreed to Rose and Ida's plans to kill him, anyway. It was the only way to be completely free of him. I told myself that Parker wouldn't have any bearing on my decision, but when I saw flashes of myself in her, I understood why Rose and Ida wanted us to meet. She was one of us. A lost girl who still had time to find herself, and she deserved the chance we never got.

Rose blew out a breath. "You have no idea how happy that makes me. We need you."

"Don't get too excited. I had no instruction on what to do with Parker—thanks. Now she doesn't trust me, either." I felt a twinge of regret and brushed it off. I liked Parker. Ida and Rose had been correct in having me meet her, but she was still one of the living. I didn't need her to like me or want to be my friend. I just needed to keep her alive.

"Give it time." Rose patted my arm. "She'll come around."

"And if she doesn't?"

Rose studied me for a few beats, her gray eyes darkening to the color of choppy lake water. I could see her mentally weighing how much to tell me. "Then we'll have to act faster."

I didn't appreciate the secrets or coded language. If she truly needed me to finish Elton, she owed me the full story. "When are you going to tell me everything?"

"As soon as I know everything. No sense in making you worry over theories." When I crossed my arms with a huff, she squeezed my shoulder. "Ida has Frankie right now. If she's successful with him, we'll have more information today."

"I want to know everything or I'm out."

"Understood. I promise you the full story once we return home." Rose hopped up on the desk, crossed her legs, and leaned back on her hands. "How does it feel being back here?"

"I don't like it." I pulled on the cap sleeves of my dress, as if the fabric was trying to squeeze the life out of me. "It feels wrong. Like we shouldn't be here."

I couldn't explain the sensation that had been scratching at me since we walked through these doors, similar to the way my skin used to feel after a sunburn, tight and itchy. At first, I thought it was old memories, a sense of mourning for my previous life. But that wasn't it. This wasn't an emotion I could put my finger on. It was more like being shoved in a thousand directions at once.

Rose held my gaze, the decades passing like shadows in her eyes. "It's time."

I looked around. "It's time for what?"

She shook her head, her shoulders bowing under the weight of whatever she'd been carrying for nearly seventy years. "It's time that makes us feel wrong in this place. It pushes at us, tries to push us out, because it knows we don't belong here."

"We don't belong anywhere."

Her explanation didn't satisfy me. I didn't feel like this anywhere else. Walking the streets of the town where I grew up should've pushed at me the same way, if time truly wanted to punish me for existing at this age in this decade.

"It's this place in particular." Rose swept her hand out. "It's as connected to us as we are to it. It's where Elton crossed that line. Where we became something other, but still what we had been before. Time doesn't like it. It disrupts the natural order of things."

"Then why does he come back here? Why this school?"

"It's a ritual." Rose turned toward the window, where a thin stream of light broke through the heavy dust. "Before the school was built in 1943, a general store stood on this land. Owned by Ida's family. She'd been working the night Elton came for her."

I ignored the shiver that crept down my spine. "Aren't rituals for serial killers?"

Rose raised an eyebrow. "Is that a serious question?"

When I didn't say anything, she pointed between us. Two of the three girls he'd already killed, on the same ground where he was grooming the fourth. He didn't even need to take a bone or a piece of jewelry to tuck away in a dark corner. He'd made us into living trophies.

I swallowed the lump in my throat. "Are we just going to wait around here for Ida?"

"You can go if you want." She waved me toward the door. "Parker takes her lunch outside, under the oak tree. You can try talking to her again." I had turned to go when she stopped me. "It's hard for me too. Being here."

"Do you feel like you're standing still?" I asked.

"No," she whispered. "I feel like I'm falling behind."

I nodded and left the classroom. As I closed the door, I turned those words over in my mind. Every second that ticked by widened the gap between us and everything else, creating a black hole that swallowed the place we should've occupied in this world. That pocket of time was where I stored all my regrets. I had enough to rip a hole in the universe.

At the back of the school, I pushed against the door and stepped outside. Breathing became so much easier once I got outside those walls. I followed an invisible path to the tree on muscle memory alone. It shouldn't have bothered me that Parker took her lunch under the same tree where I used to sit, but I couldn't *not* notice how the parallels kept stacking up between us. It made me nearly as uncomfortable as walking the halls of my old school.

The sleeve of Parker's navy, gray, and red sweater stuck out from the other side of the oak's trunk. I hesitated before I approached her. She was alone, but I didn't want her to blow me off again, even if no one was around to see it. For some reason, in the span of just one class, her opinion had become very important to me. A ridiculous notion I internally squashed. I just felt sorry for her because she'd gotten caught in Elton's web, that was all.

She looked up as I approached, shielding her eyes from the sun. "Stalking me now?"

I let out a strangled laugh that came out more like gurgle. "You wish."

"Do I?" The teasing in her voice made me recall the sensation of blushing, though that wasn't something I could physically do anymore. Fortunately.

"Is it okay if I sit with you?"

She shrugged. "It's not like I've got dozens of friends forming an orderly queue."

I sat in the cool grass with my legs crossed at the ankles. I tilted my face toward the sun. Thirty-four years ago, I sat under this same oak, under this same sun, and dreamed of the day I could leave this place behind. I thought I'd really start living my life and never look back. Yet here I was: same age, same school, same insecurities.

"This used to be my favorite spot," I said. "I think because I could act like I was rejecting the lunchroom before anyone in the lunchroom could reject me."

Parker narrowed her eyes. "I thought you didn't go to this school."

I faked choking while I scrambled to form a coherent excuse. It had been so long since I'd attempted casual conversation with anyone, my brain-to-mouth filter was a little rusty. "I don't, but I used to. Years ago. But not that many years ago. Like, last year."

That rip in the universe was welcome to come along and swallow me whole now.

"Last year, huh? Why do I think you're lying to me?" Her nose scrunched as she eyed me with less trust than I had in my old motel's "clean bedding policy."

"Do you really want the answer to that?" I held her gaze, daring her to push it. I had no idea if I'd tell her the truth or give her another vague nonresponse, but I wanted her to think about it. If she questioned me, maybe she'd also question Elton.

She stared at me, not blinking. Eventually, she turned her head. "Not really. But just so you know, it's strange how you, Rose, and Ida hang around here when you don't actually go to this school, and you're going to get found out if you keep it up."

It looked like we were just going to avoid sticky ground. Probably for the best. I plucked at a blade of grass, weaving it between my fingers. Everything inside me had gotten tangled up. I wanted to be truthful with her, for her own good, but at the same time, I didn't know if I could trust her. She certainly didn't trust me.

"I don't plan on spending a lot of time here." I paused. "Can I ask you a question?"

"I guess." She pulled out her earbuds. "No guarantee I'll answer."

"What do you see in Elton?" I knew what I'd seen in him, but Parker seemed self-aware enough. He didn't like girls who knew themselves. It took away the sense of control he relished. "Please don't tell me it's because he's hot."

"That's a nice bonus." She smiled to herself. "But it's not just that. He asks me questions. He understands my problems. He listens."

"Yeah." I thought back to all the times I'd felt alone, and Elton made sure he positioned himself as the caring boyfriend, the only one who got me. "He's good at that."

"Did you two date or something?" Parker jutted her chin like she was prepared to dismiss me as the bitter ex. And maybe I was. But she still didn't tell me to leave.

"We did. That was also a long time ago." The memory of his car kicking up dust as he peeled out of the Quick Stop without me burned in my mind. That was going to be Parker's future if she let him in. Endless towns with no roots or purpose. Aimlessly wandering at the whims of someone else, with no hope of ever building something for herself. It left a sour taste in my mouth all over again. "I'm not interested in breaking you up so I can have him for myself, if that's what you're thinking."

"I know, you want me to be safe." She air-quoted the last word. "I already got the same speech from Rose and Ida. I don't know where the three of you came from or what kind of game you're playing, but leave me out of it. I already have enough to deal with on my own."

Continuing to warn her about Elton up front clearly wasn't going to do any good, so I switched topics. "My mom had a lot of shitty boyfriends too."

"I don't even know why I told you that." She turned her head, gazing out at the open field where a couple of people kicked a soccer ball around. "That's not how I typically go around introducing myself to people, in case you were wondering."

She sat up a little straighter. It reminded me of the first time Stacey sat with me in the lunchroom, despite warnings from other people. When I wanted someone to talk to but couldn't admit I wanted someone to talk to. The only form of self-preservation I had at the time was to act like I didn't need anyone so they couldn't weaponize my loneliness. But when Stacey offered me friendship, it made me realize just how desperately I'd been in need of it.

"I didn't have the luxury of choosing with whom to share my family shit," I said. "The entire school knew, thanks to her preferred choice in partners."

"Who were her preferred partners?" Her eyes widened with interest. "Hit men and murderers? Circus clowns?"

I snorted. If only. "No. She liked the fathers of my classmates."

"Ouch. Married fathers?"

"No." I wish they had been married. Then she would've had to keep herself a secret. "She used me to bait their ex-wives."

The memory of it curdled in my gut. Most of the time, my mom acted like I was part of the living room furniture or a plant she needed to water. There, but not relevant. Until she needed to put on a show. In second grade, she made Cindy Wharton's father hoist me up and carry me on his shoulders at the county fair, right as we passed Cindy and her mom in line for the Ferris wheel. In fourth grade, she dragged Derek Milford's father to my Little League game, even though Derek was playing two fields over. If we had lived together in the age of social media, she would've posed us all in matching sweaters in front of a rotting barn, and every Instagram photo would've gotten the Juno filter with the hashtags #blessed and #lovemylife.

Sixth grade was the last time I tried to get involved in extracurriculars. The night my mom brought her boyfriend, Megan Bear's father, to my school play. She bought flowers and had him present them to me after the curtain fell, all while keeping one evil eye on his ex-wife, who had been there to support Megan. I'd never forget the devastation on Megan's face as she watched her father swing me up in his arms with a bouquet of roses. As if he had come specifically to see me. The nobody child of his new girlfriend.

I spent my entire childhood being a pawn in her one-up games. She didn't care about my play. Whenever I asked her to run lines with me, she was too busy. If I needed a ride home from rehearsal, she sent her boyfriend to pick me up. When I brought home tickets, she said she wouldn't be able to make it. She didn't take a scrap of interest in that play until she found the program I left on the dining-room table, when she noticed Megan would also be performing and found an opportunity to rub in her status as Current Girlfriend.

Unfortunately for me, Megan Bear was the queen bee of Woodward Middle School, and she put all the anger and resentment she felt for her dad onto me. She convinced the entire class to stay away from me. It soon became clear that anyone who let me sit with them at lunch would be punished, and no one wanted to test her wrath. People had gotten so accustomed to hating me, it became habit more than anything else. I didn't have a single friend until eighth grade. That's when Stacey moved to town, and she didn't give a shit about anyone's opinions.

The short swing of Parker's hair curtained her face as she looked down at her chipping black nail polish. "At least you got to stay in one place long enough for people to know you existed. I've been invisible my entire life."

"There are a lot of ways to be invisible." When people already determined your entire character based on the actions of others, they never really saw you. Every time they shot spitballs into my hair or tripped me in the lunchroom on soup day, I disappeared a little more, until I made myself so small, I didn't take up any space at all.

"Yeah, I guess there are." She chewed on her bottom lip, drawing a small bit of blood.

I inhaled sharply. I didn't need to feed quite yet, but the drop of fresh blood on her full bottom lip drew me in like a pearl on a pink oyster bed. The urge to lick the spot away caught me off guard, and I jumped to my feet, prepared to leave before I did something truly mortifying.

Her tongue dipped out, wiping the bit of blood away. Her lip was already starting to heal over. My heartbeat pounded in my ears, the vibration of it beating down, down, down until a warm glow spread through my stomach. I had a flash in my mind of running my thumb over that plump bit of skin before leaning in and . . .

Nope. I had no idea if I would've kissed her or killed her in my fantasy, and I had no intention of doing either. My job was to protect her from Elton. Nothing more.

The harmless illusion had thrown me off, though. I hadn't thought about anyone with that kind of intensity since Elton. He'd been my moon and stars since before I'd been turned, and I was still learning how to function without him. I wasn't even sure if I was attracted to Parker. Maybe I wanted to make out with her, or maybe I wanted to be her friend. Or maybe I just wanted to drink her dry. Couldn't exactly rule that one out, either.

Her brows pinched together as she stared up at me. Clearly, I'd thrown her off by acting like I was about to run for no reason. So far today I was zero for two on the first-impressions scale. If Rose and Ida expected me to be the one to convince Parker to stay clear of Elton, they were going to be sadly disappointed.

"There was a bee," I said. Though I didn't sound very convincing, even to myself.

She gave me a solemn nod. "And they're so active in October."

My lips twitched as I tried to hold back the laugh over my own ridiculousness. I didn't know Parker, and she absolutely didn't know me. I had no reason to have such a strong reaction to her. "You're messing with me again."

"Sorry, you make it so easy." She grinned, and I was struck again by her smile. It didn't just light up her face, everything around her appeared a little brighter too.

I took a step back to gather my thoughts and ran up against a hard chest. One that I knew so well, I shuddered in response. His scent hit me first, the cloying smell of musty attics, overturned earth, and overripe peaches. The sweet spice of death, with just a splash of sex.

Spinning around, I looked up at the boy who still haunted me in ways I'd never be able to change. His cheekbones were sharp enough to cut through bone. His eyes were like a frozen lake or a clear blue sky, depending on his mood. Straight nose, strong jaw, and thin lips currently tipped in a half-cocked smile that used to make my toes melt. Back before I realized he found amusement in what he considered simple-headed girls.

He tipped his head, slight enough for only me to notice. A mocking gesture that just begged me to fall into his trap. I stiffened my spine, refusing to give in and lash out. A reaction I was sure he more than expected of me.

Instead I gave him a nod, welcoming his challenge. "Hello, Elton. Long time, no see."

Chapter Six

"You just couldn't stay away, could you?" Elton circled me, forcing me to turn to keep him at my front and throwing me off balance. He always moved with more elegance than most.

"I could say the same for you." I put my hands on my hips. "Of course, a cold-blooded bastard would feel at home in the frozen north."

He tsked and prowled closer, like a sleek panther that knew it outmatched the field mouse. "You say that like you're not happy to be here."

"I'm not." Great. Now I sounded like a two year old.

"You look good, Holly." His gaze roamed over me, like I was a sheep he both wanted to shear naked and drag to the slaughterhouse. A lock of my crimped hair had come loose from my braid, and he tucked it back. "But I'm disappointed in you, you know."

Ugh. Even with self-righteousness and distain dripping from every syllable, the hard place in my heart where I stored all my ugly feelings softened. My fingers itched to run through the sweep of hair that hung over his forehead, like I used to when he'd been mine. I shook my head. He had such an impossible hold over me. I should've had more time before this meeting, more time to prepare myself against my natural instincts to curl against his body until that part of him living within me felt at peace.

"I don't care if you're disappointed." Lies. I cared, but I didn't want to care, which was as good as I could do when faced with the full force of Elton. "You have no right to be here." I glanced to where Parker eyed us with interest and lowered my voice. "Not even time wants you here. Don't you feel it every time you go inside the school?"

He flashed his teeth. "Speaking of time, have you been to see your mother?"

The sharp twist of pain took me by surprise. I'd begged him to come home for years, and he ignored my every request. At the time he told me it was because it wasn't good for me, he was protecting me from her toxicity, and I'd been so in love, I just accepted it. I hadn't even missed her, not really, but I'd wanted to check on her, if only to satisfy my own curiosity about what her life looked like without me in it. Not that it would've changed anything. Still. It should've been my choice to know.

"I haven't seen her since I've been back." I choked on the shame of those last words. I should've gone to see her, but I didn't want to feel sorry. I'd moved past that, comfortable in my righteous anger. A much more soothing balm than guilt.

The first night I arrived back in Michigan, I'd felt compelled to check in on her, in what I assumed was a lingering sense of obligation. I climbed my old tree. Its gnarled limbs stretched toward my bedroom, canopied by thick leaves. When I first started dating Elton, that tree made it easier for me to sneak out and join him in what he called "really living." Spray-painting the school, egging the homes of people who had been mean to me, running through honey-scented apple fields in the moonlight, making out under the stars. Never knowing I was actively embracing my own death. I sat on the thickest branch, sticky with maple sap, and stared into the place I'd called home, and I let the weight of my regrets press down on me.

I waited to catch a glimpse of her, wondering how it would feel to see her hunched over, with candy-floss hair and sagging skin. If I'd even recognize her. If she was alone.

It took me until morning to realize that she didn't live there anymore. Through the Facebook posts of relatives I rarely saw, I discovered she'd been moved to a local nursing home and had a strong case of dementia. She didn't remember she'd ever had a daughter.

Maybe it was better that way.

I made the decision after that not to seek her out. I had too many conflicting feelings when it came to my mom, and she wasn't in a place to shoulder any of them. So, I'd hang on to my anger. It was the only thing that kept the guilt from eating away at me.

"How have you not seen your own mother? Don't you live with her?" Parker's nose scrunched slightly when she was suspicious. I'd learned that much, since she'd been suspicious of me almost from the start. She also had the unmistakable shimmer of hurt in her eyes. "Or was all that stuff about your mom's boyfriends a bunch of bullshit?"

"It wasn't bullshit." I glanced at Elton. "It's actually a big part of the reason why I don't live with her anymore. Isn't that right, Elton? Wasn't she *such* a toxic influence in my life? Didn't I just *need* to get away from her to save myself?"

"Holly likes her stories." He took a seat next Parker, casually draping his arm over her shoulder, knowing I would notice. Making sure his territory was clearly marked. "She lives in a reality of her own making. I don't even think she means to lie. It just happens."

"Right. I'm the liar." I turned to Parker. "When he tells you that you're the only one, and he will, I hope you remember this. I hope you remember me, Rose, and Ida and think about what you'll really be giving up."

"Honestly, Holly, you were always so dramatic." He dismissed me with a wave of his hand. "It's a nice day. The sun is shining. Try to enjoy it."

He reached into his pocket and pulled out a rose petal, brushing it down Parker's nose and whispering in her ear. She giggled, closing her hand over the petal and pressing it into her book. Seeing his courting ritual from the outside was An Experience. Now that I wasn't the focus of it, I could clearly see how he staged everything for maximum swoons, like he just happened to walk around with rose petals in his pocket. Please.

It made me sick enough that I had to look away. "I'm going to go."

Rose and Ida had wanted me to try with Parker. But that didn't mean I had to stay here and watch her moon over a guy who was absolutely going to kill her within the month. If she didn't want to listen to my warning, that was on her. This was why I didn't deal with the living. They had no respect for their own mortality.

Elton smirked. "Bye."

"I wasn't talking to you," I said through clenched teeth. Rolling my eyes, I headed back to the school to collect Rose and go. If Ida was still busy with Frankie, she could catch up to us later. She knew where we lived.

"Hey, Holly. Wait up." Parker jogged toward me, panting a little as she came to stop. "I'm sorry about the weird tension back there."

"It's fine." It wasn't, but what else was I supposed to say?

"I know you two have a history." She flattened some loose gravel under her foot. "But it's hard being new, you know? I don't really have anyone to talk to about stuff."

"Yeah, I get that." Before Stacey moved to town, I'd only had myself and my stuffed pigeon, Gideon, and he was a dreadful conversationalist. My mom hadn't even gotten me a fish because they required too much upkeep. On impulse, before I could overthink it, I grabbed Parker's hand. "Do you have a pen?"

Her finger flexed a bit in my grasp, like the contact surprised her almost as much as it surprised me. Her skin was soft, the warmth such a stark contrast to my cold. My palm tingled with little pinpricks of awareness. She reached into her back pocket and handed me a pen. She frowned slightly, not annoyed, but more confused.

I turned her hand over in mine and tried not to focus in on

the way her pulse beat against her wrist. "I'm going to write down my address."

"Okay." She said it more like a whisper.

"If you ever need to talk, or just get away, you can find me there."

I didn't know what had propelled me to give her my address. For all I knew, she'd turn around and show Elton, and the two of them would share a laugh over my pathetic attempt to make friends. But it felt too final to just leave. Whenever things got tough for me at home, I could always escape to Stacey's. Parker didn't have anyone except Elton. And having been there, I couldn't think of anything more depressing.

She let out a little breathy laugh. "Can't you just put your number in my contacts?"

"I don't have a phone." There it was again. The urge to blush. Unfortunately, working part-time at Taco Bell had barely covered the cost of the roach motel where I'd been staying. I didn't have extra money for a phone. It's not like I had anyone to call, anyway.

"Oh. That's okay." Parker's cheeks reddened. "I mean, of course it's okay. Never mind. I'm going to stop talking any minute now."

I waved off her embarrassment. Being poor came with the territory of being sixteen, and it was a thousand times worse not having parental support to fall back on. "I'm staying with Rose and Ida, so it's really more like their apartment, but you're welcome any time. We can lay on the floor in existential dread and talk about our trauma. It'll be good times."

"What a coincidence. That's how I prefer to spend my Friday nights."

We grinned at each other, and for a second I forgot she was Elton's new victim, and my job here was to make sure she made it out of this alive. "Right. Well. I have to go, but do come over whenever. Or don't. It's cool."

I headed back inside the school just as the bell rang, signaling the end of lunch. Once again, I walked through the hall as if I had an invisible barrier keeping people at a three-foot distance. A guy in a blue sweater tripped over his feet to get away from me. I stopped to offer him my hand and frowned when he crab-walked away from me, bumping against a locker.

Hint taken.

We didn't interact well with the living during the best of times, but it was next level at this school. I didn't usually have people actively run from me like this. The tightness around my neck increased, and I pulled at my borrowed dress. I peeked in the classroom where I'd left Rose, but other than a garden scene drawn with remarkable precision for a dry-erase board, there was no sign of her. I added a poorly drawn bee buzzing over a snapdragon, then left. Keeping my head down, I hustled through the crowd of students on their way to their next classes and pushed through the front doors. Where I could breathe again.

If Rose and Ida were still inside, they were on their own. I'd done my part. I'd met Parker like they wanted and agreed to get on board with killing Elton. Now all I wanted was a few hours alone to process. I walked to the corner, where the city bus ran every two hours, and stopped short at the familiar face across the street wearing a frilly, vaguely pirate-like shirt and a black silk scarf. I blinked against the white spots in my vision. Before I could adjust to the sunlight dilation, the bus whooshed to a stop in front of me.

That was the second time in as many days where I thought I'd seen Stacey. She must've been in this city somewhere, in all the cities where I'd been, but I hadn't seen her once in the past thirty-four years. Not since the night I'd done the unthinkable.

Maybe my mind was playing tricks on me. Being back at this school had messed with my sense of place and time, and apparently, place and time didn't much appreciate me, either. I plugged in my return ticket and rushed to the windows, scanning the street for any sign of her wide gold eyes and frizzy black hair. Finding nothing, I collapsed in my seat with a huff. The man next to me slid down two seats.

I rested my head against the window and ran over my confrontation with Elton. I should've stayed, or goaded him into revealing himself, or anything more than trading insults and leaving like a coward. Right now he was probably holding Parker's hand and telling her to ignore me. Painting whatever picture he wanted because I couldn't stand to be in his proximity while he did to another girl what he'd done to me all those years ago.

She was already lost, and I wasn't fit to help find her.

The bus dropped me off a few blocks from the apartment. The meat market did pretty brisk business in the afternoon. This was a trendy part of town that had shops dedicated to lavender macarons and organic milk. I had no idea how Rose and Ida afforded this place when neither appeared to have jobs, and I could barely afford a shitty motel on my meager salary. It wasn't my concern, though. I trudged up the stairs to the second floor. As soon as I stepped inside, the two of them jumped up from the floor.

Rose threw her arms around me. "You made it back okay. We were just about to come collect you if you hadn't shown up."

"I would've had to ride the bus four times in one day." Ida shuddered. "I definitely would've sold one of your kidneys on the dark web for that."

"You knew where I was. Thanks for just leaving me there without attempting to let me know, by the way." I took a step back from them both. I wasn't mad, exactly. I just had a lot of anger after dealing with Elton and nowhere else to put it, so it exploded out of me. "Did you know I ran into Elton? And let me tell you, that was a real joy."

Rose and Ida looked at each other, and I wanted to knock their heads together. I hated the silent communication they were able to do. And yeah, they had decades together, where I'd just become part of their circle, but it made me feel like I was on the edge of their twosome. A convenience they needed at the moment to complete their task and discardable once I'd served my purpose. It hurt. And when I'm hurt, I hurt back.

"We knew you might run into Elton." Ida had a note of impatience in her voice, like I was being a spoiled brat about the whole thing. "It was necessary for him to be occupied elsewhere while I borrowed Frankie."

"Here's what else is necessary: me." I grabbed my suitcase and flung it toward the door, where it hit the frame and snapped open, spilling my limited supply of clothes across the floor. The urge to scream welled up inside me. "I'm necessary to your little plan, or so you tell me, but you won't let me in on anything. You just expect me to go along. Well, fuck that. I'm done."

This was why I didn't get close to anyone. At least, if all those psych books I read when I was bored and searching for meaning in my death were to be believed. Even those who claimed to be on my side were only interested in what I could do for them. Just like Elton. Even my own mother, with the way she used me as a pawn to hurt the ex-wives of her detached boyfriends for most of my life. It was why I held so tightly to my anger.

"Wait." Rose stepped forward, pushing her hand against the door to keep it closed. "You're right." Ida let out a strangled sound behind us, and Rose shot her a dirty look. "We haven't been as upfront with you because we were afraid of hitting you with too much at once."

"It's a lot to process," Ida said. "In case you missed the part about us looking out for you. We don't have time for drama, and we can't afford infighting. So suck it up, buttercup."

I glared at her, and she blew me a kiss.

"What Ida is trying to say, in her special bitchy way, is that we're ready to tell you more now, if you'll just stay and listen." Rose led me over to the floor, where they'd been hovering over some papers. "We know you know your own limits, and I apologize for trying to protect you. Tell me what you want to know, and I'll answer all your questions."

"Everything." I gazed at the papers, my eyes widening as I fell upon the word *heirloom* written in a bold script and underlined twice. "Tell me everything."

Chapter Seven

Rose scooped up the papers and put them in a neat stack. "These are just our notes. They're kind of messy, but now that we have everything we need, we can start a new log."

"What do heirlooms have to do with it?" I asked.

"Everything," Rose said.

I hadn't thought about my heirloom in years. One, because I no longer had the locket in my possession, and two, because I didn't need it once I'd been transformed. Despite popular misconception, a vampire bite alone isn't enough to complete the transformation. I'd needed to store a single drop of my living blood inside an object of my choosing. Objects held memory, and the stronger the significance, the more powerful the memories associated with the object, with silver and gold being the better conduits. The act of making it a vessel for my living self created a physical holding place for my emotions, sentiments, and self-awareness: everything that made me human and allowed me to retain those characteristics in death.

No one could survive the turning process without an heirloom. A vampire bite alone didn't do anything, since the vampire needed to redirect a piece of themselves into the one they were creating. And without the heirloom tethering them to life, the person would die. Which was why vampires generally required permission to turn anyone. Generally, anyway . . .

I rubbed at the scar on my wrist. The bite marks where Elton had sunk his teeth into me and flooded my veins with the venom that ran in his. The moment our blood mixed, he became a part of me. I thought it had been metaphorical. I'd had no idea how wrong I was.

"Elton found out about the power of heirlooms too late," Ida said. "He'd already turned me and given away his power before he discovered what a huge mistake that had been."

I swallowed. Hard. "You give away your power when you make a vampire?"

That information would've been much more useful to me thirty-four years ago. Though I didn't feel any different after I turned Stacey—other than the process itself being horrific enough to put me off the idea of ever turning someone again. If I'd given something away, wouldn't I have felt it?

"It's like a chain that links backward," Rose said. "The heirloom Ida made preserves the memory of Elton at full power. The moment he turned us, we held the power. Destroy the heirloom, and you can destroy the vampire."

"And we can't just take a sledgehammer to them or toss them off a bridge," Ida said. "We need to kill the blood stored within the heirloom at the same time. It's a whole process."

That was going to be a problem. "We need all our heirlooms?"

"Yes. Which I suspected. Even though it's rare for a vampire to make more than one, he gave up his power three times over, which means it takes three times the sacrifice to balance. I've been researching this for thirty years," Rose said.

I hadn't realized just how much time both Rose and Ida had put into this. The time and the care it took to put all the pieces together, sorting through half-baked myths and near-forgotten legends in out-of-print books. While I'd been flitting across the country with Elton, they'd been making long-term plans. Not just for themselves, but for me as well.

And I was going to be the one to ruin it.

I should've taken more care with my locket. Stacey ripped it right off my neck, and I didn't do a thing to stop her, because she was angry and I felt bad. I was still human enough at the time to let my feelings dictate all of my actions. Maybe this was the other reason I didn't get close to anyone. They all walked away worse off for having known me.

"I'm sorry I yelled at you both earlier." I bit my lower lip, piercing it with my fang. It quickly healed, and my mind instantly drifted to Parker's full bottom lip kissed with a single drop of blood. "Today was a lot. I wasn't ready to see Elton."

"It's okay." Rose laid a gentle hand on my arm. Her clean-cotton scent was like a calming balm to my internal storm. "We knew it would be tough. I had a panic attack the first time I ran into him after he ended things, but it gets easier. What did you think of Parker?"

Parker. Her name spun through my mind like a penny in a coin funnel, lightly skimming the edges. I saw so much of myself in her, protecting her had begun to feel as if it could be a do-over for me. A chance to make things right. If only we could convince her to make better choices, to live past this time when everything felt hopeless. I needed to believe there was still hope for girls who didn't have any hope for themselves.

"She reminds me of me," I said. Rose and Ida nodded. Maybe they felt the same way, like Parker had become the second chance none of us had gotten. An opportunity to forgive ourselves. "Why isn't she skittish around us like the rest of the living?"

"She's a lost girl." A shadow of grief older than time passed in Ida's eyes. I'd seen it in Rose's too. The weight that lost girls were expected to carry for an eternity. "She's not afraid of death because she doesn't think her life matters. Her world is black and gray. We're something other, so she looks at us and sees color."

The truth of her statement cut deep. Even before Elton enrolled at my school, I'd already become so good at folding myself down, making myself smaller so I wouldn't burden anyone by taking up too much space. Elton made it so easy for us to willingly embrace death. Because none of us thought we'd been worth much at all.

"Elton never loved us, did he?" It had all been for nothing in the end. "If he loved us, he never would've let us believe our lives meant so little."

"You're way late to that party." Ida paused, her expression softening. "But yes, he courted us specifically because it had been easier for him to convince us we wouldn't be missed. Funny how we had to become undead to figure out how much our lives really meant."

I couldn't think of anything less funny.

The only thing we could do now was free ourselves of Elton so we could find a way to make a life out of our immortality. That meant making nice with Stacey, somehow. I had to believe there was a reason why I was seeing her all over town now. She had to have kept the lockets. They had been our heirlooms for a reason.

"What happened with Frankie?" I asked.

"That boy will never learn." Rose let out a chuckle. "He's had a thing for Ida for years, but he won't do anything about it because he's bound to Gwen."

Gwen. Just repeating her name in my mind sent a shiver of fear down my spine. As a kid, she was undoubtedly the kind of person who pulled the wings off flies and fed them to her enemies. Beautiful in a cold and sadistic way, she took pleasure in torturing her victims before feeding on them. She often removed their eyelids first so they'd be forced to watch as she tore them apart before letting them die.

"That is all very much his problem, not mine." Ida grinned. Her smile was made of nightmares, but still carried a warmth that was absent from Gwen's. "I told him we needed to talk, and he agreed because he doesn't have a drop of common sense in his thick head."

"And he just told you what you wanted to know?" It couldn't be that easy.

"Yes." The mischievous gleam in her eye was terrifying. I had a feeling that was the last thing many people saw before she made a meal out of them. "After I tied him to a toilet-paper rack in a storage closet and ripped off his arms."

I choked and beat on my chest to clear my lungs. "You ripped off his arms?"

"They'll grow back." Ida shrugged, like she went around ripping off arms every day and this was just business as usual. "It got him to talk, so I don't want to hear any judgment."

"No judgment." I held out my hands, then glanced at Ida and tucked them under my legs. Our limbs did grow back, and rather quickly, but it was still traumatizing to lose them. Dying hadn't changed our pain thresholds. "What did he tell you?"

"We already knew we'd need our heirlooms and certain death plants to complete the burning ritual that will make Elton killable, but we didn't know if the time and place mattered," Rose said.

"It matters," Ida said. "We can burn them anywhere. The universe will throw a minor temper tantrum when we do, nothing serious, but it needs to be done under a full moon."

"That is specific." Though I supposed if making and killing vampires were easy, there would be a lot more of us. As it stood now, there were fewer than five hundred vampires in the world. And Elton had made three already.

"The moon cycles have long been a part of many rituals since the dawn of time," Rose said. "It makes sense from a historical standpoint. And it should be done at the school. To make Elton's need for his own rituals his undoing, which also seems appropriate."

"And when is the next full moon?" I needed time to find Stacey, but if we waited until the next moon cycle, Elton would have a larger window in which to turn Parker. We were walking a fine line with time.

"Three weeks until full moon," Ida said.

Three. Weeks. Panic clawed at my throat. So much hinged on getting this exactly right, and I was about to set us back, possibly indefinitely. I needed to come clean to Rose and Ida, so we could come up with a plan if I couldn't retrieve mine. "I don't have my heirloom."

"What do you mean you don't have it?" Rose raised her fist to her mouth. "Please don't tell me you lost it. Because this doesn't work without all three."

"I don't know if it's lost. It's been gone for a long time. Stacey stole it from me the night I turned her." I swallowed the bitter memories of Stacey ripping off my locket, the twin to hers, and telling me I didn't deserve to wear it after what I'd done.

Ida held out one of her palms. "Back the fuck up. First of all, who's Stacey? And more importantly, you made a vampire and didn't think that was pertinent information worth sharing?"

I sniffed. Those two had kept many more secrets from me, so they had no room to lecture. "It's not something I like to talk about."

"I don't care about your feelings." Ida paced the living room, chewing off her thumbnail, then chewing it off again when it grew back. "This changes things."

"I realize that." I knotted my fingers together. "I don't know what else to say."

"Do we have to destroy Stacey's heirloom too?" Ida asked Rose.

Rose shook her head. "Elton's power is only tied to us and our heirlooms, because he made us. Stacey can kill Holly but not Elton, because he never gave her anything."

"That's something, I guess," Ida grumbled. I tried not to cringe over her relief of Stacey having the power to kill me. "We're still screwed."

"It's not over yet. She might still have Holly's heirloom, especially if she knows its value." Rose lifted my chin and tilted her head as she studied me. "You feel guilt. Don't. Guilt can consume you. Do you know where this Stacey person is?"

"Somewhere in the city." So helpful. "I think I saw her at the bus stop outside the school, but it was only for a second, and maybe I saw her outside the piano bar the night you two found me. That might've been a trick of the light, though."

"I don't think so." Ida let out a derisive huff. "She's playing with you. Why?"

Over the past thirty years, I'd gone from city to city with Elton, never knowing Stacey had been in those same cities, not really understanding until three months ago that she would've had no choice but to follow. If she wanted me dead just for changing her, I had to imagine being tethered to me for eternity only increased that desire, and unlike Elton, she didn't need a whole trail of exes to make that happen. She only needed herself and her heirloom. Which, lucky her, she probably still had.

"She never wanted to be a vampire," I said. "I did it while she was unconscious and bleeding out. I thought I was saving her life; she thinks I damned her soul, so here we are."

I told them the entire story. Stacey hadn't trusted Elton from the start. She warned me repeatedly to stay away from him. At first, I thought it was because she was jealous, because he took away time and attention that had always belonged to her, but she'd felt uncomfortable around him the way most of the living did around vampires. The night he turned me in the school parking lot, Stacey had followed us. The moment he bit me it was too late, but Stacey charged him with a wooden stake, having no idea how useless it was against him.

He tore her neck open and left her body on the concrete.

He said he was only protecting me as I screamed and cried over her dying body. With my new heightened senses, I could feel her life slipping away. I panicked, not thinking about what she would've wanted, only of saving her. So I put a drop of her blood inside her locket and bit her wrist in the same place Elton had bitten mine.

The pain that sliced through my veins as I forced the redirection of my blood was worse than dying. Everything inside me felt as if it were being tied into knots. The process was so intense, I couldn't even scream. It felt as if I'd been ripped clean in half as a living part of me flowed into Stacey's body, while her death flowed into mine. Just reminiscing about that night caused me to break out in a cold sweat. It wasn't just the pain, although that had been unbearable, but the feeling that part of me was gone forever, and I'd never get it back again.

When she rose, covered in her own blood, her neck wound was still very much present. It had cauterized, leaving flaps of dead skin hanging wide open. Because she had died with the injury, it would stay with her for all eternity. I'd thought it would knit itself shut. Elton told me wounds healed quickly. He even demonstrated by slicing his own throat, and I watched in fascination as it barely bled before stitching back up as if it never happened. But I didn't know that only applied to after death. Anything done before death became permanent, sealed within the time gap where we all existed.

"Holy shit, that's gruesome." Ida cringed when I finished. "No wonder she hates you."

"Thanks, Ida." I patted her shoulder. "You really ought to make a living writing cheerful sympathy cards for Hallmark."

"If you want cheerleading, look to Rose. I'm the realist here." She paused, running her hand over her finger waves, a hairstyle that managed to have a modern elegance, unlike my own. "If she still wants Elton dead, though, this could be to our advantage."

"I agree," Rose said. "We should find Stacey first, then get our heirlooms next."

"What if she doesn't have it?" I asked.

"We'll cross that bridge when we get there," Ida said. "For now, we're going to function on the assumption that she has it, because it's the only option we've got."

"Don't worry yet." Rose had lined up her figurines on the counter and began polishing them with an embroidered dishtowel. She gave me a tentative smile as she held a sea-glass butterfly and rubbed it furiously enough to scrape off a layer of iridescent paint. "If I'm not worried yet, you shouldn't be worried."

Right. Not worried at all.

Stacey had to have it, though. I couldn't imagine an alternative scenario, and not just because of what that would mean for our intentions with Elton. Even if Stacey despised me, Edie Barrett's lockets meant too much to us both.

The summer after eighth grade, my mom had hooked up with Jason McCreedy's dad, so she arranged for me to stay at Stacey's while Mr. McCreedy took her on a fishing trip he had previously promised to his son. After Stacey and I spent the day at the public pool trying to get the high school boys to notice us (they never did), we dug through her attic after her mom had found some old love letters up there. The scent of sun-soaked chlorine and attic musk filled my senses whenever I thought about the afternoon we became obsessed with the previous owner, Edie Barrett. We created a whole fictional life for her based on a handful of letters, an old trunk full of moldy lace, and two matching lockets with a B carved into the tarnished silver. We believed Edie's ghost wandered the attic at night, waiting to collect the souls of lonely girls.

In a way, she had.

Stacey and I spent the rest of the summer going through every box in the attic, making up stories about Edie with each small treasure uncovered. We even made several trips to the library in the hopes that we'd stumble on an old diary or an account of her life. All we turned up was an obituary stating that she hadn't been survived by any family and passed away at the age of eighty-four. A Scrooge McDuck who had died alone with no one to mourn her or claim her lost possessions. To say it had been a letdown was a huge understatement.

When Stacey and I started high school together, we decided we'd make our own history. It might've been too late for Edie, but it wasn't too late for us. We'd been young enough to believe we could still conquer the world, not knowing the world had already decided our fates, and it wasn't kind to awkward girls who wanted, more than anything, to be loved. We vowed never to take those necklaces off, and we made good on that promise, until the night Stacey ripped mine from my throat before she ran. I never saw her again.

Until I came back to the town where it all began.

"I need some air," I said.

I went out to the fire escape adjacent to Rose's bedroom and took a seat, dangling my legs through the rusty steel bars. Rose had turned the balcony into a little oasis, with box gardens tied to the balcony spires and huge pots overflowing with bright flowers bursting with color. The back alley didn't offer much of a view, just the tin roof of the apartment across the way, broken bottles, and a few stubbed-out cigarettes that had blown into a pile of dead leaves, but this was the first place where I felt like I could breathe since I had died. If we managed to pull this off and actually kill Elton, then what? Would I just go back to aimlessly wandering, taking part-time jobs and living out of shitty motels? I couldn't stand the idea of going back to that.

The window opened behind me, and Rose joined me, leaning against the rail on her elbows with her back to the alley. "What a day."

"It's been something." I rested my forehead against the metal bars, letting the minutes tick by as I sat in the comfortable quiet with Rose and kicked my feet into the crisp fall air. "What did you want to do with your life before you met Elton?"

"What did I *want* to do with my life? Or what did I *think* I was going to do?" Rose smiled down at me as a light breeze blew the hem of her polka-dot dress. "Because those are two very different questions."

"Humor me and answer both."

"Things were different in 1954. Girls didn't have a lot of options. I probably would've either gone to nursing school or married Mike Baxter and had a bunch of babies, even though I didn't really like kids all that much."

"Kids are gross." And terrifying. I shuddered at the idea of having any floppy-headed babies of my own. "Was Mike Baxter the guy in the car? From your photo album?"

"Yeah. Our parents were friends, so they just expected us to be together. My boyfriend, my friends, my life was all just put upon me, and I was drowning in their expectations." She blew out her breath. "Once I made it clear that I wanted to make my own decisions, they stopped caring. My family did not tolerate rebellion. I'd become a lost cause in their eyes."

"Is that true? Or just what Elton told you?"

"A little of both." The corner of her mouth tilted upward. "He has a particular talent for exploiting insecurities. Though I'd like to think the rebellion was all my own." She held on to the balcony railing and tilted her head upward to face the sun. "As for what I wanted, it would've been nice to have my own flower shop one day. Nothing grand, but I love to garden. He promised me I'd have whatever I wanted once we left town. That never happened."

"He promised me a bookstore. I never got that, either." I'd forgotten about that until Rose mentioned the flower shop. That's how thoroughly my dreams had died. The bookstore I always wanted had just become another thing in a long line of broken promises.

"Maybe when this is all over, we could start those businesses on our own?"

"Maybe." But we both knew those were empty words. Banks didn't give loans to sixteen-year-old girls. Vendors didn't do business with sixteen-year-old girls. The world expected us to shoulder adult burdens but treated us like children when we needed something in return. Those were lessons we learned the hard way.

Ida joined us on the balcony, carrying a human hand that had been sprayed with a clear rubber sealant, posed as if it reached upward. Bone and muscle crunched against the balcony spire as she thrust the hand against it by the wrist. "Did I miss bonding time?"

"What is that thing?" I asked.

Ida looked between me and the hand. She took some seeds out of her pocket and poured them into the open palm. "Birdfeeder."

I made a face. "And you couldn't just make a wooden house because . . . ?"

"Rose has her flowers, you have your books, and this is my thing." Ida adjusted the hand, pulling the fingers down to make better perches for the birds. "Don't judge me."

"Fair enough." I nudged her leg with my elbow.

The sun began to set behind the horizon, bringing the temperature down with it. Despite the difficulties we had ahead, we had this moment of calm. The three of us shouldn't have been friends. We shouldn't have even existed in the same time. But in these girls, I found something I hadn't had in a really long time. Something that felt a lot like family.

Chapter Eight

A few nights later, I put on my polo with the Taco Bell logo, which always smelled like stale beans no matter how many times I washed it. Rose and Ida left me alone to get changed, as if my uniform was obscene and deserving of privacy. Which wasn't far off. My shifts at Taco Bell sucked away my will to live. An extra-impressive feat, considering that I was already dead. I twisted my terrible hair into a knot, pulling it through the back of my hat.

The bus stopped a block away from Taco Bell. Jimmy would be thrilled to see me. The 10:00 p.m. to 4:00 a.m. shift was truly a special time. Jimmy would share his coffee breath, I would share my general disdain for humanity, and if we were extra fortunate, a college freshman would throw up in the dining room. Just to keep us on our toes.

Bar-rush customers were the absolute worst.

"You're in drive-thru." A greasy lock of hair stuck to Jimmy's shiny forehead. He gave the order to my chest, as covered and shapeless as it was in my uniform. One of these days I was going to slit his throat. "Glad to see your cramps are gone."

I grabbed a headset from the backroom. "Glad to see you still haven't managed to take a shower in the two months we've worked together."

While Jimmy was technically my superior, I could not abide by giving respect to a man who had amassed an enormous collection of boogers under register four.

His expression turned sourer than the pit stains on his uniform. "Lose the attitude, or I'll find another deadbeat dropout to replace you."

"I'd like to see you try." I flashed my teeth, but he didn't even flinch. Guess Jimmy didn't have a lot to fear from death, either. "How about we just don't talk for the rest of the night. We'll make it game. You can pretend I'm smiling at customers; I can pretend you aren't holed up in your office because you want to look for porn on your phone. It's a win-win."

His upper lip, beaded with sweat, curled in disgust. Occasionally he tried to put on the boss hat and exert some authority. It was amusing at best. "You're lucky I don't have the staff to fire you tonight."

"I bet you say that to all the girls." I walked away before I did something regrettable. Like tear off his head. Jimmy irritated me on a normal basis, but after running into Elton and stressing about my heirloom, I was in no mood for even a casual amount of shit.

Stewart and Toby, the two line cooks, said hi to me, and I ignored them. After two months of working with me, they still hadn't gotten the hint that I didn't like to play those getting-to-know-you games. I stuck to my corner, rung up orders, and did the bare minimum until I could leave. That was really the most that could be expected of me, considering what I got paid.

Living in a college town meant every night had a bar rush. No one got sick in the dining room, but we did have someone pass out face-first in their Nachos BellGrande. Never a dull moment. Once we slowed down, Jimmy sent the line cooks home. The lobby closed hours ago, and I clocked out to take my dinner break with only an hour left on my shift.

Jimmy came up behind me, closer than I found comfortable from people I actually liked. I took a step forward just to put a few more inches between us, my stomach bumping up against the drive-thru ledge. I could smell the cheap whiskey on his breath and the discount TV dinner in his blood. His poor eating habits were the only thing that had saved him thus far.

"How come I never seen your parents pick you up or drop you

off?" He touched the end of my hair. "Seems like they don't care much about you."

Of course Jimmy was the type to think making me feel bad about myself was a form of flirting. "They like me enough to give me space. I'm giving you two seconds to walk away."

"I think you're lying. You know what I see under all that attitude?" He ran a finger down the sleeve of my shirt. "A scared little girl just begging for attention."

"One." I could taste his death in the air. The anticipation of the kill hummed in my veins.

"I could care about you if you were a little nicer to me." His finger reached my elbow, and he hissed in a quick breath from the chill of my skin.

"Two." If it weren't for the promise I made myself when I'd first been turned, Jimmy would've been dead already. When he chuckled under his breath, I faced him with a barbed-wire smile. "Time's up."

I grabbed him by the throat and dragged him over to the large sink in back. His eyes popped out of his head, and he scratched at my hands with his dirty fingernails. Little nicks in my skin that healed quickly. I sunk my teeth into his neck and gagged. His blood tasted like garlic salt and whatever kind of meat paste made up the McRib.

Since I didn't need to feed, I tore his neck open and watched as his blood swirled down the drain. The stainless steel turned a glossy red that would easily wash away. Nice and neat. Bubbles of air gurgled out of his windpipe. Though not drinking the life out of Jimmy made for a prolonged and painful death, I couldn't bring myself to feel any amount of remorse. He struggled beneath my grip, kicking his toothpick legs in vain, unable to scream.

Once the last trace of life left his body, I dropped him on the floor and kicked him out of the way. A slow clap had me whirling around. Ida stood beside the chicken steamer, the remnants of her own dinner glistening on her fangs. She gave me a wide grin. Blood dribbled down her chin and dripped onto the floor. She carried a dead-eyed human head under her arm like she was on her way to Gothic volleyball practice.

"For all the grief you give Rose about bringing kills home," I said, nodding at the head.

"I'm making a little something for the kids in the neighborhood, and clearly, this guy isn't alive anymore." Her voice held a note of exasperation, like I should've understood the difference. "I didn't realize you were the type to kill for sport."

"I'm not." I dug the toe of my shoe into Jimmy's flexible spine. "This one thought it would be cute to put his hands on me in the drive-thru."

"Right. Your kill code." Ida had exchanged an amused smirk with Rose when I tried to explain the nature of my kills to them the previous night. Those two had no such moral grounds and killed without restraint or remorse. Ida licked her teeth, closing her eyes with a happy sigh as she took her last taste of whoever had been on the menu tonight. "Do you need help disposing the body?"

"Nope." I hauled Jimmy's corpse into the office and dumped him in his sticky chair, then erased the security tape. "That should take care of it."

I'd have to quit, just to avoid questions from well-meaning coworkers, but at least I clocked out a solid five minutes before time of death. The police would scratch their heads over how Jimmy had gotten his neck ripped off by a wild animal in the middle of a Taco Bell, they might even wonder where I'd gone after I clocked out and why I didn't return, but they'd never suspect a five-foot-three-inch girl with bad hair and apple-dumpling cheeks could be so deadly. I was my own best cover.

"Guess you're out of a job now. That sucks." Ida looked around, jumping when some of the water popped out of the chicken pan like a deep-sea tentacle. "Or does it?"

"It's fine. I can always get another job." After I stole a new identity off an out-of-towner at one of the bars. Fast-food jobs were endless and plentiful. But now that I didn't have to rent a room at the motel, I'd be okay for a bit. "Are you here by yourself?"

"Yeah. I got hungry, and Rose is buried in research." Ida scratched the back of her neck. "She told me to fill you in on what we found, but I probably shouldn't do that here."

"Good point." Taco Bell wasn't exactly the ideal place to plan a murder.

We left the back door open and headed toward downtown. Halfway down the street, Ida stopped walking and faced me. "Just as a heads-up." She held up the head she had tucked under her arm and grinned, promptly dropping it again when I didn't return her smile. "Anyway. Rose stresses out every time you lose your shit, so try to act like you're keeping it together."

"I lost my shit one time." And I had a feeling I'd never live it down.

"Be that as it may, she thinks you're one bad bit of news away from walking, and we can't afford to lose you. We've waited thirty years for this."

"I'll keep it together, okay?" While I got that I didn't have as much time invested as they did, we all had the exact same things at stake. "I'm a partner in this, not someone you're dragging along. Don't treat me like I'm a child you have to subdue."

"Noted." She let it go, for which I was grateful.

We arrived back at the apartment to find Rose sitting on the couch, sifting through the papers she'd spread out over the coffee table. Most looked like official documents, birth certificates, bank statements, and personal rep papers. She jumped when we came through the door. "You're home early."

"I quit," I said at the same time Ida said, "She killed her boss."

"For the record, that's not my boss." I pointed to the head under Ida's arm.

"I'm not worried about the head," Rose said as Ida deposited it in the refrigerator. "We have bigger problems. Frankie neglected to tell us what happens if we destroy our heirlooms."

"Something happens?" I took a seat next to Rose on the couch. As far as I knew, we only needed our heirlooms for the transformation. Of course, I got most of my knowledge from Elton, who probably wasn't motivated to tell me too much about them.

Ida leaned against the refrigerator. "Do you know why you needed an heirloom?"

"Yes." I didn't appreciate the way she asked me that, the way a patient teacher would ask a student falling behind to slowly recite the alphabet. "It's how we retained our humanity."

Heirlooms kept us tethered to our living selves while we died by preserving who we had been at the time of death. All that we could've or would've become died with us. Not only did we physically stay the same, we never mentally aged, either. We became little more than solid-mass ghosts, wandering the world in constant stasis.

"That's part of it." Rose picked at the pimple on her chin. The one she died with and would be stuck with for all eternity. "But we retained our humanity through memory. When people die, they move on to something else. Obviously, we don't know what, but we do know their memories don't go with them. Our heirlooms remembered for us."

"Okay." I didn't quite know the whole of it, but I didn't see why that made a difference.

"You need to lay it out more plainly," Ida said to Rose. "If we destroy our heirlooms, we'll lose our living memories. That's what Frankie didn't tell us."

"Wait. What?" I didn't have the happiest childhood, but my

memories were all I had of my life. I was the only one keeping me from being forgotten forever. If my memories died, it would be like I'd never been here at all. "How is that possible?"

"The dead aren't supposed to know their living histories," Rose said. "We cheated the system, and if we want to end Elton, that is what we'll have to give up."

"We'll still have our memories from after we died." Ida wouldn't meet my gaze, opting instead to scrape her nail against some peeling plaster next to the refrigerator, letting the little flakes rain to the floor. "But the people and places we knew before will be wiped away. All we'll have left is our immortality."

Rose frowned at the mess Ida was in the process of making. "It's fair if you want to take a moment to think about what you'll be giving up."

I opened my mouth to make a joke about my memories not being all that great, anyway, but I was suddenly hit with the little things that never meant much to me before, but probably would if I no longer had them. The feel of ice cream melting on my tongue. The rare times my mom did something nice for me, like that time she called in sick to work so she could take me to see *The Muppet Movie* in the theater. The first time Stacey sat at my lunch table and made me feel like I wouldn't always be alone. All of it gone. I'd only have my memories of living with Elton and my night shifts at Taco Bell.

How depressing.

I'd been unhappy in my life. My mom mostly paid attention to me when she wanted to use me in her war against the mothers of my classmates, who then turned around and hated me, or feared people enough to pretend like they hated me, and I didn't have any grand plans for my senior year. But I also had Friday night Skee-Ball with Stacey, and Pizza Tuesdays, and Pete of Pete's Pets always let me snuggle the kittens, even though he knew I'd never buy one. I might not have been big and important. I was never going to be prom queen or in the Ice Capades, but it was my life, and it was worth remembering.

"Are you okay?" Rose put her hand on my arm, and I breathed in her clean-cotton scent.

"There's about a thousand ways I could answer that question," I said. "Did either of you suspect that you'd have to give up your memories for this?"

"No." Rose hugged her midsection. "I had no idea that's what it would cost, and I'll understand if you don't want to go through with it."

If we did go through with it, what would Rose do with her pictures? Would she keep that living tomb of regret she carried with her from town to town? I didn't have any pictures. Only my memories, but even some of those had started to blur over the years. I remembered the bad times. Those were always easiest to recall. And maybe I kept those memories closest so I wouldn't have to feel anything about the good times. It made immortality infinitely more tolerable when I could convince myself I hadn't left anything behind.

"What about you?" I nodded to the photo album. "Won't you miss them?"

"I already miss them. Every day. Maybe it'll be better, not knowing what I gave up for the love that turned out to be a lie. Maybe it won't hurt me anymore."

"Maybe." I touched the edge of the blue cover, the daisies painted on it with so much care. Rose had complicated feelings about her family, but she loved them. "Or maybe it will always ache. Like a phantom limb."

"I'm scared." Rose's simple statement touched on my own fears in the most visceral way. Everything about immortality scared me, but the memory of myself had been an anchor to keep me grounded. Without it, I didn't know what I'd become.

"I'm scared too." I squeezed her hand.

"Me too." Ida pulled the living-room chair closer and placed her hand over ours.

"I'm scared I'll open my photo album and it won't mean anything to me," Rose said. "I'm scared it will, and I won't know what to do with those feelings because I can't remember. Before today, I questioned if it was worth it. I still don't know if it's worth it."

"What about Parker?" I asked.

Ida held my gaze, her dark eyes heavy and serious. "If we don't go through with it, you know what will happen. That song always stays the same."

"I don't think we have a choice then." It wasn't just about getting free from Elton. Parker was one of us. She became one of us the moment Elton set his sights on her and mistakenly targeted her as weak. We were all hurting in different ways when Elton found us, and we wanted so badly to believe the pretty lies of a pretty boy, but that didn't make us any less deserving of having a full life. Wanting to love and be loved wasn't a weakness.

Rose tipped her head to the side, resting it against my shoulder. The three of us sat there until the sun came up, with each of us holding our memories in our hand.

As we watched them run between our fingers like water.

Chapter Nine

We spent the next few days poring over Rose's research, looking for a way out of losing our memories, when a knock at the door made all three of us jump. We weren't expecting company, let alone in the early hours before dawn. Ida put a finger to her lips and motioned for us to get behind her. While she'd been confident Frankie wouldn't go to Elton with information about what we were up to, I didn't trust anyone in his coven.

Rose gripped my wrist, and I bent my knees, ready to spring, but Ida's posture visibly relaxed once she looked through the peephole. "It's just Parker."

Ida opened the door, where Parker stood in the dark, her shoulders slumped. She looked sadder than a wet box of free kittens. "I'm sorry to bother you."

Rose gave her a warm and welcoming smile. The same smile the wolf probably gave Little Red Riding Hood when he was dressed up like grandma. "You're not bothering us."

"Yes, you are." Ida crossed her arms, and Rose swatted her.

I just stood there staring. I told her she could come over anytime, but I hadn't expected her to actually take me up on it. "Why are you here?"

"Oh." Her cheeks pinked. "I guess I should explain myself. My mom's still at work, third shift, but she gave her ex-boyfriend the key, and he decided to use it. When he stumbled into my room, drunk off his ass, I left." She shook her head as I widened my eyes. "Nothing happened. He didn't know it was my room,

I don't think he even knew it was his ex-girlfriend's apartment. He was pretty wasted." She lifted her hands and let them fall at her side. "I don't know anyone else in town."

"You know Elton," Ida said.

"I don't know where he lives, and I didn't want to see him right now, because he doesn't—" She swallowed. "It's okay. I can go."

"No. Stay." I took half a step toward her, rethought that idea, and took a step back, so I ended up in some kind of weird shuffle dance. Because, apparently, I was going to be forever awkward around this girl. "You can hang out on the couch for now. Or we can go somewhere?"

"Ida." Rose jerked her chin toward her bedroom. Shaking her head, Ida followed Rose out to the balcony, leaving me alone with Parker in the living room.

I shifted my stance, not entirely sure what I was supposed to do. It had been a long time since I'd entertained the notion of "having company." We didn't even have anything to offer her to drink. Thankfully. "Should you call your mom or something?"

"I'm eighteen. I don't need her permission to be out," Parker said.

"I was just suggesting it so she doesn't think you got murdered, but okay."

"Do you like breakfast?" Parker blurted out the words in a rush, like she'd psyched herself up to ask and had to push it out all at once before she lost her nerve. "Because there's a little diner I passed on the way over here, and I could go for some pancakes."

I didn't know how to respond to that. I didn't eat, but I had a feeling that wouldn't be a good lead in, especially because she looked about two seconds away from combusting. "I could go with you?" I phrased it more like a question, giving her an out if she'd only said that so she'd have a handy excuse to leave. "I like the smell of pancakes."

I like the smell of pancakes? For fuck's sake. I wished I still ate food, so

I'd have something handy to stuff into my mouth to stop the talking. Just because my body was dead, didn't mean my brain was too.

"That would be great." She gave me a relieved smile, and oh, no. It was a good thing vampires couldn't be killed by sunlight, because that smile had the power to ruin me.

After letting Rose and Ida know we were leaving, and waving off a dozen questions from Ida, we walked down to the diner between the pharmacy and the consignment shop. It opened at six, and the place already smelled like ninety-nine-cent coffee and Bisquick. We took a seat on brown vinyl seats that had cracked with age. The diner was called Momma's House now, but it used to be called Dave's. The walls that had once been an olive green were now painted butter yellow, but the booths hadn't changed. Stacey and I came here a few times after Friday nights at the arcade. We would order water and eat the free crackers left on the table for soup, and we probably made all the waitresses want to do a murder. Another memory I'd be losing.

Parker pulled the jelly holder in front of her and began making a tiny pyramid out of the strawberry and grape. "I don't think Ida likes me."

"Ida doesn't like anyone." I closed my eyes, and for one brief second, I let myself believe this was just another Friday night with Stacey. It still smelled and sounded the same. The old vinyl crackled beneath my seat, and I opened my eyes to the real world. "Do you want to talk about why your mom is giving your apartment key to drunk men?"

"I'd rather not." Parker pulled a bowl of individual creams in front of her and began adding them to the pyramid. "I feel bad enough showing up on your doorstep so early."

A waitress wearing jeans and a jean shirt came by to take Parker's order. Her face was rough and lined with age, but I still recognized Megan Bear underneath that leathered exterior. The girl who had made my life a living hell in middle school. Time and tanning beds had not done her any favors. Still, my heart raced, and my palms began to sweat on instinct as I glanced between her and Parker, like Megan still had the power to keep people from sitting with me.

She took Parker's order, then paused when she got to me. She tapped her pen against her order pad, and I sunk lower in my seat. Just like I had in school. Back when I tried to shrink myself until she stopped seeing me.

Her gaze roamed my face, flickering between confusion and recognition. "Forgive me, sweetie, but you look familiar. Do I know your momma?"

She knew my momma all right, but I very much doubted she meant the woman who had once dated her dad. "I don't think so. I'm new here."

"Sure. You just look like someone I used to know." She shook her head, her helmet of sprayed curls staying in place as she tapped her order pad again. A bold move on her part to keep the same hairstyle she wore in high school by choice. "What can I get you?"

"Water." Even though I wouldn't be drinking it.

Once Megan left, Parker tilted her head. "She looked at you like she knew you."

"You know how it is in towns like this. Everyone thinks they're supposed to know everyone." I tried to laugh it off, but I sounded more like a strangled cat.

"You're not new here." Apparently, Parker was in the mood to press this morning. "Why didn't you tell the waitress you used to live here?"

"It's complicated and not worth spending time on." My fingers brushed against a loose thread of vinyl on the torn seat, and I wrapped my finger around it. "Why do you care about what I choose to tell strangers about me?"

Parker ran her thumb over the chips and scratches on the table. "Because she didn't look at you like you're a stranger. Have you ever been to this diner before?"

"No." I pulled the string around my finger tighter. "Maybe she saw me at the store or something. I don't know why she recognized me."

"I would've been willing to buy that"—Parker gave me a smug look that would've been annoying on anyone else—"if you didn't look like you recognized her too."

"Look." I rested my hands on the table, and Parker's eyes widened as she stared at them. I glanced down, realizing I ripped half my finger off on the vinyl thread. Shit. I snatched it back under the table. It was like a paper cut, something that didn't really hurt until you noticed it. "Maybe I recognized the waitress because she lives around here. Who knows?"

"Your finger." Parker's voice shook, and she'd gone pale.

"What about it?" I put my hand back on the table, where it had already healed. I turned them both over and only felt mildly bad for lying. It was for her own good.

"I. You." She opened her mouth and closed it again. Though she appeared willing to let the missing finger go, she had something in her craw she was trying to work out. "How do you, Rose, and Ida live in that apartment?"

"I don't really live there." I didn't really live anywhere at all. Elton liked to move, and money for a place had always been hard to come by. The dingy motel I rented by the week had become more my home in the last three months than anywhere else.

"Semantics," Parker said. "Where is your mom? Or theirs? How is it that three high-school girls can live on their own, and no one thinks that's weird?"

"Why do you think that is?" I sat back, crossing my arms. She asked a lot of questions for someone who didn't want answers. "What do you really want to know?"

Megan came back with my water and Parker's coffee. She frowned as she set my water in front of me but didn't try to place my face again. Her eyes kept flicking to my hair, though. She spit enough wads of paper into it to recognize the awful crimps. Or maybe I was reading too much into it, and she was just hoping the '80s were coming back so she could relive her glory days.

"You never went to Glen River West, did you?" Parker asked as soon as Megan left.

"I did a long time ago. Longer than anyone there would remember, except maybe Mr. Stockard." I stared at the cars slowly meandering down the road, like they hadn't fully woken up yet. "So did Elton, but you're a smart girl. I'm sure you've figured that out already."

"You didn't order anything for breakfast. I've never seen Elton eat, either. Normal people won't go near him, and they go out of their way to avoid you, Rose, and Ida too."

I shrugged. "Are you looking for an apology for that?"

"I'm looking for a reason." She slammed her hand on the table, rattling the silverware. "You say Elton is dangerous, but why? Why does it feel like you're all playing some kind of sick joke on me? I've got enough going on in my life, in case you haven't noticed. I don't need this."

"You know what we are." I lowered my voice as I leaned forward. "Deep down, you know, and it scares you. It should scare you."

Parker took a large gulp of her lukewarm coffee, which she'd watered down with two creamers and six sugars. "If you are . . ." She stopped, and I could see her gathering thoughts as her gaze darted around the diner, landing anywhere but on me. "What do you want?"

"I want you to stay safe. Until we can do what we need to do."

"Which is . . . ?"

I flashed my fangs as I smiled, and she shuddered. The first sign of fear she'd shown around me. "I like you, Parker."

"You do? Why?" She groaned and stared up at the ceiling. "I swear, I'm not begging for compliments. Could I possibly sound more pathetic?"

"You're not pathetic." I smiled to myself, once again struck by how much she reminded me of me. "I like that you're self-aware, but you're not an asshole about it. You seem kind, and not the fake kind where you're trying to get recognition." I cleared my throat. "But that's just an observation. I don't know you that well."

She blinked a few times. "That's the nicest thing anyone has ever said to me."

"That's really sad."

She brightened up. "Isn't it?"

I closed my eyes again, but this time I didn't imagine I was back in this diner with Stacey in 1987. I wanted to be exactly where I was now. It was so easy to be around Parker.

Megan dropped off Parker's pancakes, and this trip through, she avoided eye contact altogether. I had a feeling I wouldn't be getting an e-invite to the class reunion any time soon.

I used to dream about meeting Megan again, when I first left Glen River. Funny enough, it had been in this type of scenario, where she'd be serving me in some capacity. Now that it was happening in real life, though, it was a thousand times less satisfying. Like most fantasies I'd pictured in my mind. While I wasn't sorry to see life had been hard on her, I found myself more indifferent to her than anything else. Even if my emotions didn't move on from the time I died, some things inevitably changed with distance. This was one.

My untouched water glass dripped condensation while Parker finished her food. After she took her bill to the register, we stepped outside. We both turned toward the horizon, where the last of the night sky began to wink out with the daylight.

"You don't have issues with the sun." She said it as a statement, as close as she'd come to admitting what I was. "It makes me second-guess what I think I know."

"Don't believe everything you see in the movies." A half smile tugged my lips, the closest I'd come to confirming her suspicions. "Are you heading to school now?"

"Yeah." She tucked her hands into her pockets. "What about you?"

"I'm not going to school." I'd rather shave my bikini line with a chainsaw.

"I didn't think you would. Should I tell Mr. Stockard you said hi?"

"Please do." He might not have been the cool teacher any more, but he'd mourned me when I left. There weren't many people who could say the same. "And if you see a girl with frizzy black hair, pale as death, with gold eyes that look perpetually surprised, tell her I'm looking for her. She'll probably be wearing a scarf or a turtleneck."

"Oh, you mean the fake vampire?" Parker rolled her eyes.

I grabbed her arm, with a little more force than I intended. "What do you mean?"

"That's what she calls herself, anyway. She hangs around the dirt hill by the school, where all the smokers go." She glanced down to where my fingers had a firm grip on her upper arm but didn't try to release my hold. "She has a small following, mostly the people who wear all black and shop at Hot Topic. She goes by Lilith but forgets to answer to it half the time."

"She hangs out at the school?" That didn't sound like Stacey. She hated school when she was required to go. She wouldn't go for fun. What kind of con was she trying to pull?

"I don't think she goes to Glen River West." Parker pursed her lips. "In fact, I'm sure she doesn't, but she definitely has friends who go there. I hear them talk about her in class."

Vampires didn't have mortal friends. I glanced at Parker. Okay, vampires didn't usually have mortal friends, but these weren't usual circumstances. Whatever Stacey was doing at the high school, I was certain she didn't intend to endear herself to the class of 2022.

Looked like I'd be headed back to the school after all.

Chapter Ten

Parker took the bus to school, and I waited until she made it on safely before running back to the apartment. I flung open the front door with so much force, the knob punched a hole in the wall. "I found Stacey. Or at least, I know where she'll be today."

Rose looked up from her notes. "Excellent. We've run into problems with my heirloom. Ida's is easy to get but much more unpleasant, so we could use some good news."

"What problems?" We didn't need problems. We had enough problems just trying to track down my heirloom. With only a few weeks to collect everything we needed, we couldn't afford to have any more setbacks.

"It's in a safe-deposit box. I paid for a hundred years, at First National up the road. My grandmother's silver combs were the most valuable thing I owned. It made sense at the time, but they won't let me in without ID, even if I have the key."

"ID is a thing banks usually require."

"Well, that wasn't a thing they required in 1954." Rose stacked her notes with a huff. "Believe me, if I'd known how vital those combs were going to be, I never would've put them in that box. We can't risk them thinking I'm dead, so we'll have to find another way in."

"Are you saying we have to break into a bank vault? Before the full moon?"

"Yes." Rose used her most prim-and-proper-lady voice, and I wanted to scream into the void. The rolling dumpster fire just kept picking up speed.

I pinched the bridge of my nose, where a headache would surely be forming if I were still capable of getting headaches. "And Ida's heirloom?"

"That's not my story to tell." Rose glanced at Ida as she came out of the bedroom. "I'm going to wash up. The two of you should talk."

"I heard you found Stacey. Good work." Ida took a seat on the couch, her black-cherry scent trailing in her wake. "I assume Rose told you the complications with her heirloom."

"She did." I hesitated on my next question. Ida struck me as more of a private person. Rose had been warm and open from the start, but Ida didn't share anything of herself unless she got something in return. "She also told me yours will be unpleasant but didn't say why."

"I appreciate her trying to protect me, but I'm not that sensitive about it." Ida twirled the chain around her neck, which had a finger bone hanging from it. "It was a long time ago."

When she didn't say anything else, I pushed a little more. "What is your heirloom?"

"A glass-and-silver figure of a horse, made for me by my younger sister, Bea. She was the sun to my clouds." The ghost of a smile touched her lips, but sadness lingered there. "We always thought her hobby fitting, seeing as how she was also fragile. Born small and never really quite caught up. She died shortly after I'd been turned."

"I'm sorry." The universal empty words to give someone when you weren't quite sure what else to say. Even though her sister would still be dead, even if she lived a full life, losing someone you cared about had to hurt. Not that I was overly familiar with those feelings. "Did you get a chance to say goodbye?"

"In my own way." When I didn't say anything, she glanced at me like she wasn't sure if she wanted to go on. I had a feeling no matter how much she told me today, she'd still keep the more personal details to herself. "We hadn't left town yet when she caught a bad cold that turned into pneumonia. I couldn't face my family after what I'd become, so I snuck into the funeral home after dark to pay my respects. She was my heart. The person I thought of as I was dying. So, I placed my heirloom inside her coffin."

I covered my mouth with my hands. "Oh, God."

"Yep." Ida gave me a grim smile. "That's pretty much the reaction I expected."

"We have to dig up her grave?" While she likely wouldn't be much more than dust at this point, the idea of violating that space made my stomach churn.

"We need to do it soon." Ida pressed her lips together, her dark eyes like hardened steel. "Elton knows what I did with my heirloom, and I can't count on Frankie holding out information from him forever. He doesn't always like Elton, but he won't help us kill him."

"Should we go to the graveyard first?" Even though I wanted no part of this, I wouldn't make Ida face that alone. "We can track down Stacey later. Elton doesn't know she has my heirloom."

"He doesn't?" She blinked at me in surprise. "Didn't you turn her the night you were turned? He must've seen what happened."

"He threw a temper tantrum over me mourning someone who allegedly tried to kill him, even though we both knew she never stood a chance."

I could still feel the spray of water on my face as he stamped his foot in a puddle and demanded we leave at once. When I refused, he had the nerve to act like the injured party. It never occurred to him that I could've had feelings for someone other than him. That should've been one of many, many red flags.

"I could've had any girl in this school, and I chose you."

That was how he phrased it to me when he left in a huff. Like I was *lucky* to have his attention, like I was *lucky* I'd given up my mortal trappings for a life spent at his beck and call. Not once, not one time, had he ever considered himself lucky to be with me.

"That sounds like Elton." Ida stood and squeezed my shoulder, the most outward affection she'd ever shown me. "I shouldn't even be surprised by his shit anymore, but for some reason, I always am. As to your question, no, we shouldn't go to the graveyard yet. We'll need the cover of night. You know where to find Stacey. We'll deal with her first."

What she didn't have to say was that she also needed time to mentally prepare for what we had to do. She might've waved it off like it was a long time ago, but I recognized that emptiness in her gaze, the place deep within her that still hurt for a girl who was dead and buried a hundred years ago. Maybe I was closer to Ida than I'd thought.

Rose came out of her bedroom in a fresh dress with a cherry print in the rockabilly style she tended to favor. You could take the girl out of 1954 . . . "Are we ready to head out?"

"I'm all set." I turned to Ida. "You'll be thrilled to know we're taking the bus again."

She groaned. "One of these days, I'm going to kill someone in broad daylight on that thing, and then you'll both be sorry."

"Come on." I hooked my arm through hers. "You'll be able to sit close to people and make them really uncomfortable on purpose. Should be fun for you."

The bus hadn't been terrible. Ida flashed her fangs at three people and only threatened to kill one, so all in all, a pretty tame ride. We made it to the school with ten minutes to spare before the first-period bell rang.

"Parker said Stacey would be by the dirt hill where everyone goes to smoke." Nothing like that existed when I went to school here, so I hoped it would be easy to spot. I had to assume it wouldn't be much more than some dirt in hill form. I eyed the school, looming like a brick mausoleum across the street. "Once we end this, I'm never coming back here again."

"I wanted to come back once." Rose's gray eyes became soft as summer nightfall. "He said no, but I wish I'd pushed him harder." She shook her head and her expression returned to that of polite disinterest. "I suppose it doesn't matter now."

"You're right, it doesn't matter," Ida snapped. "There is nothing here for us, and anything we used to feel for this place will be gone with our memories."

Before the two of them could start an argument, I pointed to the hill straight ahead. It wasn't entirely dirt. A few sad weeds clung to the surface. But the real giveaway was the little tendrils of smoke that peeked over the top before being whisked away by the wind.

If Stacey was behind that hill, these would be the first words we spoke to each other in over thirty years. What did I say to someone who had known me inside and out but was now little more than a stranger? How would I be able to face her with the weight of all that time between us? The guilt was always there, a gentle tap on the dark corridors of my mind, a reminder that there were pieces of me missing. Pieces I'd given to another.

I steeled myself for the confrontation I'd never be fully prepared for as I rounded the other side of the hill. Stacey had her back to me, but I had no trouble recognizing her frizzy hair, which had been pulled into a smooth knot at the base of her neck. She wore a red scarf decorated by tiny skulls. Guilt, guilt, guilt; it slammed into me in waves, washing over me, threatening to drag me under. She had been the only person I could count on before Elton moved to town, and I did this to her. I made her into whatever she'd become while trying to survive.

She had her hand wrapped around the neck of a kid with black eyeliner and a spiked collar. He dropped his cigarette as Stacey sunk her teeth into him and drank deeply. Though he must've been in pain, his face was pinched in a way that suggested he was doing his very best to convince himself he liked it. He'd be dead within minutes. Once the final strings on his lifeless body had been cut, she kissed his cheek before dumping him in the dirt. It reminded me of how she used to make little snowmen out of her mashed potatoes before biting their heads off.

"After all these years, still playing with your food," I said.

Stacey turned around slowly, and I sucked in a sharp breath. Disinterest flickered over her features. The distance of every single decade stood between us. That moment right there was as close as I'd ever get to feeling the fifty years I'd walked this earth.

Her features hadn't changed since the night she died. Same jutting cheekbones, narrow nose, and protruding amber eyes that always looked surprised. But the way she carried herself, her expression, not to mention the heavy black eyeliner and dark-maroon lips, were all brand-new. The all-black ensemble clashed with the image I had of the girl who used to wear more neon than a crossing guard. I didn't recognize the person before me, even if she technically wore my best friend's face. She hadn't just accepted the vampire life; she was thriving in it.

"Holly." She licked the bloody point of one of her fangs. "Wish I could say it's good to see you, but we both know I'd be lying."

"Stacey." I inclined my head, keeping my gestures nonchalant, even as a storm of emotions lashed through me. "Or should I call you Lilith now?"

"Been spying on me, have you? I didn't know you cared." She pouted, her thin mouth still glistening from the leftovers of her kill. "You just had to crimp your hair the night you died, didn't you? What a pity."

"Not nearly as much of a pity as your neck."

Her eyes flashed. That chasm between us grew wider. I shouldn't have made that comment about her neck, but she didn't seem to have any interest in playing nice, either.

Maybe I should've been buttering her up, considering she likely had possession of the one thing I needed most, but I couldn't stand the way she looked at me with that disdain. I saved her life, damn it. And this whole time I thought she'd been wandering around, horrified by what she'd become, when in actuality, she seemed to be relishing it. Yet in all the cities we'd lived in, over all the years, she never once tried to contact me.

I smothered the hurt with anger. A survival tactic I'd learned long before I ever became a vampire. As my gaze hardened on Stacey, Ida drilled her elbow into my back. I'd forgotten about her and Rose for a moment.

"You brought friends." A cruel and bloody smile touched Stacey's lips. "How adorable."

"This is Rose and Ida." I motioned to them like I was a flight attendant and they were my exit doors. "They're also exes of Elton."

"How did that guy manage to sucker three of you? Jesus, he wasn't that good-looking." She sneered at the three of us. "But then again, I guess the desperate aren't that picky."

"Can I pull off her arms now?" Ida whispered beside me.

"If you came here to taunt me, I'm afraid I'll have to pencil you in for next week." She checked her watch. "I'm very busy these days, and I don't have time to reminisce."

"Yet you've had time to stalk me all over town." I gave her my sweetest smile, the one that promised I'd see her in hell, but I'd bring a dessert to pass.

"I wanted to know why you dragged me back here." Her clipped tone was sharper than the razor edge of her fangs. "Thanks for warning me that I'd be stuck trailing behind your sorry ass for all of eternity, by the way. It was real fun figuring that one out."

Part of me wanted to apologize for all the things I should've known or considered before I turned her, but the other part of me just wanted to get my locket and be done. "I'm not here to fight with you, Stacey. I'm in a situation that might be of interest to you, but we can't really talk out in the open. If you'll come with us—"

"Nope." Stacey held up a hand. "I'm not going anywhere with you. How do I know the three of you won't tie me up and starve me?"

"I'm not going to starve you." I couldn't keep the exasperation out of my voice. Even though we hadn't stayed friends, she knew me better than that. I had no interest in becoming more of a monster than necessary. "I can't say more out in the open, but would you feel more comfortable if we went to your place?"

She was alone now, but I had no idea if she'd hooked up with a small coven. I sincerely hoped she operated alone. Offering to walk into her nest with no guarantee that she even had my heirloom wasn't my brightest idea, but I had no alternatives. She obviously didn't trust me, and I wasn't willing to say more than this so close to where Elton spent his days. I had to take the chance.

Stacey stared at the three of us for a small eternity before finally relenting. "Okay, fine. We'll go to my place. But if you make trouble for me, I will find a way to starve you all."

I breathed out a sigh of relief. We'd just gotten one step closer to ending this.

Chapter Eleven

Stacey heaved the dead-eyed Goth boy over her shoulder and carried him to the river, where she dumped his body. I was long past caring what would happen to the people we left behind. It used to bother me. Killing had been one of the hardest things to get used to when I first turned, but I found a system that made it easier for me. These days, I hardly gave it a thought anymore. Just part of the food chain.

Stacey took us on a meandering route through a residential neighborhood, close to where she used to live. A toddler with haunted eyes sat on the uneven steps of a front porch wearing nothing but a full diaper and drinking Mountain Dew from a bottle. She watched us pass without so much as a flinch. Too young to already be so jaded.

I recognized the area but didn't want to confirm my worst suspicions about where we were going, so I kept my mouth shut while we trudged toward a more wooded part of the neighborhood. A small forest grew wild behind the houses on this street, unable to be leveled because of the wetlands at its center. At the end of the cul-de-sac, overgrowth swallowed the remaining sidewalk. The rooftop of a house peeked over the tangle of short trees and bushes out front. It wasn't until she pushed open a gate choked with ivy and vines that I recognized the place I'd thought of as a second home while I'd been alive.

The white siding had turned gray. Fat flakes of peeling vinyl littered the ground like ash. Broken windows smeared with dirt watched over the scraggly yard like dead, filmy eyes. A crooked shutter creaked in the wind. Not even the haunted house that went up every Halloween on the east side of town could as effectively create the creepiness that oozed through every crack. It wouldn't have surprised me to learn that actual ghosts had taken up residence there.

"What happened to your house?" I walked up the front steps where I'd once spent long and lazy summer days drinking lemonade. The dry wood splintered beneath our feet.

Stacey gave me a look that could've melted the skin off my bones. Apparently, her anger hadn't cooled a bit since our happy reunion. "A kidnapping and double murder tends to bring down the property value."

Stacey and I both lost enough blood the night we became vampires to be ruled a double murder without our bodies, and since Stacey's mom left the slider unlocked, the investigators determined we'd been kidnapped. If Stacey hadn't followed me, everyone would've assumed I'd been a runaway. Which had been my original plan when I left her house with a backpack full of clothes.

My spine stiffened. "I hope you're not seriously suggesting I take responsibility for this."

Stacey whipped around and grabbed my throat, her movements so swift it took me by surprise. Pain radiated through my neck, and a burning sensation fused the muscles in my back to my spine as she snapped my bones. "If you had stayed at home instead of sneaking out of my house to meet your boyfriend, none of this would've happened. Do you even know what life was like for my mom after we died? She blamed herself for our deaths. She never got over it."

I didn't know because I made it a point to never look back. I chose death. This was my eternity now. And taking on more regret wouldn't do a thing to change that. Ida broke Stacey's wrist, forcing her to release her hold, and my neck healed within a minute. I tilted my head from side to side as the lingering soreness drained out of me.

"Please don't tell me your mom still lives here," I said.

"So nice of you to ask about my mom, but you're about thirty-fours years too late to give a shit." She clenched her jaw, wearing her molars down to nubs as she looked like she was fighting an internal war with herself. "She died ten years ago. I couldn't even go to her funeral because I'm attached to wherever you are, and you were in Texas."

"I'm sorry." I thought a lot about the consequences of immortality over the years, but not enough about the ripples that rolled over everything we left behind. "If you had come to me—"

"You would've what? Talked your boyfriend into coming home?" She faced me with fangs bared, like she might rip out my throat, and I wasn't entirely sure if I'd try to stop her if she went through with it. "Tell me, when did he ever do one thing that wasn't for his benefit?"

Never. When we first moved to New Orleans, he killed a couple in the French Quarter so we could have their honeymoon suite for the week. He drew a bath, added some candles, and made it seem as if he'd gone to so much trouble to make me happy, like I owed him a favor because he turned on the hot water and lit some matches. In actuality, he set me up with the bath so he could have fun on Bourbon Street without having to drag his girlfriend along. We got in our first fight the morning he came home smelling like he'd spent the night rolling around in a pile of mortals, and he still wouldn't admit any wrongdoing. He didn't need to check in with me. It was my fault for being worried. I was too sensitive.

From that point on, I learned every one of his grand gestures came with a condition.

"No one bought the house? I know it's a fixer-upper, but . . ." Ida put her hand on the molding around the front door, and it crumbled to dust at her feet. "Okay, forget I said anything."

"It used to be in better shape, but it's been a tough sell since it's rumored to be haunted by my ghost. Which is just ironic enough to amuse me." Stacey smiled at the sky, cracking the blood that had dried on her chin. "Anyway, it's technically for sale, but I'm not concerned about a realtor showing a loving family with two point five kids the open floor plan."

She opened the front door, and I gasped. Actual loss of breath. All my memories of searching for clues about Edie's life or curling up on the couch to watch MTV went out the window. Nothing of the house I'd known existed. Stacey had transformed the place into some kind of over-the-top vampire den from every cheesy B movie ever made. Red velvet curtains covered half the walls, black iron candelabras dripping black wax sat on a dusty piano with missing keys. A coffin had been propped in the corner. Where did one even procure a coffin in this economy? Gauzy sheets of black satin covered a four-poster bed that had been shoved into the corner. Skulls that looked like they'd come from a natural-history museum gift shop were piled in the fireplace. It was as if Stacey had watched every vampire movie ever made and vomited out the contents.

It was so gaudy, I didn't know where to look without making a face.

Two teens dressed in all black were making out on a second mattress with red satin sheets that had been dumped in the middle of the living-room floor. Three other teens dressed in—surprise!—all black passed around a crumpled can that smelled like skunky dirt, while another teen sat huddled in a corner crawling with black mold. He'd just pierced his lip with a rusty safety pin and it was already swelling and turning an unpleasant shade of green. Stacey took stock of them all with a hungry gleam in her eye, the way a farmer might assess their cattle.

She clapped her hands once, bringing her tiny cult to attention. "Leave us at once." Her voice had taken on just a hint of Transylvanian accent, and Rose had to slap a hand over her mouth to keep from laughing.

The teens shuffled out, but not before they stopped to lavish Stacey with praise and kiss her outstretched hand like she was queen of the damned. It took every ounce of willpower not to roll my eyes. Rose eventually lost her battle to hold in her laugh and ended up snorting through her nose. The ridiculousness of these wannabe misfits was over the top. It was one thing for Rose to bring her kills home, but at least she didn't treat them like pets she had to house train.

As the last teen left, Ida rubbed one of the curtains between her fingers. "You really leaned into that whole vampire thing, didn't you?"

Stacey sniffed as she lifted her nose in the air. "It keeps me occupied."

If she needed to stay busy, why not collect stamps? Or do a puzzle? Or get a Netflix subscription? This went way beyond being bored. She was collecting kids and keeping them on hand like a living buffet. "What the fuck, Stacey?"

"Oh, please. Do not even think about using that tone on me." Stacey sashayed over to the red satin mattress and lay back on it, propping herself up by her elbows. "It's called making the best of a shitty situation. At least I'm not walking around all, 'Boo-hoo, my hot boyfriend didn't love me forever after all, and now I have to sling fast food and live in a roachy motel.'"

That was so not what I sounded like.

And how dare she throw Taco Bell in my face, like there was an abundance of jobs for teenagers out there. "First off, I'm just trying to get by. Secondly, you hate all things vampire."

"You haven't seen me in over thirty years; you don't know what I'm into anymore." Stacey stood and paced the length of the living room. The carpet crunched beneath her feet from whatever had soaked in and dried there. "You did this to me, so you don't get to judge how I spend the eternity I never asked for."

"If it wasn't for me, you would've died in that parking lot." She had the nerve to guilt me, acting like death would've been preferable to being a vampire, only to turn around and embrace the worst clichés like she took lessons from the Count on *Sesame Street*.

"Keep telling yourself that." Stacey whirled on Ida, who had moved in closer, staring intently at her neck. "What do you want?"

"Nothing." Ida twirled a lock of hair around her finger. "Just minding my own business."

"Okay." Rose stepped between us, fully in her element as the peacekeeper. "I think we need to take a minute here. Clearly, you two have unresolved issues."

That was putting it mildly. Clearly, Stacey had learned to adapt to immortality, even if it was in an incredibly crude way. The only reason she kept blaming me was so she could hold it over my head. Not because she was actually sorry she was alive. "I made the right call in turning her, and if she wants an apology for saving her life, it's not going to happen."

"You don't think you owe me an apology for this?" Stacey ripped off her scarf, revealing the gray flaps of skin hanging limply around a gash covered by a thin layer of pinkish scar tissue.

"Cool," Ida breathed. "Can I touch it?"

"No, you can't touch it." Stacey backed away, her face twisting in disgust.

"Knock it off, Ida." Rose grabbed her by the elbow. "Now is not the time to be you."

Just looking at Stacey's torn neck activated my gag reflex. "I suppose I should've gotten your permission before I turned you." I toed at a patch of dry blood on the floor. "But what would you have done in my shoes? You were dying, and I had the means to stop it."

I had a lot of resentment mixed with my guilt when it came to Stacey. Maybe I screwed up, but there was no way I could've let her die. I was a handful of weeks from saying goodbye to every positive memory I had of us, leaving me only with today and the night I turned her, and no understanding of why she'd been so important to save. I didn't need to be her best friend again, but we had to deal with this old wound before it was too late.

"You want to know what I would've done?" Stacey crossed her arms. "I would've listened to you if you had told me a guy I was dating was bad news."

And that's what it would always come back to. She wasn't really mad at me for turning her, horrific neck flap notwithstanding, but she would never forgive me for letting her get killed in the first place. If I'd just walked away from Elton because he made everyone else uncomfortable, we both would've been fine. She'd never understand that's what had drawn me to him in the first place. He had played into that mysterious loner persona, making me believe we were two souls who didn't fit anywhere, except with each other. What a joke.

"We all made that mistake," Rose said quietly. "And we regret it deeply. But how long are you going to keep her feet to the fire over it?"

Stacey turned on Rose, her eyebrows rising with her incredulous expression. "She stayed with him. He murdered me without a second thought, and she stayed."

"I was in love." It was a terrible excuse, but I still couldn't admit the deeper truth out loud. It still shamed me to my core. Yes, I'd been in love, but I'd also been terrified of being alone. As I was dying at his hands, I had regrets. I wanted to stop the process and rewind. But it was too late, and I was too afraid to attempt surviving on my own. "But you were right. He didn't really love me, he just wanted to have me, and now I'm on my own. Feel better?"

"Believe it or not, no." Stacey swatted at Ida, who had lifted a hand like she was going to poke at her neck. "You came here for a reason, so what is it?"

The time had come to show my hand. If she didn't have it, we were screwed. "I need my locket. The one you ripped off my neck the night you died."

Stacey narrowed her eyes. "Why?"

"We need to kill Elton." I could only hope her hate for him endured and that would appeal to her more than withholding something I wanted out of spite. "My locket is a necessary component to get that done."

Stacey paused for a moment, running her finger over a rusty nail poking out of the fireplace mantel, letting it slice open and heal over and over again. "Good one. You can't kill a vampire, though. Something that would've been nice to know before I attempted to stake Elton."

"You can kill one. It's complicated, but not impossible." I ran my hands through my hair, pulling at the roots. "Look, I know you hate me, but don't let that override your common sense. We can end Elton and break the bond that forces us to be in his proximity."

Her nostrils flared. I'd said something to set off her temper again, though I couldn't guess what. After thirty years of zero communication, we were bound to think the worst of each other. "I don't have it," she said.

"You're lying," I said. She wouldn't get rid of Edie's locket. She had to have some level of sentimentality left. She never would've been able to live in this house otherwise.

For the first time since we arrived, Ida tore her gaze away from Stacey's neck. "What did you do with it? It's imperative that we find it."

Stacey turned her back to us, resting her arms on the fireplace mantel. "I tossed it in a rubbish bin in New Orleans. It's probably buried thirty years deep in a landfill."

If I'd had any blood in my face, it would've drained clean away. I recovered quickly enough, schooling my features into casual indifference. I refused to believe she'd tossed my locket away like that. She would've put it somewhere safe; if not for me, then for Edie.

I pulled a nail out of the mantel and scratched our address into the wall. "Now you'll know where to find us if you were mistaken and the locket shows up."

I grabbed Rose and Ida by the elbow and dragged them out the door into the hazy fall sunshine. They sputtered and tried to fight me as I pulled them across the front yard to the sidewalk. As soon as we made it a safe distance away, Ida yanked on my arm hard enough to nearly pull it out of the socket. "What the hell was that?"

"We had to get out of there," I said. "I think she knows where my heirloom is; it might even be somewhere in that broken-down funhouse where she lives."

"Neat." Ida glared at me. "So why did we leave again?"

"Because I pissed her off. I'll explain on the way home."

Withholding my heirloom after I let her know how much I needed it was the easiest way to hurt me. If I had any chance of getting it back, I had to let her make the next move. And I could only hope she still hated Elton more than she'd grown to hate me.

Chapter Twelve

It took some convincing to get Rose and Ida on the bus. Ida wanted to storm back into the house, overpower Stacey, and steal my locket. But if Stacey didn't keep it in the house, we'd never see her, let alone my heirloom, again. She needed a few days to cool off. Ida and Rose didn't trust her, but I knew Stacey. Buried under the thick eyeliner and black clothes was the same girl who collected bells, loved cold-case mysteries, and thought you could never be too old to catch fireflies. No amount of dressing up and playing mistress of the dark to a feeding ground of clueless worshippers would change that.

"That girl has serious issues." Ida pulled a brain out of the refrigerator and plopped it down on some newspaper she'd spread out on the dining-room table. "There's something not right in her head to make her act that way." She took out a steak knife and began carving into the brain, setting aside the sections she'd cut away. "Are you sure something didn't break in her when you did the transformation?"

"It's not like she's the only one with issues." I eyed the pale and squirmy brain on the table. Even when I was furious with Stacey, I still felt the need to defend her.

"To whom are you referring?" Ida plunged her knife into a section of brain, held it up, and grinned as fluid ran down the blade and curled around her wrist.

"Never mind." We all had our own ways of coping with death. "The more important thing here is that Stacey either has my locket or knows where it is."

"How do you know?" Rose had her dishrag out again, and she attacked the beveled glass cabinets with fervor. "Forgive me for being skeptical, if she does that's wonderful news, but I don't want to get my hopes up again."

"I just know, okay?" When Stacey and I were fifteen, we stole some of her mom's vodka because we wanted to see what the big deal was about being drunk. Her mom wouldn't have noticed. Still, as soon as she got home, Stacey acted weird and twitchy until she finally blurted out, unprompted, that someone had broken into the house to steal drinks from the liquor cabinet. Stacey absolutely sucked at lying.

"I still say it was a bad idea to leave so soon." Ida peeled apart the brain, tilting her head as she studied the places she'd carved away, then carefully cut a circle around the top. "There are three of us. We could've taken the heirloom and been done with this."

"And if it's not in the house? Or she somehow got away? We'd never see that locket again." I opened a window over the kitchen sink to let out the foul scent of rotting brain. "This way I still have a chance of talking her into giving it to me."

"I'm going trust that you know her best." Rose grimaced. "I'll feel better when we have the locket in hand, but if you think this is the way we need to go, I'm willing to wait."

What she didn't say, but heavily implied, was that Stacey was on a deadline. If she didn't give us the locket soon, there wasn't anything I could do to stop Rose and Ida from going after it. I didn't even want to think about those consequences.

"Fine." Ida went back to her brain carving, dismissing us both entirely as she focused in on whatever she was trying to do with that thing. "I can wait too, but not forever. If we don't have it in three days, we'll retrieve it ourselves by any means necessary."

"Should we move forward with next steps?" I really didn't want to say, *Let's go dig up your dead sister.* Tiptoeing around it was horrific enough. "Or should we wait until Stacey shows up with the locket?"

Ida set her knife aside, and by the look she gave me, I had a moment where I was pretty certain she debated whether or not to use it on me next. "I'd rather we have a guarantee."

"We'll go in three days," Rose said.

Ida pounded her fist on the table. "We will not go without the locket."

Rose stared Ida down, part warrior, part Disney princess. The portrait of a young 1950s housewife, one broken Jell-O mold away from snapping. "A vote then, if you don't want to be reasonable. Those in favor of getting Ida's heirloom before Frankie sells us out to Elton and he snatches it from under our noses, raise your hand."

Since she put it like that . . .

I tentatively raised my hand, while keeping a careful eye on Ida's knife.

"That settles it." Rose gave a curt nod. "I've been watching the security rotation of the graveyard for two weeks now. They are lightest on staff on Sunday nights. It's our best chance of getting in and out without alerting anyone to our presence."

"Cool." Ida got up, leaving the misshapen brain to ooze on the table. "I need toothpicks and a candle. Don't expect me back any time soon."

She slammed the door on her way out.

Rose pressed a hand to her midsection. "That went better than I expected."

While I agreed with Rose's reasoning, I still sympathized with Ida. Stacey had been the only person I really loved in life, not counting Elton, and if she'd died in the parking lot that night, I would've been hard-pressed to dig her up again. "For the record, I hate all of this."

"It's no picnic for me, either." Rose stared down at Ida's half-finished project before shaking her head and pulling out all the cleaning supplies from under the sink.

I curled up on the couch with a Tessa Dare book, thankful they'd picked an apartment right around the corner from the library. Books had always been my bright spot away from the dark. I couldn't concentrate, though. The constant swoosh, swoosh, swoosh of Rose cleaning and polishing every surface began to drill into my head. My heart started to skip in rhythm, and the urge to feed beat in my veins. I'd always been a stress eater.

After half an hour of staring at the same page, I couldn't stand it anymore. I set my book aside and rose to my feet. "I'm going out for a while."

I needed space to be alone and think, and there were few places I felt more alone than in a crowd of strangers. The apartment was only a few streets over from the bigger college bar scene, though the earlier hours were generally populated by the middle-age crowd who were still trying to find a work/Tinder balance in their lives. Early dinner dates before they had to get home and put the kids to bed, or work on an office project, or try to get their basement craft breweries off the ground. All those adult-type things I'd never fully understand.

As I turned down the street where I'd chosen to do my hunting for the evening, the sun had just started to set. The crisp scent of fall twilight always made my pulse hum. A wooden stand on the corner sold hot apple cider, and a fire pit at the center of a multi-bar courtyard popped and crackled. I was weaving my way through the older couples who window-shopped and waited outside for a table at the new sushi bar, when I spotted a familiar bald patch. Mr. Stockard, out on the town. I tapped him on the shoulder to say hi.

"Oh. Hey, Holly." He gave me a lukewarm smile, like the very effort of it made him tired. "Do I want to know what brings you out tonight?"

"Probably not." I scanned the crowd for someone I could pick off easily. "How is class going? Seems like you have some pretty decent students this year." Which was not my roundabout way of asking about Parker. Because I had no reason to ask about her. None at all.

"They're students." When I just blinked at him, he shrugged and took a sip of what I'd bet my heirloom was a pumpkin spice latte. "I'm not sure what else you want me to say."

"When did you become like this?" I waved a hand to encompass his general aesthetic. Crooked tie peppered with dryer lint, coffee-stained teeth, sad droop to his red-rimmed eyes. This wasn't the same guy who jumped on desks and threw Jolly Ranchers, or gave kids who were struggling on the outskirts books they'd actually want to read.

"I'm not uncaring . . . not completely." He scrubbed a hand over his five o'clock shadow that was well on its way to becoming a six o'clock. "Look, you're still young, so you might not understand, but when you get older, you begin to see the world through realistic-colored glasses. You approach life a little less idealistically."

It took everything in me not to roll my eyes. I'd lived through things he could only imagine, but because I was a teen girl, my experiences weren't nearly as valid as his worldly perspective from a single classroom. "You stopped caring. That's what I'm hearing."

"The kids stopped caring long before I ever did." He gave me a sympathetic look, like I truly couldn't understand, and tossed his latte in the nearby trash bin as he turned to go.

"Bullshit."

He stopped, narrowing his eyes as he faced me again. "Bullshit? Forgive me, but you haven't been a student for a long time. You have no idea what it's like anymore."

"I know what it's like to be sixteen because I'm always sixteen. I know what it's like to be alone because I'm always alone. And I damn well know what it looks like when someone gives up on me before I have the chance to show them what I'm really made of." I'd raised my voice to the point where a few people had stopped to stare. "It shouldn't be up to the kids to care when faced with someone who's already written them off."

When he didn't say anything, I left. It wasn't my job to make him a decent teacher again. I had bigger problems to worry about, finding someone to eat being at the top of my current priorities, but a piece of me hurt for his students. They deserved better than someone who had stopped seeing their worth.

Out of respect for what he'd done for me when he'd been my teacher, I wouldn't feed on him. But I'd considered it. Instead, I worked my way to the end of the street, which opened up to a large park with an amphitheater. A few people milled around the concrete steps while a terrible band played a cover of the Beatles' "Let It Be." I kept my eye out for the first person to look at me funny, but the guy who grabbed my butt would do. Peeking over my shoulder, I gave him a wink and expected that would be enough for him to follow.

Guys like this were so predictable. It was almost too easy.

I walked into the more heavily wooded area at the edge of the park. The fresh fall of leaves crunched beneath my feet. The air carried the smell of a world preparing for hibernation. I thought about running to let off some energy, knowing he would chase, but I ruled out that idea. He'd been drinking, and he was already half walking, half stumbling over the roots and forest floor's growth. He'd probably break his neck if I made him move any faster.

"What's your name, honey?" He finally deigned to speak to me. The rough scratch of his voice made my skin crawl. "You here all alone?"

"Do you care?" I asked.

He chuckled, like I was just. So. Amusing. Once we'd gotten far enough under the cover of the trees, I turned to him. The gleam in his eye made my predatory pulse beat harder. The stress of everything I needed to do echoed in the pit of my empty stomach. I almost didn't want to give this one the opportunity to run.

"Why'd you bring me all the way out here, huh?" He stepped closer. His breath reeked of protein shakes and hard cider. I anticipated this one tasting like a hot-dog-eating contest.

"I was hungry." No point in lying. He'd be dead soon, anyway. "But I made an oath to myself a long time ago, so I'm going to give you two seconds to run."

He laughed. "That's cute."

I closed my eyes and counted in my head. *One Mississippi, two Mississippi.* When I opened them again, he stood even closer. What a shocker.

"One of these days, one of you will run and surprise the hell out of me." I wrapped my hand around his throat and crushed his windpipe. "But today is not that day."

He ended up tasting like sugar cubes. The hard, grainy kind farmers fed to their horses. Not what I'd been expecting, but I'd had worse dinners. His legs scrambled against the dry forest floor, kicking up a river of red and gold leaves as the earthy aroma battled with the ripening scent of his death. Borderline poetic.

I left his lifeless body in a heap with just enough of his own blood exposed to attract whatever prowled these woods. Animals would make quick work of the fresh meat.

Licking my lips, I enjoyed the last of the sugary aftertaste as I slipped back into the crowd that had gathered in the park for more bad Beatles covers. Adults out on dates mixed with families with small children mixed with college students mixed with high school students desperately trying to pass for college students.

A few older people had brought out lawn chairs, and they sat on the edge of the open grass field, exchanging gossip and people watching.

The scene reminded me of a puzzle I'd done once. I'd bought it during a rare bout of homesickness because it reminded me of this place. Music nights in the fall had been a Big Deal when I went to high school, and it made me oddly happy to see some things hadn't changed.

In the middle of the park, drawing a small crowd, was Parker. She waved her hands in the air, whipping around like she was trying to dance but had never quite learned how. I bit the inside of my cheek to hold back a smile. It was so awful it had crossed over to adorable.

She stumbled over her own feet and swayed to the side. That's when it hit me that she wasn't exactly sober. People elbowed one another and laughed as they pointed at her when she stumbled. I wanted to snap their necks. When she tripped over a loose stick, I rushed forward to grab her before she took a header into the ground.

Her soft brown eyes were hazy and unfocused as she looked up at me. "I knew you'd be the one to catch me if I fell."

Then she turned her head to the side and vomited into the grass.

Chapter Thirteen

"I'll be quiet if you just let me lie down." Parker weaved into me, then veered to the edge of the sidewalk. "Don't make me go home."

"You're not going home. I've got you." It was like trying to navigate a raft over white water. I'd direct her left; she'd veer right. I'd lean right; she'd keep going. "How did you end up in the park? Did you go there with friends?"

She let out a loud, snapping laugh, like lightning cracking across a stormy sky. Full of just as much turmoil. "It's funny how you think I have friends."

It really wasn't that funny.

"How did you get the liquor?" The only access I'd had to liquor in high school had been through Stacey, and I didn't really count those three sips we took from her mom's vodka.

"Stole it from my mom." She hiccupped. "She brought the bottle home to celebrate, drank half of it, and passed out. I stole the rest and just kept walking."

"You walked all the way over here?" Parker lived on the west side of Glen River, which was a minimum of ten miles from here, if not more.

She shook her head. "Uber. Can I lie down now?"

I'd seen the public-service movies in health class. If she fell asleep, she'd choke on her own vomit and die, at least if the movie was to be believed. "Just a little bit farther now."

Hauling Parker around made me very glad I'd never managed to get drunk. I had terrible impulse control while I'd been sober. I could only imagine the horrifying things I would've let Elton talk me into if I'd barely been able to walk.

I dragged her around the corner, where she attempted to run headfirst into a stop sign, then helped her navigate the stairs beside the meat market. Halfway up to the second floor, she wanted to stop and rest. I rubbed her back while she hung her head between her knees, but she didn't throw up again. Finally, we made it to the front doorstep. Ida's finished brain project greeted me. She'd cut a face into it and hollowed out the inside, where a small candle burned, lighting up the toothy grin. It slightly resembled a blobfish. I hit the door with my elbow in order to keep Parker upright.

Ida flung open the door, carving knife pointed at my chest. "Oh. It's just you." She dropped her arm and stepped back to let me in.

"What is this supposed to be?" I poked at the blob with the toe of my shoe.

"Brain-o'-lantern." Ida grinned. "Something cute for the kiddies if we get any trick-or-treaters this year. What did you do to Elton's latest victim?"

"I didn't do anything to her. I found her in the park this way." I flung Parker's body forward, and Ida scooped her up on the opposite side. Parker managed to do a great imitation of a corpse as we dragged her into the living room. "This is so far above my pay grade."

"You worked at Taco Bell," Ida said. "Everything is above your pay grade."

Rose came out of the bedroom, her black-and-white-striped rockabilly dress swishing around her knees. "Oh my God. You killed Parker."

"She's not dead." I let go of her once I was reasonably sure she could stand on her own, and she promptly tripped over the coffee table and fell face forward. "Yet."

"Hello? Is someone there?" Rose's bedframe thumped the wall while the guy she brought home begged for mercy. "Help me. Please.

I think she's going to hurt me."

I rubbed my temples. "Did you have to bring home another kill?"

"I didn't know we were going to have company." Rose looked between Parker sprawled out on the floor with her mouth hanging open, and her bedroom, where the guy she tied up continued to scream and beat against the wall. "Hold on."

Rose disappeared behind the door. The cries of the guy she brought home became more insistent and louder as he pleaded for his life, with real fear in his voice. Rose's low murmurs sounded soothing as the guy's voice became more muffled, as if he had a pillow over his face. With a final thump, he went eerily quiet.

Parker lifted her head. "Who turned off the music?"

"I like her." Ida grinned. "She's fun."

"Yeah. A great time." I grabbed Parker's arm and helped her to the couch. She slumped to the side with her eyes closed, and I poked at her, pulling up her eyelid. "You have to stay awake, okay? No sleeping."

"Did you give her a concussion?" Ida grabbed Parker, who put up zero resistance, and twisted her neck from side to side as she examined her head. "I'm not seeing any bumps."

"She's drunk. Won't she choke on her vomit and die if she goes to sleep?" I asked.

Ida let out a barking laugh. "Where do you get your information?"

"Health class," I muttered.

"Oh, man. No wonder Elton keeps enrolling in modern high school. That's hilarious." Ida shook her head. "Lay her on her side, and let her sleep it off. She should be fine."

"I chloroformed the guy." Rose came out of her bedroom and licked blood off the end of her finger. "I couldn't resist having a little nibble, and he's delicious. French toast and fresh strawberries. Have you killed Parker yet?"

This night was testing what little patience I had left. Keeping in mind what Ida had told me about upsetting Rose, I took several deep breaths, counting to ten before I responded. "Why would I kill her if we're trying to protect her?"

"I don't care if she lives or dies, so long as she doesn't become a vampire." Rose shrugged. "Anyway, I'm not super hungry, so you're all welcome to the guy in my room."

"Wait." I held up a hand. "You don't care if she lives or dies?" For some reason, this personally offended me, even though I didn't typically care much for the living, either. "Why not just kill her, then? Why go to the trouble of being friendly with her?"

"Don't kill me. I probably taste like cheap vodka," Parker slurred from the couch where she was half asleep with one arm flung over her head.

She was a pretty cute drunk. I had a feeling I'd be one of those messy drunks who ran naked in the streets before collapsing in a puddle of my own tears. I swept a loose piece of hair away from her face, tucking it behind her ear. She shivered, and a liquid warmth pooled in my stomach. Rose and Ida gave each other a look I didn't appreciate.

"What?" I asked.

"I can't believe I didn't see it before," Rose said.

"I hope this isn't going to be a problem," Ida said to Rose.

"It shouldn't be," Rose said.

Their coded communication had me gritting my teeth. I stood in front of them both with my hands on my hips. "You know I hate it when you do that."

"Forgive us," Rose said. "I assumed you knew we were discussing you and Parker. Specifically, you liking Parker."

Why was that even a discussion? "So? Ida said she likes her too. What's the big deal?"

"You *like her*, like her," Ida said.

Oh.

"I do not." The denial came quickly. Too quickly, from the way Ida raised her eyebrows. "I think she's a nice girl, and funny, and I relate to her a lot. That's all."

"Sure." Ida smirked. "Whatever you say."

"It's fine if you like her." Rose's expression softened as she squeezed my shoulder. "My last relationship was with a mortal girl I'd met in New Orleans, and she's not the first mortal I've been attracted to over the years."

"Not me." Ida waved her raised hand like class was in session and she really wanted an A in Not Sleeping with Mortals 101. "I'm still figuring myself out. And since I have all the time in the world, I'm in no rush. I don't think I'm sexually attracted to anyone, but I'm romantically attracted to the idea of someone I haven't met yet."

"Okay." I hadn't expected to talk about all this, but it didn't surprise me. A lot of vampires left heterosexuality behind, much like exercising for fun, an appreciation for abstract art, and all those other things mortals lied about enjoying. Sexuality became much more fluid when you had an eternity and no longer felt obligated to conform. "Since we're sharing, I'm bisexual, but I've never been with anyone except Elton." I hated that I felt the need to overexplain myself, as if my identity was a dress that made me feel cute, so I had to downplay it by explaining how I got it on sale. If something felt good and right to me, I protected it the only way I knew how: by acting like it didn't matter so no one could hurt me with it. "That doesn't mean I'm into Parker, for the record."

"Who you're into isn't ever a factor." Rose squeezed my hand. "There isn't a litmus test or a certain number of boxes you have to tick. How you feel and who you are is yours. It's not for anyone else to decide or question."

The tightness in my chest eased. I hadn't realized how tense I'd become until I rolled my neck and felt the muscles unclench. Like I'd been waiting years for someone to say my feelings were important. I'd been alone for a long time before Elton ever left me.

"We get you." Ida dipped her chin in acknowledgement.

"And we never really intended to kill Parker, if you were worried about that," Rose said. "If we did, Elton would just find a replacement and turn her before we could do the ritual. But we wouldn't be mad at you if you turned her after this was all over."

"Or killed her," Ida said. "I'm not believing for a second she tastes like vodka."

"No one is killing or turning Parker." I looked at the couch, where she breathed evenly, her long eyelashes pillowed on her cheek like inky trails of stardust . . . which was a perfectly normal thing to think about a friend. Fuck. "I want her to live and have a future beyond her high school years. The way we never got a chance to."

"Then we need to get those heirlooms," Rose said. "The quicker, the better."

The next morning, after Rose finished off the French toast guy and disposed of him in the dumpster at the end of the alley, I decided to wake up Parker. We didn't have any aspirin or glasses for water in the apartment, so I ran down to the pharmacy and grabbed what she'd need. According to health class, hangovers were worse than death.

Rose and Ida didn't give me any more grief over my feelings for Parker, for which I was grateful. I wasn't entirely ready to examine those yet. Yes, she was beautiful, fun, and I enjoyed her company, and if Elton hadn't currently set his sights on her, I might've considered her a nice distraction from everything else going on. But I couldn't afford to catch feelings for a mortal. Feelings for other people always ended up making me careless with myself.

I nudged Parker, and her lashes fluttered. Thankfully, she didn't puke again. I didn't have a lot of experience in babysitting drunk people, so I stayed in the living room, keeping one eye on my book and one eye on her, to make sure she didn't choke in her sleep.

Ida called me creepy. But I wasn't watching her sleep because I lacked boundaries; I was just trying to make sure she didn't die in the middle of the night, for fuck's sake. Even though Ida had assured me that my health class had been—and I quote—scare-tactic bullshit.

She was alive at the start of Prohibition and still had strong opinions on the matter.

"Good morning." I pushed the bottle of water closer to the edge of the coffee table. "You're alive." I cringed as she peeled open one lid, revealing a bloodshot eye. "Sort of."

"How did I get here?" She sat up quickly and immediately clutched her head. "Oh, God. Everything hurts. Please don't tell me I showed up on your doorstep last night. I barely remember leaving my apartment."

"No, I found you in the park. You were . . . I'm not sure if I can call it dancing, exactly, but you were flinging yourself around to music."

"I'm never drinking again." Pressing her palms into her eyeballs, she moaned. "How can my mom stand that stuff? I feel like I've been run over by a truck."

"I'm sorry?" My mom hadn't been a drinker, so I wasn't familiar with these types of family issues. Ida said no bright lights or loud noises, so I kept the curtains closed and tried to keep my voice down. "What, uh, prompted the bottle stealing?"

"She said we're moving again."

"What?" My heart raced. On one hand, it would get her away from Elton. On the other, we'd just started to become friends, and I didn't have many of those. "How soon?"

"Not so loud." She rubbed her fingers over her eyelids. "She met a guy online, of course, and he lives in Tennessee. She said we're leaving in a few weeks."

Right around the time we'd be doing the ritual. Maybe she'd be okay after all.

"I'm not going with her." Parker sat up and swallowed some aspirin, drinking down half the bottle of water in one gulp. "I never get to stay anywhere long enough to make friends, but this place is different. I actually have people here now. I'm not leaving again."

"What are you going to do if you don't go with her?"

"Move in with Elton. He called me last night when I was on my way to the park, and he said I could move in with him." Her cheeks pinked. "He told me he was in love with me."

"He's lying." Elton didn't love anyone but himself. "He loves control. He loves having power over people. That's not what love is supposed to be like."

"You're just bitter because he broke up with you." Even as she said the words, she didn't look like she fully believed them, and it gave me a small bit of hope.

"You know that's not true," I said quietly.

"I have no other choice." She crossed her arms. "Unless you have a better idea?"

I had a million other, better ideas. "You could go with your mom, at least for a few weeks; you could move out on your own; you could stay with us for a little while."

"There are three of you and two bedrooms." She stood, stretching her arms over her head, revealing just a small bit of skin between her jeans and T-shirt. "I like you, but Elton wants to be my boyfriend, and the weird dynamic you two have already makes it hard to be your friend. I appreciate you letting me crash on your couch, but please don't push me on this."

She grabbed her gray peacoat off the back of the couch and

headed for the door.

"You're leaving?" I jumped to my feet. "You're just going to drop that and leave?"

She couldn't walk out after that. There had to be something I could say. She could have Ida's room or Rose's (if we could get her to stop bringing kills home); she could have anything she wanted if she stayed. This wasn't supposed to be happening yet. Elton was moving more quickly than he had with any of us. We needed more time.

"I have to get home. For all I know, my mom is packing right now, and I need to start transferring my stuff out. One time when we were living in Oregon, she moved to Seattle and forgot to take me, so I sat in our empty apartment for two days waiting for her to come back."

"No offense, but your mom sounds like a mess." My mom ruined my formative years and made it nearly impossible for me to have a normal childhood, but at least she never left me in random cities by myself. I guess I could thank her for that.

"Now you see why I've got to go." She looked around like she wanted to linger, but didn't really know how. "Anyway. Thanks again."

I didn't say anything as she walked out. I just stared at the door, wondering how this could've all gone so wrong. I thought we'd been making progress. Yesterday morning at the diner, I'd been so sure things had changed. I'd hoped she had at least considered stepping back from Elton, but not likely, when she still seemed to be flattered by his attention and his false declarations of love. At this rate, he'd turn her by the end of the week.

"We heard everything," Rose said as she came out of the bedroom with Ida trailing behind. "We have no choice. We move on to the graveyard tonight."

Chapter Fourteen

This was poorly planned out from the start. None of us wanted to take part in this. Ida laid her sister to rest a hundred years ago, and she'd done her grieving, she'd learned how to move on from it. This was just going to dig it all up again. Literally.

While Rose laid out a map of the cemetery, complete with red lines and times for the security rotations, Ida stepped out for a few hours. She returned with a bloody stump that turned out to be a human leg. Or, as she liked to call it, an art project.

"Are you sure midnight is the best time?" I asked. "Wouldn't security increase at that time, seeing as how we're so close to Halloween and people are fools?"

"You'd think." Rose shrugged. "This is when they do shift change. I don't make the rules. Lucky for us, the older graves are in the back and don't get checked as often because they generally don't have family around to complain if something isn't right."

"Ida?" I looked over to where she'd set out her leg, having already washed it, dried it, and covered it in clear rubber sealant. She painted little black diamonds in a crisscrossing pattern up the thigh. "Do you have any thoughts on what time we should get there, since we'll mostly be taking direction from you?"

Even though Rose and I agreed to do all of the digging, because of the mental toll it would take on Ida, we still wanted to make sure we were doing what she felt was best. My feelings toward my mom were ever complex, mostly tinged with resentment, and I still couldn't stomach the idea of opening her coffin years after she died.

I couldn't imagine what it must've been like for Ida to do this with someone she loved.

"I'd rather not make decisions on the details." Her bottom lip stuck out as she kept full concentration on the pattern she drew on the leg. "It's bad enough that I'll have to stand guard while you dig her up and act like you're not putting your gross, undead hands into her coffin."

"Fair enough." I turned back to Rose. "Midnight is fine."

After we put the finishing touches on our plan for the night, we took a trip down to the hardware store to use my last paycheck to buy some shovels. I'd have to get another job soon if I wanted to put away a small amount of money while I stayed with Rose and Ida for free. I had no idea how they managed to have such a nice apartment when neither worked. I made a mental to note to ask one of them later.

A newspaper rested on the edge of a trashcan, and I picked it up when I read the headline "Wild Animal Makes the Night Manager a Fourth Meal at Taco Bell." The tactlessness of it tickled my funny bone. Apparently, Jimmy had been fined in the past for trying to purchase a jaguar to keep in his residential neighborhood. Police assumed it was an illegal big-cat deal gone bad. No longer my problem. I tossed the newspaper into the next bin.

In the hardware store, the cashier, with a look of horrified fascination in her eyes, snapped her gum as she watched us walk up and down the aisles. We grabbed a couple of shovels plus the lampshade and hot-glue gun Ida had requested. The cashier shuddered as she handed me the change for a twenty by giving me another twenty. I wasn't going to complain.

On the way back to the apartment, I slipped into the antique shop next to our apartment and bought Rose a fish-shaped paperweight made out of carnival glass to add to her collection as a thank-you for taking me in. I'd grab a random body part off my next kill for Ida.

When we got back, Ida had sewn together some fringe and finished painting what looked like a fishnet stocking on the leg. She'd put one of Rose's black heels on it.

I handed her the lampshade we brought home. "I'm afraid to ask."

Ida took the lampshade and hot-glued the fringe around the bottom, then stuck it to the bloody stump, where it had been ripped out of the hip socket. She held it up, her expression like a proud kid who just took the first place trophy on field day. "What do you think? It's the leg lamp from *A Christmas Story.*"

"You are seriously demented," I said.

Ida batted her lashes. "Please stop complimenting me, I might remember how to blush."

"If you're both done screwing around, we should probably go." Rose had changed into a little safari outfit with hiking boots, olive pants, and matching shirt knotted at the waist. She'd tied her short bob into a red bandanna. It took an impressive amount of skill to turn our mission of digging up Ida's dead sister into a costume party. Yet there we were. "It'll take us at least two hours to walk there."

"Why are we walking?" Ida whined. "Why can't we take the bus?"

"Oh, now you're a fan of the bus," I said.

"We can't take the chance of anyone tracking us to the graveyard if things go sideways tonight, okay?" Rose thrust one of the shovels into my hands. "You both should put on better shoes. It's a six-mile hike."

Once we changed our shoes, and did a little more bitching just to annoy Rose, we headed out. It wasn't so bad walking. We had plenty of stamina since our bodies didn't require rest, and the dark fall night was actually soothing. Leaves scuttled down the street on a phantom wind. The streets were near empty on a Sunday night. It was still warm enough to be comfortable but with a hint of a chill just beginning to snap in the air.

We made it to the edge of the graveyard at just after 11:30 p.m.

For a place that had bodies going back two hundred years, I expected a lot more ambiance. Black iron, spiky spires, and a creaky gate that opened by itself at the stroke of midnight. None of that was present. It was just a stretch of neatly trimmed grass dotted with headstones of varying sizes.

"This is it." Rose glanced at Ida. "You okay?"

"Fine." Ida took a deep breath. "Let's get this over with."

We made our way to the back of the cemetery. The dark pressed in on us as we moved farther away from the edge of the road. The open expanse of space dropped the temperature by ten degrees. Trees, near leafless already, had twisted branches that reached for the starlit night.

We had gotten almost to the end, where a small forest of birch trees marked the cemetery's property line, when Ida flung out her arm, bringing us to a halt. "Right there. That's where Bea is buried."

We set our shovels down and wandered closer to the grave. Bea had been buried in the third-to-last row under a birch tree. A few golden leaves still clung to its bone-white branches. The headstone was flat and plain, with a small angel carved into the granite. It read: BEATRICE RADLEY, BELOVED DAUGHTER AND SISTER, 1907–1921.

"She was only fourteen." I dipped my head in silent respect for the girl who would've been long dead now regardless, but still left a dull ache in my heart for her sister who had been left behind to carry the grief past a lifetime. "I'm so sorry, Ida."

"I appreciate the condolences, but I can't treat this like a second funeral." Ida hugged her chest and turned her back to us. "I barely survived mourning her the first time."

I'd opened my mouth to offer more meaningless comfort when Rose shook her head. "Let her be." She tossed me a shovel and plunged the spade of hers into the grave. "The best thing we can do for her now is to make this quick."

Without another word between us, we dug. It was slow, painful work. Even with my immortal stamina, my muscles quivered. Each shovelful was heavier than the last. Clay threaded through the dirt made each crack into the earth feel like chipping through a frozen lake. Hours later, my spade hit a hard surface with a thunk. I kneeled down and brushed away the crumbling rubble, running my hand over a dull and dirty surface that had once been polished.

"Found it," I said to Rose.

"Good, because I'm ready to drop dead. Again." She came to me, tapping the earth with her shovel until we got the dimensions. "We'll uncover the top enough to get the lid open."

"Nicely done, ladies." We both looked up to where Elton prowled the edge of the hole we'd dug. He gave a slow clap, and once again my blood hummed while I simultaneously wanted to rip out his throat. "Thanks for doing all the hard work."

"You bastard." Rose flung her shovel at his head, which he dodged with ease. He moved with the natural grace of a dancer, and he'd been very good at using those moves to seduce us.

"Come on now, Rose." He crouched, reaching into the grave to grasp her chin and rub his thumb along her jaw. "You're better than that, love."

"I'm not your love." She scrambled out of the grave. "Why are you here?"

"You ought to know." He was so heartbreakingly beautiful, like a Renaissance painting in motion. Too fluid and water-like to be real. Mischief lit his eyes, and it was as if the gods of sarcasm had blessed his smile with an edge of mockery. "I heard you're collecting your heirlooms. Though I can't think what on earth you'd need them for."

"We didn't want it to come to this." Rose took a step toward him, as though she couldn't help the pull she felt, even as disgust etched her features. "We tried to tell you to back off of Parker, but you wouldn't listen to reason."

"Ah, yes. Parker." He rubbed his thumb over his bottom lip. "She is lovely, isn't she?"

"You—" A scream split the air, and Rose swung around. Her face froze as she took in whatever happened while she'd been busy arguing with Elton.

Fearing the worst, I clawed my way out of the grave with more speed and energy than I should've had in reserves. Gwen had Ida tied to the birch tree at the head of her sister's grave. Both of Ida's arms were already gone and her torso had been ripped open, allowing her intestines to spill onto the ground like a tangled web of bloody snakes. Ida's body would heal itself within minutes, but the pain would be unimaginable. It was Gwen's favorite brand of fun.

I lunged for them, and Frankie wrapped his meaty arms around me, pulling me to the side. "Don't give her reason to tear you apart too," he whispered in my ear.

"You did this," I hissed. There could be no other explanation. He had to have sold us out to Elton. No one else knew we were searching for heirlooms.

"I didn't say a damned thing." His muddy brown eyes held an ocean of feelings, and I didn't buy a single one. "Keep your mouth shut if you want to be spared pain."

"Hey, Holly. Not surprised to see you slumming it with the other castoffs." Gwen, tall and lithe, still wore her bleached hair in the 1970s feathered style. She picked her fangs with her sharpened nails. "It's so sad how the three of you couldn't just move on."

"Not as sad as your belief that Frankie is loyal to you because he wants to be," I said.

Frankie's grip on me tightened, but he didn't say a word. His attention was too focused on Ida. He looked as if he was in nearly as much pain, even though his intestines remained perfectly intact. My sympathies were extremely limited.

"Such a pretty girl." Gwen circled Ida as if debating which chunk of her to cut away next. Her green cat eyes lit with malice as she tapped Ida's left leg. "I can't knock Elton's taste."

I had to look away, but I'd never forget the sound of tendons snapping and Ida's tortured scream as Gwen tore off her leg. We should've come here first. The first day we learned about the heirlooms. This was a mistake we'd all have to own.

"We can keep hacking away at my first love, though I hate to see her in pain." Elton leaned in closer to Ida and kissed her cheek. If I'd had a living stomach, I would've vomited the entire thing up. "Or you can give us her heirloom, and we can all leave here in one piece."

I glanced at Ida, who had already reformed her arms. Noticing the regrowth, Gwen ripped them both off again, throwing them into a nearby bush, where they'd turn to ash and blow away on the wind. While Ida screamed and thrashed against the birch, Frankie began to cry. It pissed me off enough to break free of his grasp. I dug my nails into his eyeballs, and as warm fluid and blood gushed over my fingers, he snapped my neck. My entire body flooded with pain as he dropped me to the ground like a discarded doll.

"You're a monster." Rose, tiny and soft and the source of all things beautiful and soothing in my world, bared her teeth to Elton. Her entire body vibrated with unleashed rage. "You created this situation, but we no longer live on your terms."

"I'm the monster?" Elton chuckled, which sounded more like a low growl. "The three of you want to kill me. The one who gave you eternity. Where is my thanks?"

Would this be what I'd be like once my memories were gone? Would I be as cold and selfish as Elton and Gwen? Did losing their living memories cost them what little humanity they had left? The thought shook me down to my core, freezing my skin to near numbness. I couldn't become like him. I could never be that heartless.

My neck healed, and I stepped up beside Rose. While I'd given my mortality to the boy before me who would never be a man, I'd walk through a thousand fires for the girls who took me in with no questions asked. "You never told us the cost. You brought this on yourself."

"I brought eternal death on myself?" His aghast expression nearly made me laugh. It was so Elton to have such a narrow, selfish view. He couldn't see any possibility where he wasn't the constant victim. "What have I done to any of you besides break up with you? We had a good run, but we weren't meant to be. It's not my fault you can't get over it."

"You manipulated us and made us believe you were the only one who loved us." Rose shoved him, and he stumbled back a step. "You didn't let me come home when my mother got sick. You didn't let me go to her funeral, knowing full well I had no power to do so on my own."

He shrugged, his expression disinterested, like she was overreacting. I recognized the gesture well. Treating us like we were hysterical and dramatic was his favorite form of gaslighting. "She stopped being your mother the moment you died. You made that choice."

"Don't you dare put this on us." A rage like I'd never known rolled through my veins, pumping my blood at the same speed it whispered *closer, closer, closer*. "It wasn't a real choice when you never told us there were others, or that we'd be tied to you even after you left us, or that people cared about us. We were missed."

"And most of those people who missed you are dead, while you live on." Elton smoothed down his freshly pressed shirt, ever concerned about appearances. "I'm bored with all this, so we're going to take the heirloom and go now."

Elton angled himself toward Bea's open grave, knees bent, ready to jump. Ida let out a bloodcurdling scream, temporarily distracting him. Rose gave me a tight nod. Before I could process what she intended to do, she launched herself at Gwen, a tiny ball of fury and flame. Frankie began shouting, and I used the opportunity to grab Elton's throat.

He broke my wrist, but I quickly recovered and caged his temples between my hands. I had half his head torn off—his neck resembling Stacey's the night he killed her—when he backhanded me, sending me sprawling across the grass. As I dug my nails into the earth, he wrapped my hair around his hand and yanked me off the ground.

He dangled me in front of him while I swung my legs out, trying to catch him off balance. "What is this, Holly? Foreplay?"

"Maybe." I went limp under his grasp. "I've been so lonely since you left Tulsa."

"Really?" He gave me a slow grin as his eyes tracked my body. "I'm not sure if I should believe you. Why don't you get on your knees and show me you're sorry?"

Ugh. Gross. As soon as he loosened his grip, I swung forward, knocking him to the ground. He tried to flip over, but I was already on his back with his head in my grip. He smiled as I pulled, like he'd really come to enjoy pain. His skin tore in layers until I had his head all the way off. A muffled laugh bubbled out of his mouth as his eyes rolled to the back. Stringy bits of flesh and veins hung from his serrated neck. I crushed his skull between my hands.

His head would grow back, unfortunately, but without eyes, his arms and legs flailed about uselessly. Rose had torn Gwen to ribbons. Normally, Gwen outmatched us all in skill, but she'd underestimated Rose's adrenaline-fueled anger. Frankie hefted Gwen's temporarily broken body over his shoulder and took off running.

The two of us quickly untied Ida, who dropped to the ground, half healed and wincing. Rose stroked Ida's sweaty forehead. The pain left Ida's face as her limbs grew back, but her skin remained clammy.

I left the two of them and bound Elton's body to the birch tree. By the time I turned around, his head had grown back.

Ida stood on shaky legs, but she had enough strength to grab Elton by the hair and pull his face up to meet hers. "I'm going to take so much pleasure in killing you."

"Don't think you've won yet. I know for a fact you can't do a thing to me without all three heirlooms, and Holly lost her locket years ago. But keep collecting them if you must." He sent an air kiss to Rose. "Good luck at the bank, love."

Underneath that flippant exterior, his pale skin vibrated with unchecked rage. He'd expected to waltz out of here with Ida's heirloom, that it would be easy for him to take what he wanted, and it ate away at him that it wouldn't be happening. I tilted my head as he held my gaze. That pull to him thrummed in my blood, but I couldn't see anything of the boy I'd been drawn to. He'd been soft once. Did something happen to make him this hard, this unyielding? Or had he always been this way, and I just had failed to see it?

Rose stuffed her bandanna into his mouth to keep him quiet.

While Ida rested against a headstone, Rose and I uncovered the rest of Bea's coffin. I lifted the lid, not really knowing what we'd find. It wasn't a lot. Some teeth and a tiny glass horse with a silver mane and tail stuck in some waxy substance. Instead of waiting to see if Ida wanted a moment with her sister's remains, I plucked out the horse and shut the lid again. She didn't need to see what was left of Bea.

I wiped off the wax and handed the figurine to Ida. "I got it."

She held up the horse, and the tiny drop of her living blood encased inside its body shone in the moonlight. "Thank you." Ida palmed her horse, tucking it into her pocket. "Let's fill in the grave and go. I don't want to be here anymore."

Rose and I picked up our shovels. Ida helped, a sense of peace overcoming her features as she pushed dirt back into the grave.

Maybe she needed this part. Some time to say a proper goodbye to her sister and lay her memory to rest for the final time.

Once we finished, the three of us held hands while Elton struggled against the metal cables that held him bound to a tree. It was so tempting to rip off his head again. Frankie would probably come back to untie him; that boy had serious conflicting loyalties, but I had a feeling we'd need him eventually. Ida bowed her head and whispered words to Bea's grave that I couldn't hear and weren't for me, anyway. We left with a soft and calming breeze blowing over the grass.

"He didn't try that hard." Ida kicked a pop can lying in the gutter. "With Gwen and Frankie at his side, he should've been able to take us. Did you see the way he was laughing? He doesn't think we'll be able to finish him."

"We got lucky," Rose said.

"Only because he thinks my locket is lost." I never did tell him Stacey took it the night I turned her. He seemed really interested in what had happened to it, to the point where I believed he would've hunted her down if I told him she'd stolen it. I figured I'd put her through enough already. "As long as he never finds out Stacey has it, we should be okay."

When we got back to the apartment, we found Stacey leaning against the front door.

"It's about damn time you all came home." She gave a light sniff. "The three of you smell like dirt and old death."

"It's been a long night." I sighed. "What do you want?"

"The real question should be, what do *you* want?" She reached into her pocket and pulled out my locket, letting it dangle between her thin fingers.

Chapter Fifteen

The silver locket had tarnished to near black, but I could still make out the ornate letter B carved into the surface. If I flicked open the small latch, I'd find a drop of my living blood stored inside. Sealed away for all these years. I reached for it, but Stacey pulled her hand back.

"Not yet." She tucked my heirloom into a black leather bag she held in her clenched fist. "First, there are things I want in exchange."

"Can we do the negotiations inside?" I was covered in grave dirt, my fingers were still sticky from decomposed body wax, and I just wanted a hot bath and a fresh meal. Maybe there was something to Rose bringing kills home after all. "I need to change."

Rose pushed open the front door, swept out her arm, and allowed us all to pass. Now that we had Stacey here, we wouldn't let her leave again without giving up that locket. I went into Rose's room and changed into jeans and a cozy sweater I'd stolen out of the college dorms. After a detour into the bathroom to wash my face and hands, I returned to the main room to find Rose and Ida guarding Stacey, both wearing matching scowls.

Stacey walked in circles, examining the space I'd come to think of as home. She stopped in front of Ida's leg lamp and tilted her head. "Cute."

"I'd offer you something to drink, but I don't have anyone on hand right now," Rose said.

Stacey curled her lip. "Do you normally keep bodies on hand?"

I opened my mouth to point out her little feeding ground of minions but promptly shut it again. We had plenty of time to argue after I had possession of my heirloom.

"So what if she does?" A muscle ticked in Ida's jaw. Which nearly made me laugh, considering how much she hated it when Rose brought her kills home. "You wanted to talk. Let's get to the point, then."

"You're killing Elton." Stacey held my gaze. "I want in."

Ida let out a short laugh. "There's nothing you can do. It has to be us."

"I assumed." Stacey gave Ida a bland stare. "But I still think I can help. I can spy on him at school. He probably won't remember me; I was just another dead body to him, which is an advantage if you want to find out how he plans to retaliate."

"How do we know we can trust you?" Rose asked.

"Because I'm going to give Holly her heirloom. And mine as well, as a show of good faith." She removed both lockets from her bag and pressed them into my palm. A jolt went through me at the contact. Standing here with both Stacey and our lockets, it was like that first summer again, but this time we'd become the ghosts we'd chased. "I'm not a hundred percent ready to forgive you."

"What do you want?" The tarnished silver was cool against my already cold hand.

Stacey's locket opened on the left while mine opened on the right. They linked together by a small latch on the opposite side. They'd been sister lockets. From what we'd been able to uncover, Edie's sister died a few years before her. The lockets had been a gift from their father.

"Once it's done, I never want to come back here again," Stacey said.

"I think we can all agree to that." I looked to Rose and Ida, who nodded in return. The first confirmation I'd had that when this was over, maybe we wouldn't have to go our separate ways. They'd become like family to me in this short time, and the idea of being on my own again made the large expanse of immortality near unbearable. "What else?"

Stacey trailed her hand over the dining-room table. "I want equal input on location and a vote in the final decision. Also, no moving on a whim without notice."

"I can agree to that." It didn't seem fair that Stacey got stuck dragging behind me anymore than it was fair for me to be at the mercy of Elton's whims.

"Excellent." Stacey clapped her hands together. "Now, tell me what your plans are, because I'd love to get the hell out of Michigan as soon as possible."

"Aren't you going to miss all your new friends?" I smirked because I couldn't resist taking a dig at her bizarre lifestyle, though I found it more perplexing than disturbing.

Stacey clenched her fist tight enough to turn her knuckles translucent. "You're right, I absolutely love living in my dead mother's house, which is falling apart because the state can't find anyone to buy the place with a history of a kidnapping and double murder."

I knotted my fingers behind my back. "Even though I still maintain that wasn't my fault, I'm sorry it went down like that. I had expected to be labeled a runaway."

"But that's not what happened, is it?" She glared.

"Look, we can spend all night rehashing the past." I held out my palm, dropping the argument before it spiraled again. "But I won't even have that soon enough, so it all feels kind of pointless." I ignored Stacey's quizzical look. I still wasn't sure how much I wanted to tell her about killing Elton, even though she'd handed over the key to ending him. "What really matters is how we're going to stop it from happening again."

"I wasn't supposed to be here." Stacey kicked her foot against one of the wicker chairs. "I'm not really a part of this, but I'm in. I'll do it for who I used to be." She swallowed as she looked up at me. "And I'll do it for who you used to be too."

"Thank you." It wasn't forgiveness, exactly, but I'd take it. "We don't have a lot of time left. Let's figure out where we should go from here."

We worked into the night, deciding how to use Stacey and what steps to take next. Ida and Rose wanted me to be honest with Parker and talk to her about the real-world consequences of immortality, but I was hesitant. Even though I was sure she suspected the truth, it was a huge risk, opening up myself that way.

I had to be careful.

Since Stacey volunteered to spy, we worked out a plan to put her in action. We spent a few hours arguing over whom she should follow and what she should do, but eventually we couldn't put it off any longer. When the sun rose, the four of us took the bus back to the high school. We'd decided Stacey should follow Frankie over Elton. We knew what Elton's plans were, but Frankie was a wild card. He claimed he cared about Ida, but he still sold us out. We needed to know if he could be flipped, and if so, what purpose we'd use him for.

I'd put on my locket, and it surprised me how fast I'd become attached to it again. It felt as though it were a part of me. It belonged on me. While I'd been separated from it, I hadn't given it much thought beyond the memories I associated with it. But now that I had it back, it molded against my skin like it couldn't bear to be separated from me again. Maybe when I died it had become something other too.

We stopped by the school, and Stacey held us back before crossing the street. "If they figure me out, don't let them starve me."

"We'll come for you." I'd failed Stacey once. I wouldn't do so again.

As soon as we crossed the street, time began to push at me again. My clothes got tighter, and my skin shrunk against my bones. I stretched my arms out, like I could shake it off.

"What are you doing?" Stacey let out a short laugh.

I scrunched my shoulders. "Don't you feel it?"

"The extra gravity?" Stacey smiled as she shook her head. "Yeah.

It's weird, but it's probably just ley lines or whatever. Something we're sensitive to in our undead state."

"It's time," Rose said. "It's trying to shove us out because we don't belong here."

The smile died on Stacey's lips. "That's disconcerting."

"It's fine. You'll get used to it." Rose shoved Stacey through the front door. "Follow Frankie. He's the ox-shaped guy with caterpillar eyebrows and a bowl cut."

As soon as Stacey made it through the metal detectors, Rose turned back to me. "Keep an eye on her. We're going to the library. We need to double-check the info Frankie gave us, since we're not sure if what he told us can be trusted."

Before I could open my mouth to protest, Rose and Ida hurried down the front steps and headed down the street. Traitors. With a long-winded sigh, I pulled on the neck of my sweater and pushed open the front doors of the school.

It wasn't just time pushing at me. Students jammed the halls like a pack of rats in a narrow sewer, their different scents mingling with the overt sweetness of sweat and body spray. There hadn't been nearly this many people in the halls when I went here. No one wanted to get near me, so they shoved other people into my path, bouncing me against the wall of lockers.

I made my way to the senior hall, near the abandoned classroom where I'd met with Rose the first time we came here. A pair of hands shoved me into a room from behind and slammed the door shut. Fangs bared, I spun around, prepared to make a meal out of whoever thought they could play, and stopped short at the sight of Parker's shaking frame, her face twisted in rage.

"What are you doing here?" She attempted to push me again, but I was prepared this time and adjusted my stance. "You said you weren't coming back. It's not safe for you here."

She flung her hands out again, and I grabbed her wrists. "Worried about me?"

Her eyes widened as her pulse picked up beneath my grasp. I let my thumb move, slowly, trailing it over that tiny beat of life in her wrist. She sucked in a sharp breath, and I released my grip, shoving my hands into my hair as I turned away.

She put a tentative hand on my shoulder. "I don't know what you're planning to do, or what heirlooms have to do with it, but you're my friend. So, yes, I'm worried."

I grabbed her arms, backing her against the wall. "What do you know about heirlooms?"

"I overheard you and Rose talking about them the night I crashed at your apartment. I asked Elton about them, but he got really quiet and wouldn't say. It scared me."

God damn it. I ground my teeth hard enough to chip one, and it grew back before I could spit out the shard. Frankie hadn't sold us out after all. Parker had. Unknowingly, but still, Elton could use her questions about heirlooms as an opening to show her just how they worked.

I narrowed my eyes. "You said you couldn't remember anything that night."

"I lied." She ducked her head and blushed. "I was embarrassed, and I heard some things I'm still trying to process."

Fuck me. Rose and Ida had a whole conversation about my feelings for Parker. Feelings that I was still figuring out, regardless of their ideas. It wasn't like I noticed the way she bit her full bottom lip or how soft her mouth would feel against mine or . . . I shook my head. We'd also talked about killing her, so there were multiple things to process.

"What things?" I searched her expression for some clue of how to proceed.

"I'm supposed to move in with Elton," she said. "I need a place to live, but I don't know if I want to be his girlfriend anymore."

My heart sped up. This was good news. If she could put him off for another week and a half, we might be able to pull this off. So long as he didn't pull her back into his web. "Is it because you've finally seen that he's a manipulative asshole?"

"A little." She lowered her gaze to her feet. "And I think I like someone else."

I'd become very aware of how close we stood, my leg positioned between hers, my hands still wrapped around her arms. I slid my grip upwards, over her shoulders. My fingers trailed along her neck. Little goose bumps dotted her skin, and I badly wanted to sink my teeth into her tender skin. Not to hurt but to feel her. Taste her.

"Who?" That word hung in the air like a dandelion seed, soft and light.

She stood two inches shorter than me, and she tilted her face up to meet mine. "I think you know already."

"Maybe." I'd gotten the feeling Parker was teasing me, and I didn't wholly mind. "But it's still your move. What do *you* want?"

She wrapped her arms around my waist and pushed up on her toes. With her lips a breath away from touching mine, she paused. "Are we really doing this?"

"Only if you want to." I choked on the last word. My fingers and toes tingled. My entire body was taut, poised, waiting for her answer.

She closed the distance.

Her lips, softer than I imagined, parted and her tongue swept over mine. My fingers got lost in her hair. I tilted my head, deepening the kiss as I pressed my body against hers, wanting closer, more, everything.

I'd done a lot of kissing in thirty years, some of it nice, and some of it not as nice, but this—None of my kisses had been like this. I never wanted to do anything else, be anywhere else, but right there with Parker's delicate touch slowly undoing me.

She pulled back and blinked at me. "Wow."

"Yeah. That was . . ." I had no words for what that was. I'd never felt every single one of my nerve endings all at once before. It overwhelmed my senses. "Should we do it again?"

A smile curved her lips, and I groaned as she took my mouth again. She flipped me around, surprisingly strong for someone so small, or maybe I'd just gone weak and pliable. My back hit the cinder-block wall. Rough brick bit into my skin as she pushed her hips against me, and I moved as if I'd never get close enough. My entire body burned. If I caught fire right then, I seriously doubted I would care. Her fingers teased the hem of my sweater, and I kissed her harder, wordlessly begging her to put her hands on me.

The doorknob turned, and we instantly broke apart. Parker's hair looked like she'd ridden in the back of a pick-up truck over wild country roads. Her sweater hung off one shoulder, and she breathed heavily through her swollen lips. I imagined I must've been in a similar state. From kissing. If we had taken it any further, I had a feeling we would've torn each other apart.

She absolutely had the power to be the end of me.

Stacey rushed into the room, slammed the door, and leaned against it. "We have to go. I followed the big dude, but Elton recognized me, and now he has some girl with mean eyes and bad hair trailing me."

Gwen. She'd torture Stacey for days. We couldn't stay here.

"Don't tell Elton anything. Act like everything is normal between the two of you." I gave Parker an apologetic look. "We'll . . ."

What could I say? We'll pick this up later? I'll call you? None of that would work. We wouldn't work. This had been wrong, all of it. I was supposed to be protecting her, not hooking up with her. This made everything a thousand times more complicated.

"It's fine. Go." She seemed to have the same thought as me. "We'll talk later." I turned to go, but she grabbed my hand and pulled a pen out of her back pocket. She scribbled down her address, like I'd done to her with mine. "There. Now you know where I live too. My mom mostly works second and third shifts, if you ever want to stop by."

"Okay." I said it as casually as possible, even with my heart hammering in my chest. Going to her house wouldn't be a good idea. We had to stop this before we really got started.

Even though it wouldn't stop me from wanting to feel her lips on mine again.

Chapter Sixteen

After we ducked into a storage closet to avoid Gwen, we managed to sneak back out of the school without a confrontation. I had to believe Parker would be safe, as long as she continued to see the truth about Elton. I knew how smooth he could be, though.

"You have a goofy look on your face." A strong gust of wind blew Stacey's scarf into her face, and she swatted it away. "What happened?"

"Nothing happened." Something had definitely happened.

I touched a finger to my tingling lips, where I could still feel the press of Parker's mouth against mine. It had been different than Elton's kisses. His had been firm and demanding, like I owed him something. Parker's had been like a question she let me answer. It had been wild and frenzied, but also sweet and a little insecure. It had been real. Kissing Parker had been what I'd always imagined kissing was supposed to be like.

"You can trust me, you know. Even though I have zero interest in romance, you can still talk to me about that kind of stuff." Stacey's mouth formed a downward slash, and her thin eyebrows pinched together. Her signature annoyed face. At least one thing hadn't changed in thirty years. "I'm putting my neck out here for you."

"I'm not ready to talk about it yet." Parker and I couldn't go anywhere. Our entire plan to kill Elton revolved around keeping her mortal, but I'd always know what it felt like to kiss as if it were my last, and I'd never settle for less again. "And neck puns are beneath you. We've got to go that way." I pointed to the left, in the direction of the library. Rose and Ida needed to know Frankie hadn't sold us out.

"Okay." Stacey rubbed a hand against her heart. "When you want to talk, I'm here."

It almost sounded like she cared, and I didn't know whether or not to trust it, so we walked in silence.

Everything had changed. Once upon a time I could've walked these streets blindfolded, but now every corner held reminders that I no longer belonged here. The ice cream shop where we used to get slushies after school was a bank. The convenience store that had been family owned was now a Walgreens.

Stacey nodded to Bab's Bakery, which was miraculously still in business. "Remember when we made that bet with Bab?"

I smiled at the memory. Bab had been in her seventies back then, she was probably dead now, but she made the best glazed doughnuts. Made to order, so they were always hot. Stacey once bet her that the two of us could eat four orders—forty-eight doughnuts—in one sitting. If we won, she'd put our picture on the wall and give us free doughnuts for a year.

We both ended up puking in a bucket after our ninth doughnuts. But it inspired Bab to start the Forty-Eight, giving challengers forty-eight minutes to eat forty-eight doughnuts. The winner got free doughnuts for a year, their picture on the wall, and a T-shirt. I peeked in the windows as we passed. New pictures had been added since the last time I'd been there, but it was nice to see that some things stayed the same.

I stuck my tongue out. "Please tell me that's not our living legacy."

"Nope. I found our real legacy a few months ago." Stacey crossed the street and motioned for me to follow.

We cut through an alley next to an auto body shop, through the tall grass growing behind it, until we came to a dirt field covered in scraggy weeds. Tucked next to a short bush with a few clinging red leaves sat a cracked brown bench. Years of initials and signatures had been scratched into the sun-weathered surface.

I walked around the impromptu campsite. A firepit, crushed beer cans, and fast-food wrappers littered the area. "Is that . . . ?"

"It's the bench from the dollar theater." Stacey clasped her hands under her chin. "They tore the theater down twenty years ago. I have no idea how this got all the way out here, but I found it when I first started wandering around town."

I touched the place I'd carved with a safety pin. HOLLY + STACEY BFF4EVER. It had faded with time and damage, barely visible anymore, but my fingers still found the grooves in the plastic. "God, remember how we used to live there?"

We didn't even like half the movies we saw there, but it was something to do in our sleepy town. We'd get frozen Cokes, split the smallest bag of popcorn, and kick our feet up on the back of threadbare chairs while we added our own commentary to the worst releases of the year. Another series of memories I'd be losing forever.

"That's how I knew we were meant to be friends," Stacey said. "Even when the movies were bad, I still had the most fun watching them, because I was with you."

"Why did you sit with me at lunch? That first day in eighth grade?" Sure, Stacey had been new, and I had an empty table in the lunchroom, but she'd been warned to stay away from me. She sat with me anyway.

"Because you were alone, and you looked like you didn't want to be."

It had really been that simple for her, to sit with someone who needed a friend, and screw whatever everyone else thought. I'd never been that kind of brave. My whole life, I'd always cared too much about what other people thought. Starting with my mom, then the kids who bullied me all through school, and eventually Elton. I let their opinions of me color the opinions I had of myself, and when they decided I hadn't been worth much, I let them convince me it was true.

"I never did thank you for that," I said. "For outcasting yourself."

"That's not something I want thanks for." Stacey hugged her chest as she stared across the barren field. "It wasn't a hardship to be your friend, Holly. It didn't require a sacrifice on my part to care about you. After all this time, is that still how you see yourself?"

"Maybe. Not on purpose." I thought I'd come a long way since my days of pining over Elton and letting his moods dictate my feelings, but apparently I still had work to do. "I've only recently gotten past thinking I didn't need anyone. It might be a minute yet before I accept that people might need me."

Stacey nodded, staying quiet for a while, before she said, "I'm sorry I left the night you turned me. I was angry for a long time, but then I missed you, and I didn't know how to tell you that. I wish I'd been there for you when he left."

I wished I'd been there for her too. The first few weeks after Elton left me had been terrifying. I didn't know where I'd end up, what I'd do once I got there, or when I'd be up and forced to leave again without warning. And Stacey had been living through the same fears. Alone. For over thirty years. I'd been so focused on the night everything went wrong and the implosion of our friendship, I didn't stop to think of all the ways I should be supporting her now. If I kept shutting her out, would I be any better than Elton? I owed her more than that.

"I'm sorry I didn't listen to you when you tried to warn me, and I'm sorry I didn't leave Elton the moment he revealed himself to be a monster." I thought saying the words would only make them weigh more and be more difficult to accept, but I felt lighter as I let that part of my past go. "I'll never be sorry I saved your life, though."

"I'm not entirely sorry you saved my life, either." Stacey took her scarf off. "I'm really sorry about this neck situation, though."

The corners of my lips quirked. I fought very hard to keep a straight face, but I couldn't hold it back any more. Tears pricked the corners of my eyes as I let out a horrible cackle. It was so wrong and awful, but I couldn't stop laughing.

Stacey retied her scarf, navy blue stitched with tiny silver stars. "It's fucking hilarious."

"I know it's not funny." I held out my palms, still laughing. "But I swear I didn't know your neck would stay that way."

"Obviously. I'll never forget the look on your face when I rose from the dead." She sniffed as she tried to hang on to some of her dignity. "Anyway, I brought you out here because this bench meant something to us. Those shitty dollar movies meant something to us. And I never forgot. You made me mad as hell when you let Elton become the center of everything, after he told you that your life wasn't good enough, but I still loved you."

I grinned at her, and the years between us became a thin mist I could almost—almost—reach my hand through and touch the living girls we used to be. "I love you too. Even when you act like you stepped out of a Vincent Price movie."

"I knew you wouldn't let that go." She rolled her eyes. "I did it the first time as a joke, but after I'd been on my own for so long, it was nice being around people who thought I was something special."

I thought back to all the time I spent alone in my awful motel room, thinking that was as good as it was going to get for me. "I can understand why that would have appeal. Still a weird way to go about it, though."

"Shut up." She gave me a playful shove.

We cut through the same alley, and I glanced back at the bench. My living legacy, left to rot in this barren field that would probably be a gas station in the next thirty years. Seemed fitting. We crossed the street and walked the rest of the way to the library, which was tucked next to the bank where I opened my first account, back when I thought I'd have money one day.

We approached the table where Ida and Rose had a dozen books spread out. Ida tapped away on her tablet, while Rose was so buried in a book, her nose touched the pages. "Did you find anything to make you think Frankie lied?"

Rose looked up. "No. But I didn't really expect to. It took us twenty years to find out we needed to destroy our heirlooms and the list of death plants to burn with them."

I slammed my hands on the table. "It doesn't matter, because Frankie didn't tell Elton we were looking for our heirloom. Parker did, by accident. So I think we can trust what he told us."

"Thank God." Rose slammed her thick book shut. "Does this mean we'll have to kill Parker after all? Such a shame. She was a nice girl."

My heart leaped to my throat, even though I was half certain Rose was joking. "She overheard one of us mention the heirlooms when she was drunk, so she asked Elton about them. That's what tipped him off. It was an honest mistake that could've been avoided if we'd been more careful with our conversations."

"It also could've been avoided if she hadn't told us she blacked out," Ida said.

Touché.

"Either way, it's done. Elton knows. But Frankie was loyal." Which made me feel really bad about tearing out his eyeballs. That couldn't have been pleasant. "We should decide how we're going to use him, because I don't think he'll stand in our way."

"Let's go back to the apartment," Rose said. "There is too much being said in the open."

The four of us took the bus. Ida and Stacey sat at opposite ends and took bets on who could make the most people uncomfortable.

Ida nearly had her beat, but then Stacey took off her scarf, and when an old man puked in the aisle, it was game over.

Back at the apartment, someone had kicked in the door. They had spattered Ida's brain-o'-lantern against the inside walls, leaving a grayish sludge sticking to every surface. Rose's ceramics had been pushed to the floor. Glass shards cut her hands as she scooped them up and held them against her chest. Her photo album had been ripped to shreds. I picked up a torn picture of Rose, the 1954 laugh frozen on her face. All the books I'd brought with me had been ripped apart and tossed around. Including the library ones, which pissed me off even more. Following the path of destruction, I checked both bedrooms. All the bedsheets had been sliced, and the closets completely emptied out, with the contents flung everywhere.

The only place I'd been able to call home since I died. Completely destroyed.

"Bastard." Ida punched a hole in the wall. "This was so unnecessary. Did he really think we'd leave our heirlooms lying around?"

"No." Rose shook her head as she picked up pieces of her album, holding her black-and-white memories in one hand while her other bled and healed as she clutched shards of colored glass. Everything she had been, the last fragments of her living self, ruined beyond repair. "He knows we'd keep them on us. This was a warning."

"He's throwing a temper tantrum because we got the best of him at the graveyard," I said. If Frankie and Gwen hadn't been there, he might've let it go. But Elton couldn't stand to lose face. He'd consider this fair retribution.

"What if he comes back and takes one of us?" Ida clenched her jaw, no doubt thinking of all the ways Gwen would make her suffer for days on end, just for fun.

Stacey put her arm over my shoulders and squeezed. "Grab your stuff. All of you. I know my house isn't as nice as this place, but it's secluded. You're all welcome to stay."

It was a nice gesture, but I just wanted to curl into a ball and hug every inch of this apartment to my heart. This was ours. We'd made this into someplace we could be without him, where we could put our broken pieces together and make something whole.

"Come on, Holly." Stacey gave me a little nudge. "It won't be so bad, staying at my house again, will it?" A trickle of doubt cracked her voice. As if she was afraid I'd say no. How many nights had shadow memories haunted her in that house?

Ida hesitated but gave a short nod and disappeared into her bedroom. Rose soon came out of her room with her suitcase and mine. I went out to the balcony, hoping to find a few flowers for Rose to take with her, but they'd all been smashed and shredded. Elton knew exactly where to hit hardest. Without another option, we headed back to the other side of town.

Chapter Seventeen

Stacey opened the front door. The creaking hinges set off the neighborhood dogs, and a pane of glass slid out of a window, shattering on the front porch. Home sweet home. In the main room, Stacey's loyal followers, sad kids in black, were sprawled out everywhere. Like human roaches, they emotionally suckled off the filth and dreary atmosphere.

"Attention." Stacey gave a single clap. With a change in posture, she had gone from the girl who had seen *Pretty in Pink* five times in the theater to a discount Dracula. "I have invited a council to join us this evening. Initiation begins in five minutes in the basement."

The six teens scrambled to their feet, tripping over one another as they shoved their way toward the basement entrance. All over the opportunity to die. They were so hungry for it, for the beauty they thought came with immortality. They had no idea how ugly it could be. The scent of their desperation snapped in the air. They'd probably taste gamy, like deer and bark.

A girl with two lip rings and fishnet gloves hesitated at the door. She pulled her store-bought black hair over her shoulder as she examined the four of us with fear glazing her eyes. The promise of immortality no longer appeared as appealing when staring down actual death. She had a chance to change direction. To live fully. She looked at me, and I mouthed, "Run." With a final glance at Stacey, she booked it through the sliding glass door and disappeared.

"Smart girl." Stacey gazed out the open slider like a proud mother bird who had just pushed a baby out of the nest. "I always did like Alyssa. It would've been a shame to eat her. Make yourselves comfortable while I deal with the others."

The metallic scent of rust and standing water wafted up from the basement as she headed down the stairs, which groaned with each step she took. I was surprised they hadn't rotted out completely. The five teens who had clamored to get down there probably shook with anticipation, thinking they'd soon be joining the ranks of the undead.

Poor things. What a terrible place to die.

Ida dumped her suitcase by the front door. She stepped on the carpet, and it crunched beneath the pressure. Her delicate nostrils flared as she sniffed the air. "Good God, it's even worse than I remembered."

"Don't be rude, Ida." Rose clasped her hands, looking every bit like a big-eyed bunny facing a gothic house of horrors. "A little fresh air, a little Lysol, and this place will clean up nicely." Her smile faltered as a mouse scurried across the living room and into a hole in the wall. "It was very kind of Stacey to let us stay here."

"We could always get another apartment," Ida said.

"How did you find the last apartment, anyway?" The rent on that place must've been double what I made at Taco Bell in a month. Unless Ida had a secret business selling her art projects on Etsy, I couldn't figure out how they afforded it.

"We killed the landlord." Rose had a way of making murder sound like peaches-and-cream innocence, and she gave the sweetest smile at the memory. "He owned six properties, lived alone, and charged enormous late fees. He still hasn't been reported missing."

"Huh. Good idea." That was so much more economical than trying to scrape together enough money for rent. When I lived with Elton, we mostly stayed in hotels or off-season cabins. It had never occurred to me to secure housing for more than a few days at a time. Just another way I hadn't been properly prepared to live as an adult.

"Now that that's done, a few warnings." Stacey dusted off her hands as she came out of the basement. "The second floor is beyond repair, don't go up there. The backyard butts up against the woods. You can dump your kills back there, not too close to the house, though, or it'll attract animals. My mom's house isn't a palace, but I don't think Elton knows about it."

She looked to me for confirmation, and I shook my head. I never did tell Elton where Stacey lived. She insisted it would be the end of our friendship if I ever told him personal details about her. If only I'd listened when she tried to warn me. A thought that had become a constant spinning loop in my mind on nights when I'd been left alone. The nights that had become all too frequent near the end of our relationship and should've signaled the writing on the wall. I didn't realize until much too late that he didn't like her because he didn't like any threats to his full attention. My job was to feed his ego, and Stacey threatened my dependence on him, which he'd so carefully honed over months of subtly eroding my confidence.

I shook off the shame and regret that always accompanied thoughts of Elton. We were ending this soon. I had to keep reminding myself of that. "What did you do with your cult?"

"Tied them up in the basement." Stacey opened the door near the kitchen, where the horrified screams of the teens floated on the air like a symphony of dark delights. "There are enough to last the three of you a week. In case you need to lay low."

"That was considerate of you." Rose shot a warning glare at Ida, who had groaned. "I might nibble on one or two, but we'll be on the move quite a bit over the next week. There are a few things we need to take care of before the full moon."

We only had a week left. A week to get Rose's heirloom and say goodbye to our memories. Another week of keeping Parker alive. It didn't seem like enough time, but at the same time, it felt like too much.

I understood Parker's resentment for her mom. Hell, I still carried mine around over thirty years later, when it shouldn't have mattered anymore. I even understood her desire to set down roots somewhere after I'd spent all that time moving around with Elton and never getting attached to anything. But if Parker left, I'd be able to breathe easier.

"I'm sorry I wasn't much help with the spying." Stacey walked around, picking up discarded paper, plastic cups, and other trash. "Elton recognized me, which was surprising."

"I'm not surprised," I said. Stacey had challenged Elton the way very few did. She didn't shy away from him, and she wasn't enamored by him, either. It got under his skin.

"I do think I can help with the bank situation, though. Breaking in might not be necessary." Stacey held out her hand to Rose. "Can I borrow the ID you've been using?"

"Sure." Rose gave her the license that had belonged to a Kristin Helms, before Rose made a meal out of her, took her wallet, and assumed her identity. "What are you going to do?"

"Back in high school, I used to forge parent signatures for money," Stacey said. "I was pretty good at it, remember, Holly?"

I'd completely forgotten. She'd done such a good job of faking parents' signatures, her own mom thought she'd signed Stacey's report card, even though she couldn't recall ever seeing it. Her forging business kept us in cheap dollar movies and arcade money for most of the year.

"Can you put together something that would allow Rose to get into the box?" I asked.

"I can try to put together something official looking." Stacey tucked Rose's current ID in her back pocket. "I'll need a few hours at the library."

"Excellent." I bounced on my toes as I clapped my hands together. It would make my entire week if we could get out of the bank-heist portion of this mission. I did not want to spend the full moon in jail. "What about Frankie? What should we do with him?"

"I'll go talk to him." Ida put her hand on the front door and gave a meaningful look to Rose. "Not. By. Myself. Remember what happened at the graveyard?"

"Oh. Right." Rose jumped to attention. She'd already gotten one of her dishrags out, fully prepared to stress-clean until her problems became more manageable. "We should find out if he had a hand in ransacking our apartment and see just how close he is to Gwen these days."

When Ida left, with Rose trailing behind her, Stacey turned to me. The two of us in this house was like moving through a dream, familiar yet all the details were wrong. It wasn't until I clenched my fist and felt the pull of my skin over my bones that I realized time didn't like it, either. The two of us alone in this house didn't belong here.

"I need to get going on that paperwork, but you're welcome to stay." Stacey loosened the knot on her scarf, as if it was trying to choke her. "One of the kitchen cupboards has a stack of books. I don't know if there are any romances, though."

Stacey hurried out the front door, bending over and breathing out a sigh of relief at the foot of the porch stairs before disappearing toward the adjoining neighborhood. I stared around at the moldy walls, jars of greenish liquid with bits of gray meat floating inside, and unidentifiable stains in the carpet. If only I got some sense of peace from cleaning the way Rose did, I'd be able to find my calm. The muffled screams of the kids in the basement hummed on the dusty air. I couldn't just sit around and read. I had too much restless energy, and everything about this place depressed me.

My mind went back to Parker, because it always seemed to go back to Parker. She'd be fine. She wouldn't tell Elton we kissed. She had no reason to tell him about that. But still, it would probably be better if I made sure . . .

Closing the front door behind me, I set off for the one place I really shouldn't have gone.

I rubbed my palms against my jeans as I stood outside Parker's apartment. The complex wasn't that far from the school. Blue and brick-colored buildings with eight units apiece surrounding a pool and clubhouse. It was a smaller complex, but nice enough. Generic. Easy to leave behind and move into another complex in another state just like it.

I pressed my nails into my palm as I worked up the nerve to knock.

"Just do it already," I whispered to myself.

It wasn't that weird for me to show up. She'd be happy to see me. Maybe. Probably. I needed to get over myself. I was a vampire. Undead, immortal, powerful. I would not be brought to my knees by a mortal girl with a gorgeous smile and terrible dance moves. I straightened my spine and knocked, wincing as it echoed through the empty hall. No taking it back now.

Parker flung open the door. It hit the wall, and she jumped. "Hi."

The left side of my mouth curved up in a grin I tried to suppress. I couldn't help it. Everything about her made me smile. "I came over to make sure you were okay."

"Why?" She tucked her hair behind her ears. "I mean, do you think I shouldn't be okay? Because I'm totally okay. Fine. Why?"

"Uh-huh." I strolled around her living room, careful to keep my distance. A couple of generic floral prints hung on the walls, an iron clock, cheap and trendy couches with bright throw pillows. No pictures anywhere. The entire apartment screamed impersonal and transient. "So. This is where you live."

"For now, anyway." She tugged on the fraying hem of her sweater.

"Did you make this?" I held up a lumpy pottery sheep.

"In third grade." She grabbed it from me and put it back on the bookshelf.

"Has it always been you and your mom?" I asked. I didn't know why I kept firing questions at her, except being in her space made me want to wrap myself in her and know all the pieces that made her tick. I wanted every part of her, not just the ones she chose to show me.

"Yeah. I don't know who my dad is." She lifted a shoulder, as if to say it wasn't a big deal. "To be honest, I don't think my mom knows, either."

"My mom told everyone my dad was dead so she could get sympathy widow points."

My father took off right after I'd been born, a scandal in the early '70s. So my mom moved to Glen River and told everyone she was widowed, including me. I didn't find out my father was alive until she confessed it to me in middle school, but by that point, I just kept the lie going because it was easier. Stacey was the only person who knew the truth. I never even told Elton. Of course he never asked, either, because it didn't center on him, so he didn't care.

Parker let out a choked laugh. "Sorry. I shouldn't laugh. That's really fucked up."

"It's kind of funny." I grinned at her for what felt like way too long to be considered normal. Playing with the clasp on my locket, I turned back to the bookshelf. "Are you a reader?"

"Yes. Historical and fantasy, mostly. I like going someplace that isn't here. Do you want anything to drink?" When I raised my eyebrows, she shook her head. "No, of course you don't. Silly me. Why are you here?"

"I can . . ." I gestured at the door. This was turning out to be way more awkward than I'd anticipated, and I hadn't anticipated this going well. "I'm not even sure why I came over."

Other than wanting to see her, which was a problem. I didn't need to involve myself in her life or feel things while standing in her sad apartment because her mom never gave her anything close to stability. And I absolutely did *not* need to notice how cute she looked as she bit her bottom lip and knotted her fingers behind her back.

I had no place here.

I started to march across her living room toward the door when she reached out and grabbed my hand. Her palm was warm, and her pulse thumped in a skipping beat until it matched my own. "Wait." Her soft brown eyes met mine. "Don't go yet."

"This is a bad idea." I swallowed. "You should tell me to leave."

Her gaze swept my lips. "But I already invited you in."

"That's not a thing."

I kissed her, and oh, God, it was just as consuming as the first time. I'd never kissed with this much urgency before. Tangled tongues, teeth bumping, completely lost in this girl. She guided me to the couch and backed me into it so I fell against the cushions. As she straddled me, I gripped her hips, pulling her closer, needing more.

A knock at the door had us both pulling back. "Parker. Open up."

Elton. My heart leaped into my throat. If he suspected anything . . .

Parker rested her forehead against mine. "I'll get rid of him."

"No." I grabbed her arms to hold her still. "If he thinks there is something going on with us, he'll kill you. Act like everything is fine. This will be over in a week."

Her eyes widened. "What do you mean, he'll kill me? Is that a joke?"

"You know what it means." I moved her off my lap and adjusted my sweater, retied my messy bun, making sure everything was in the same place it was when I came over. "If you want to keep living in denial, that's your choice, but do not think for a second that Elton is just some harmless high school boy."

"I've never considered high school boys to be harmless." Parker straightened her own sweater and smoothed down her hair. "I wish you would just tell me the truth."

"I wish you'd say it first." I gave her a mocking bow. "And I'd be happy to confirm."

Her expression hardened as she stared at me. Elton knocked again.

"Coming," she said as she kept her eyes on mine.

I tucked my locket into my sweater, and she flung open the door. Elton, in all of his black leather jacket, windswept glory, stepped into the living room like it was a stage and we were an audience who existed just for his entrance. My stomach clenched, an involuntary reaction, as my blood rushed through my veins. Still so beautiful. My fingers itched to trace the lines of his face, even as my mind screamed at me to run. His grin sharpened as soon as he laid eyes on me.

"Holly. How nice to see you all cleaned up." He slung his arm over Parker's shoulders and nuzzled her ear. The sharp point of his fang traced the shell, and her shoulders hunched in response. "Grave digging is such dirty business."

Parker's brow furrowed as she glanced at me. "Grave digging?"

"Don't listen to Elton." I glared at him. "He seems to have lost his head."

"Yet here it is, fully attached." He picked a piece of lint off his button-down shirt. "By the way, while I appreciate you sending that frizzy-haired menace to check up on me today, it's truly unnecessary. We're old friends. I'm sure we can settle our differences on our own."

"Is that what we're calling them now? Differences?" One more week. Then I could rip off his head in a more permanent way. "What do you want?"

"I'm sorry." He put a hand to his chest as he looked around.

"Do you live here? My mistake."

"I was just leaving, actually." I rammed my shoulder into Elton's as I passed. "Obviously, my presence here is unwanted. Be careful," I said to Parker.

"This tired conversation again?" Elton let his icy eyes fill with pity, an act he'd perfected over the years. "You need a new angle, Holly. I know our breakup hit you hard, but you're starting to look desperate at this point."

"And you're starting to look . . ." I waved my hand up and down. Honestly, it was a crime for him to be so pretty. "Whatever. I'm done here."

"I'm sure we'll see each other again soon enough." He gave me a little wave.

I slammed the door and blew out a breath. Hopefully Parker would play along. If she broke up with Elton, he'd probably think it a fun little game to win her back. But if she told him she was ending things because she wanted someone else . . . I didn't want to think about what he would do if she broke his delicate ego. We only had to keep this up for another week. Then Parker would be free to move on with her life, I'd be free to leave Michigan, and we'd never have to see each other again.

That did nothing to comfort me.

By the time I got back to Stacey's house, Rose and Ida had returned. Ida had another art project. She sat at the dining-room table with a length of long blond hair, which she knotted to form a thick rope. She hummed a tune I didn't recognize. Lost in her own world. Rose had already tied up four bags of trash and had one corner of the living room scrubbed to a gleaming polish. If I looked at that one corner, and blocked out my peripheral vision, I could almost shut out the rest of the disaster around us.

"Did you talk to Frankie?" I asked Rose.

"He was with Gwen. We couldn't get him alone." Rose pulled out the last rusty nail from the fireplace mantel and got to work on the surrounding marble. "He could be useful, though. We'll have to set up a time to meet him where we can all speak freely."

"I saw Elton today." I told her about my visit to Parker's, minus the kissing, and what Elton had said to me before I shut the door in his face. "I think he might try to ambush us on the way to the bank, so we need to be cautious."

"He won't know what direction we're coming from, though." Rose had put some wildflowers in a mason jar and arranged them on the mantel. "That's an advantage."

The front door banged open, kicking up a fresh round of dust, and starting the chorus of screams in the basement anew. Stacey walked in with blood staining her lips and a board game under her arm. "Anyone want to play Monopoly?"

I raised my hand with much more enthusiasm than I felt. Only because Stacey loved board games. If I shut out the crumbling walls, the faint scent of dried blood, and the shrieks of terrified teenagers, it could've been 1987 again. But as I glanced between Rose and Ida fighting over the thimble, it occurred to me that not everything in my present needed to be compared to the way things used to be. I had things worth fighting for now, and maybe it was time to let my past go, before it let me go.

Chapter Eighteen

The sun rose over the trees as I stood on Stacey's back patio. An old swing with rusted hinges and faded cushions still managed to stay upright at the back of the property. I walked through the yard, where a chilling mist wound around my ankles, and a light frost coated the grass. The gazebo where I spent lazy summer days reading had fallen apart, now no more than a pile of sticks with chipped white paint and overgrown weeds. Her backyard bumped up to the woods where Stacey and I waited half the night for the Fisher brothers, who never showed up because they'd been caught sneaking out of their bedroom window. Another memory that came to me out of nowhere, but soon would be burned away the moment Rose, Ida, and I sacrificed our heirlooms to kill a boy we all once had loved.

Ida stepped outside. "It's almost time."

While Stacey, Rose, and I had played Monopoly all night, Ida quit after the first round to work on her human-hair rope. She stayed silent and moody. At around one in the morning, she'd gone off on her own, not returning until now. The closer we got to ending Elton, the more withdrawn she'd become. I worried what losing her memories would do to her state of mind and what trauma still lingered from the graveyard.

Not for the first time, I considered if it was all worth it. Protecting Parker had becoming important enough for me to say yes, but Ida had no such attachment, and her memories felt so much larger than mine. I didn't have a sister who had been my sun. I had a mother who'd consistently put her fragile ego before me and a teacher who had stopped caring about his students. When I put it like that, I wondered if I was really making any kind of a sacrifice at all.

I approached Ida as the last of the morning mist burned off with the sun and rubbed my arms. "Are we doing the right thing? Is killing Elton worth the cost?"

"Yes." She grabbed me so fast, I was nearly thrown off balance. "You're not having second thoughts, are you? Because we've passed the point of no return already."

"I'm still on board. I'm just . . ." I lifted my hands and let them fall uselessly at my sides.

"Just what?" Ida's black-cherry scent sharpened as her ancient eyes bored into me. "We don't have room for doubt, so you better spit out whatever you're thinking."

"I'm in, that's not going to change." Like always, Parker was at the forefront of my mind. The way she scrunched her nose whenever she was trying to figure me out, her adorable ramblings, the way she'd let out a soft sigh the first time we kissed. Every memory I had of her, I'd be able to keep, and making sure she made it out of this safe and alive made it worthwhile to me. But Ida would be losing Bea. It felt like she'd been asked to pay significantly more than Rose or I had, and I hated the unfairness of it all. "I wish there was another way."

"Believe me, so do I." She released me and hung her head as she leaned against the gray, splintered siding. "I'm the only one left who remembers Bea. When my memory goes, she goes with it. Permanently. There are no pictures, no recorded history. She'll just be wiped away. As if she'd never been here at all."

For some odd reason, jealousy rose inside me, snapping its bitter teeth. I couldn't help but wish I'd had family I'd loved like that in life, who had loved me in return. Maybe I wouldn't have made the choices I had with Elton. Or maybe I would've gone through with it anyway, and I would've felt worse. That was the problem with constantly looking back. I could spend the rest of my eternity running over every choice I'd made and convincing myself I'd done everything wrong. Regret was the kind of burden that managed to get heavier with each passing year.

Ida had her own burdens, some she shared and some I only knew as shadows that lingered in her dark eyes. "What's the one thing you wish you could keep?" I asked. "If you could have just one memory?"

"The summer Bea turned thirteen and the fair had come to town." Ida fired off the memory without a second thought or consideration. As she smiled, it melted away all the hard angles of her sharp face. "She had a crush on a farmhand named Tommy, who had been in charge of keeping watch over Mr. Harrison's prize pig. I lured Tommy away from the judging pen, while Bea sneaked out the pig so she could spend the afternoon with Tommy looking for it."

I chuckled. "That sounds like a terrible plan."

"Oh, it was." Ida let out a small laugh, edged with the weight of knowing just how far and long those days were gone. "That damn pig caused the biggest ruckus around the food tents. I laughed so hard I ended up puking. The three of us managed to corral the pig before Mr. Harrison found out, and Tommy bought us both popcorn fritters for our trouble."

"Hold on a minute." I rushed into the house to dig through my suitcase, tossing clothes around until I found the notebook where I kept track of all the books I've read. I grabbed a pen off the sticky countertop and went back outside. "Give me the sights, sounds, and little things you don't think matter. I'll keep the memory here. If you ever want it, all you have to do is ask."

For the next hour, she gave me everything she could remember. Corndogs dipped in hot oil, the screams from the top of the Ferris wheel, the hay and flies and animals with blue ribbons. Every taste and texture from the 1920 Allegan County Fair. I wrote until my hand cramped, filling pages and pages of details. She wouldn't have the exact memory, and the feeling could never be replicated, but she could go forward knowing that in these pages, it would always be there. A record of her and Bea on their best day.

Once I finished writing, I put the cap back on the pen and closed the notebook. "Should we get ready and head over to the bank?"

"Might as well." Ida turned her gaze to the unkempt lawn. "Thank you. For taking the time to write all that down. If you want to go ahead and tell Rose that we'll be ready to leave soon, I'll be along in a minute."

I stepped inside, leaving Ida alone with the memories she wouldn't have for much longer. For the last couple of hours, Rose continued with her quest to tidy up the main living area. Despite her best efforts, it still looked like the set of a post-apocalyptic vampire takeover. Not that it mattered. Per my agreement with Stacey, once this was all over, we'd never set foot in Michigan again.

I found Rose in the downstairs powder room, putting the finishing touches on her powder-perfect makeup. She reminded me of a porcelain doll, delicate features set within a sweet face made for tea parties and picnics. A lovely façade to conceal the vicious predator beneath.

"We should leave soon," I said.

"Where's Ida?" Rose dabbed a little gloss on her lips. "By the way, I took a look at the bathing situation, and we'll be better off using the hose outside to shower."

"Ida is coming in a minute." I looked Rose over. She'd put on another polka dot, fifties-style dress that she favored but paired it with gloves, like a lady about to go out for a Sunday drive. "You know people don't dress up to go to the bank anymore, right?"

Rose turned up her nose. "Just because the rest of the world is content to do their business in Hello Kitty pajamas doesn't mean I have to follow suit."

"If you say so."

Ida came back inside, her eyes a little wetter than when I'd left her, but I didn't mention it. Stacey had gone out after we finished playing early this morning and hadn't returned. She'd left the forged paperwork stating that Rose was dead and Kristin Helms was the personal rep for her estate. Since Rose had the key, we hoped it wouldn't be too much of a fuss for her to get into the box.

I passed by the basement, where the feeble cries of the teens filtered through the cracks in the door. Their pleading had become weaker over the night. Either they had accepted their fate, or Stacey hadn't been giving them enough water. After going so long without mortal nourishment, it was easy for us to forget how frequently they needed to drink.

"Should we bring some water down to those kids in the basement?" I asked.

"No need," Rose said. "I took care of that earlier this morning when I went down for a little snack. But I must say, if they're all going to taste like toast and rubber, I'd rather Stacey just let them go. It's too much responsibility remembering to feed and water them. This is why I'll never get a dog."

"Stacey is probably keeping them all on a steady diet of her favorite food." I mimed gagging. "Grilled cheese sandwiches made with that fake stuff you spray out of a can."

Rose furrowed her brow. "I don't understand."

"Never mind. We can ask her about it when we get back." I didn't like the idea of keeping a corral of kids on hand, either. Especially since it remained important to me to allow my victims a chance to run. I headed to the front door, with Rose and Ida behind me.

Sunlight had cleared most of the early-morning frost, but the grass still crunched beneath our feet, and we cut through the yard and into the neighborhood. The bank where Rose kept her heirlooms wasn't far from the high school. Just two streets over from where she'd grown up, in an area that was now considered retro and trendy for young families.

"Have you gone to your house since we've been back?" I asked.

"Why would I?" Rose asked. "My family is long dead. I have no reason to call on the strangers who live there now."

"Just wondering." The closer we got to ending our memories, the more I wanted to know about Rose and Ida while they'd been alive. If only so I could remind them once they could no longer remind themselves.

The bank was in a smaller building off the main road. Rose told us it had been called something else in 1954, but they still had their safe-deposit boxes in the vault. We had a few minutes until they opened, so we pretended to window-shop at the clothing store in the nearby strip mall until the manager unlocked the doors at exactly nine. No sign of Elton or Gwen on our walk over, or hovering around the entrance. An uneasy feeling settled into the pit of my stomach, but I brushed it off. Maybe he expected us to come at night.

As soon as we walked through the door, Gwen stood behind the teller line, wearing a name tag that said DEBBIE. "Welcome to First National."

She gave us a deadly smile and a prom-queen wave. Her robot-voiced greeting made me shudder. I couldn't think of anyone on the planet less suited for customer service.

We should've anticipated this. There was no way Elton would let us just waltz in here without having someone on guard. While we took a seat in the lobby, Gwen tapped the manager on the shoulder. She pointed to us, then looked directly at Rose and licked her lips.

Gwen was a sadistic beauty who never should've been made into a vampire. Elton once told me her maker had turned her after he found her squeezing the heads off kittens in a remote barn. He had hoped to use her to handle his enemies. She did as he asked because she took pleasure in the pain of others, but when she met up with Elton a year later, she killed her maker and did as she pleased. When she lived with us, I barely ever saw her, much to my relief. She made it a point to be gone whenever I was around. She'd done the same with Rose. Gwen didn't play well with others, except Frankie, whom she had created to be a plaything, and Elton, who was her narcissistic kin in every way that counted.

"There are three of us," Rose said. "She can't do anything when there are three of us."

I would've had a lot more confidence if her voice hadn't wavered. Though Rose had managed to overpower her in the graveyard, it was only because she had the element of surprise. Gwen was mean, strong, and had no fear. It made her a dangerous enemy.

The branch manager came out from behind the teller line. "Can I help you?"

His voice dripped with disdain. He had one of those mustaches that looked like a broom, and he wore a three-piece suit with gold cuff links. He was the kind of person who carried himself with an air of being Very Busy and Very Important, and three teenage girls who clearly didn't have any money weren't worth bothering with manners.

Rose told him our reason for being there, and as he took her over to his office, Ida leaned into me and whispered, "Can we just kill him and skip all this?"

"If only." I kept a close eye on the manager as he examined Rose's forged paperwork. He wore a polite, if disinterested, mask but didn't appear to suspect her of lying.

Until he left his office.

He walked over to the fax machine with the personal-rep papers Stacey had drawn up, and Gwen pulled him aside. While he recoiled from her touch, his gaze remained intensely focused as she pointed at the paper and waved her hands around. His frown deepened.

Whatever Gwen was telling him wouldn't work out in our favor.

Their voices were too low to overhear, so I stood and went over to the office, where Rose sat with her hands folded in her lap. "Why isn't he letting you in the box?"

"He said something about faxing the paperwork to legal. I don't know."

"Did you see that Gwen's talking to him?"

"I'll handle it." She shot a worried glance over her shoulder. "Go."

I went to the lobby and flopped back in my seat. "I don't like this."

"I'm going to see if I can get closer." Ida stood and walked past the check-writing stand, dumping a stack of deposit slips to the ground as she passed.

While I crawled on my hands and knees to pick them up, the other teller came out to the lobby to help me. Ida took advantage of the distraction to slip behind the teller line and position herself behind the vault door. I kept the teller too busy to notice, but within a few minutes, Ida rushed over to where Rose was still seated in the office. The two of them argued, then Rose got up, and they both motioned for me to follow them outside.

"What's going on?" I asked as soon as we hit the sidewalk.

Ida looked both ways before picking up her pace and running. "Gwen called our bluff. She convinced the manager to get on the phone with the police."

"Are you serious?" We cut through a neighborhood, running between the unfenced yards on the way back to Stacey's. "What do we do now?"

"We go back to the original plan," Rose said. "We'll have to break into the vault."

"We have three days," Ida said. "That's the soonest they can get their locksmith in. Gwen told him that Rose's death certificate is real, but Kristin's personal-rep papers are forged. They're going to drill the box and send the contents to the state."

"I need to do more research on bank vaults," Rose said. We slowed down once we got to Stacey's street. "I should've planned for this. Elton knows my heirloom is at that bank; I should've expected he'd station Gwen there to keep an eye out for us."

"You couldn't have known." I laid a hand on her arm. "I mean, who would hire Gwen?"

Ida let out a snort. "They must be really desperate for employees."

"Be that as it may, I need to go to the library today." Rose wrung her gloved hands together. "Maybe they have some old plans on the bank. We'll have to do it tomorrow night."

"So soon?" I didn't want to do the break-in at all, but with such short notice, it was bound to go wrong. "Shouldn't we take time to plan?"

"We don't have time," Ida said. "If they get their locksmith in sooner, all will be lost. I agree with Rose, it has to be tomorrow."

Great. Three girls with no experience in breaking and entering were bound to be successful. We couldn't count the odds though, because the box was for sure getting drilled, and we needed those combs out of there before that happened. Better if we could do it without Gwen around.

We walked into the house, completely deflated, to find Stacey had returned. She stood in the center of the living room with the bodies of the teens at her feet. A fly landed on one of their open and sightless eyeballs. Blood soaked into the carpet, and Rose groaned behind me. It had taken her hours to get the living room into habitable shape.

"Okay, this is way worse than anything Rose has done with her kills." Ida lifted an arm of one of the bodies and tilted her head, like she was contemplating what kind of secondary use it might have. "Were you really that hungry?"

"I don't normally kill where I sleep, but when you three said you weren't going to eat them, I had to get rid of them somehow.

They were becoming a nuisance." Stacey's tone suggested it was our fault she'd piled up four bodies in her living room. We never asked her to keep her cult captive. She could've let them go the first night, but it wasn't a point I wanted to spend any amount of time arguing.

"Bad news," I said. "Your paperwork didn't get us in."

"No problem." She licked a bloody finger. "I already came up with a backup plan."

"What kind of backup plan?" I asked.

She looked at the angelic face of one of her victims and, with a wicked smile, she turned toward the sliding glass door, where Frankie had just stepped in from the backyard.

Chapter Nineteen

"What is he doing here?" Frankie hadn't sold us out at the graveyard, but from his sour expression, he hadn't forgotten about me tearing out his eyeballs, either. Or maybe his face just always looked like that. It was hard to tell.

"I caught him following me," Stacey said. "We had a nice little chat."

"I wanted to see Ida," Frankie mumbled to the floor. If he could blush, his face would've been on fire. "And say I was sorry for what happened at the graveyard."

"I'm standing right here." Ida had already removed one of the teen's arms and bent it back and forth at the elbow like a seesaw. "But your apology is unnecessary. We know you didn't tell Elton we were gathering our heirlooms."

Ida turned her back on us and wandered over to the fireplace, measuring the arm she'd just collected against the mantel. I didn't even want to ask what horrifying project she had in mind. Frankie frowned. He had to have been deluding himself if he expected more than a brush-off from Ida. She had no interest in him and had never expressed otherwise.

"Is that all you wanted?" Rose wrung her hands as she glanced at me. She didn't like the idea of Frankie knowing where we were staying any more than I did. He didn't sell us out, but that didn't mean we were ready to start braiding one another's hair.

"No." Frankie shook his head like he was clearing out the small family of bats who resided there. "I can help you get into the bank."

Ida dropped the arm she'd been holding against the fireplace.

"Are you serious?"

"See why I brought him back here?" Stacey gave us a curtsy. "You're welcome."

This was getting a lot more complicated than breaking into a high-security vault, and we hadn't expected that to be easy. Frankie looked at Ida with longing in his eyes. It gave me a bad feeling in the pit of my stomach, but if he really could get us past Gwen and into the bank, we'd need him. We didn't have any options at this point.

"Did you know Frankie here is good at picking locks?" Stacey rested her elbow on his massive shoulder. "He told Elton he could get into Rose's safe-deposit box without her key."

"What?" Rose asked. "How?"

"Don't worry." Stacey tapped her on the nose. "He's going to help us get into the vault before it ever comes to that."

"I . . . ah . . ." Frankie cleared his throat. "Gwen gave me the security code to the building and the combo for the vault. I told her I'd go in tonight and get Rose's heirloom."

This could work. It scared me how much hope I had at the moment, but this had to be better than straight-up breaking in. If we could bypass the security alarms, we could be in and out without being detected. I looked to Rose, who gave me a thumbs-up.

"We'll let you three talk while we clean up in here." Stacey nudged Frankie, and they each grabbed a body to dispose of in the woods.

As soon as they stepped outside, Rose turned to us. "What do you think?"

"I don't know." Ida grimaced as she took in the last two bodies in the living room. "I still maintain there is something very wrong with Stacey, and the thought of her coming up with a decent plan that might actually work makes a little piece of my soul shrivel up and die."

My spine stiffened. Even if something had corroded in Stacey over the years, she'd been nothing but generous and helpful. A miracle, considering the kind of resentment for me she was absolutely entitled to. And if her idea worked, we'd have everything we'd need.

"I think this is a great plan," Rose said with a heavy dose of cheer. Probably because she sensed my rising annoyance and wanted to defuse it before it became an issue.

"I didn't say it was a *bad* plan," Ida grumbled. "This is our best shot at getting into the bank, and I think we should do this, even if the idea did come from Stacey."

With that settled, I gestured at the remaining bodies. "Should we . . . ?"

"Good idea," Rose said.

The two of us each hefted one over our shoulders and took them out to the woods in the back, passing Stacey and Frankie on the way. Sunlight filtered through the red and gold leaves. If we weren't dumping a bunch of bodies that had already begun to stink of rotted meat, it would've been beautiful. The blank, empty face of a sixteen-year-old girl stared up at nothing. It was really too bad. Her only mistake had been thinking vampires were sexy, and really, who hadn't been there?

We continued to plan well into the afternoon. Frankie shared with us that Elton had been in a mood ever since the graveyard, which didn't surprise me. He also told us about Elton's growing frustration with Parker's continued distance from him. Of course, he blamed us. The thought gave me a considerable amount of joy.

"Has Elton always been like this?" I asked.

It was more a rhetorical question, a way for me to voice my fears about what losing our memories might do to us, but Ida set aside the arm she was trying to fashion into some kind of a wall sconce. "His parents spoiled him but also ignored him. He grew up entitled and insecure, and it made him feel like he had to be important."

"I guess." My mom ignored me most of the time, but it didn't turn me into a controlling asshole. "How does he justify himself, though?"

"He thinks he has genuine feelings," Frankie said.

"He thinks of us as his," Ida said. "And the problem is, he doesn't know how to love anyone other than himself. He was selfish when we were kids too, but I let him get away with it because I knew his home life sucked, and I felt sorry for him."

Frankie choked on a laugh. "He would not appreciate your pity."

"I'm aware." Ida went back to her latest art project. "He might've had a shot at being decent once, but immortality gave him a lot of power that went right to his head."

After living with Elton's whims and tantrums for so many years, I'd learned he was the type of guy who would've pushed everyone else out of the way to grab a solo lifeboat on the *Titanic* for him and all of his possessions. I couldn't bring myself to feel guilty for wanting him dead. Only sad that it had come to this, and that I hadn't seen his true colors decades ago.

Frankie left but wouldn't tell us where he was staying, which made me question whether or not we could really trust him. But if he got us Rose's combs, I wouldn't care whose side he was on. With our plans for the bank set in place, I had the rest of the day to do what I wanted, and what I wanted was to eat. My pulse started its irregular beating, and my stomach grumbled. There had to be a jogger or someone I could pick off in the nearby park.

Unable to take another second of sitting in this house, I stood. "I'm going out."

I glanced at Ida, and she gave me a small nod of acknowledgment. The story about the county-fair pig had been the most personal thing she'd shared with me. It was a shame I'd never know more about her life before it was gone. With us all being one day closer to losing our memories for good, the best thing we could do for ourselves was to settle our pasts.

"If you happen to go hunting on the east side, can you stop by the apartment and grab my heirloom notes?" Rose asked. "I think I left them in the hidden drawer in my dresser."

"No problem." I just so happened to be heading that way.

I took the bus over to Shady Pines, the nursing home where my mom had been ever since her dementia had gotten bad enough that she could no longer live on her own. Elton must've known about it long before I ever did, but he never told me. I had to find out about it on Facebook, of all godforsaken places. But he had to have known. He told me a long time ago that he kept tabs on her but wouldn't ever give me updates. For my benefit, he said. So I wouldn't feel obligated to tie myself to her when that was no longer my life. Like it was up to him to decide what I needed based on what *he* said I needed. His opinion had become so ingrained in me, I hadn't even realized I was still giving it weight long after he was no longer a factor.

At the same time, my mom had consistently made my life harder because of her careless choices. She screwed up all the time. I was so angry with her, and I loved her. I could hold those two opposing facts in my mind, but I was still trying to find a way to settle them.

Shady Pines was a sprawling complex with assisted living and full-time care all on the same grounds. Cheerful plants in fall colors bordered the walks. An old man with a plastic gnome tied to his walker held a finger to his lips as he passed me and sneaked out the front gates. Far be it for me to stop him from trying to live his best life before he died.

I walked through the main entrance, which had the look of both an apartment-complex clubhouse and the front desk of a hospital. Maroon carpets with gold threading, plastic potted plants, and a fountain with cracked plaster made up most of the ambiance. The nurse behind the desk looked like she'd rather be handing out free enemas.

"I'm here to see Marie Liddell." I tapped my fingers on the counter, debating if I should go through with the visit or run while I still had the chance.

The nurse eyed me with part fascination, part revulsion. The typical mortal response, though I would've thought she'd be more accustomed to facing death, working in a place like this. "Are you family?"

"In a way." I hadn't considered my mom family since I'd been turned. It jarred my senses to claim her with that kind of title. "I haven't seen her in a long time."

"She might not recognize you." She gave me a kind smile with tired eyes. "It's nice for her to have visitors. I don't think anyone's come by since she's been here."

Guilt and indifference hit me with equal force. I spent my entire childhood raising the person who was supposed to be raising me. I tried time and time again to save her from herself, to stop her from playing games with the ex-wives of men who never tried to make her feel secure in their relationship. She never listened, never changed, no matter how many times she promised. At the same time, she was dying. Alone. As her memories slowly eroded away. No one deserved that, not even neglectful mothers.

The nurse led me down the hall. Death lingered in the air, so much more potent than the dark alleys and shadowed corners where I claimed most of my victims. The scent of antiseptic stung my nostrils. Hopelessness clung to the muted white walls. I'd been to hospitals in the past, but it wasn't the same. People didn't come here with the expectation of getting well.

At the end of the hall, the nurse left me at an open door and let me know she'd be up front if I needed her. I'd expected my mom to be older. Maybe a little more wrinkled, her bones a little more brittle.

Nothing could have prepared me for the end stages of a hard-lived life.

My mom sat in a padded rocking chair, staring out the window. Her skin now hung in sallow sags off her birdlike frame. Wispy curls framed her hollow face like a cheap Q-tip. She used to have a laugh that would draw the attention of men within a ten-mile radius; bold, bright, and so self-assured. None of that remained. She stared up at me with empty eyes.

"Holly?" Her voice cracked as I entered the room and took a seat on the edge of her bed. She squinted at me. The papery skin around her eyes folded in on itself. "What year is this?"

"Hi, Momma." I took her hand, and she shivered as she pulled it away.

"You're not here. You died." She turned her head toward the window. "I remember. They think I can't do that anymore, but I can. I remember everything. This isn't real."

"It's real, Momma. The night you thought I died? That's not exactly what happened. I left town with that boy my teacher tried to talk to you about. I became something else." It didn't hurt to tell her the truth. She wouldn't remember I'd been here, anyway.

"No, you died. They found all that blood, most of it belonging to that sweet girl you used to run with. You remember her, don't you? Bug-eyed little thing, but such a nice friend." Her eyes widened, and the wooden legs of her rocker screeched across the linoleum floor as she pushed her chair away from me. The glaze over her eyes cleared for a fraction of a second. "Why are you here? What did you do to yourself?"

"Something I regret, but I'm trying to make sure it doesn't happen again." I stood and walked around her room. She didn't have many personal possessions, but she kept a silver frame with my junior-year picture. The same one they'd put on the side of milk cartons for a few weeks, hoping I hadn't been killed after all. "Pretty soon, I'm going to forget everything. This might be my last chance to say the things I should've said while I'd been alive." I exhaled, letting out the words I'd been hanging onto for decades. "You hurt me, Momma."

My throat tightened. The truth was always so much harder to say than the lies I told her when she asked if everything was okay. Her selfishness hurt me over and over, and I let it go because it was easier to hope she'd stop remembering me altogether on the days she wanted to trot me out to play happy family with her new boyfriends. She wouldn't have cared if I'd said I was anything other than "fine." She wanted the peace of mind, the reassurances, and the pats on the back while I quietly died inside.

Elton hadn't been the start of it for me. He hadn't been the one who trained me to feel small. I'd been learning how to shrink my entire life.

"I know this isn't real." She shook her head. Even in what she thought was a delusion, she still couldn't bring herself to take responsibility. "Who are you, really? Why are you wearing my daughter's face? She's dead, and she's not coming back."

I crouched in front of her, this woman I loved and hated with my whole heart. My very presence made her recoil, and even in her last days, I was glad to see she hadn't stopped seeing the world in color. A glimmer of that bold and brash woman still lived within her deteriorating mind. "I wish you had been better."

"What is this nonsense?" She'd gone back to 1987. I could see it in her posture, the way she held her head high, and the haughtiness in her voice. I didn't talk back in 1987. I didn't demand more from her as a mother back then. "Don't you have homework to do?"

I took her hand and pressed it to my cheek. "I'm sorry I don't have words of comfort to offer you now when you probably need them most, but I wish you had cared more about both of us when you had the chance."

"How can you say I don't care? Who buys your clothes? Who is always picking you up a new book when I do the shopping? Who works double shifts so we can live in a decent neighborhood?" She lifted her chin. "My personal life is not your concern."

"Don't you see that it is, though?" I let go of her hand. "School was so much harder for me, because you never once thought of me when it came to your life."

"I'm sorry." Tears swam in her old eyes as she moved in and out of focus. We'd shifted back to her thinking I wasn't really here. "If I could do it all over again, I would've never given those men the time of day. They all fucked me over in the end. I was so hurt when your daddy left, and I kept trying to find someone to fill that role. Not just for me, but for you too. I went about it all wrong, though. Forgive me, Holly. Please."

I could've had my final say. I could've lowered the hammer and refused in these last moments we had together. I might've even been able to convince myself I deserved to have my turn, but it would've given me only a moment of triumph, and that's not really why I came here, anyway. "I forgive you, Momma."

She turned back to the window, a small smile disappearing into her folds of wrinkled skin. Her shoulders relaxed as she took in the sunset. I'd leave, and she'd probably convince herself this was all a dream, but it was a dream she'd needed.

Maybe it was a dream I needed too.

I left the nursing home, not necessarily with a sense of closure, but I'd done the best I could do. Though the resentment I carried for my mom wasn't gone by any means, it was time for me to let go. I hoped in death she'd finally find the peace that had eluded her in life.

She hadn't been a good parent, but I no longer needed her to be.

Chapter Twenty

The sun had just begun to set as I made my way over to the apartment above the meat market. I wasn't exactly eager to get back to Stacey's and sit around that moldy tomb until it was time to go to the bank, so I stopped to grab a bite to eat. The guy who told me I'd be pretty if I smiled tasted like a mix of tomato paste, noodles, and metal. It reminded me of SpaghettiOs.

Rose had given me instructions on how to unlatch her hidden drawer, and I was eager to look over her notes myself before bringing them back. Maybe there was a loophole to the memories. Something she had overlooked.

Elton and Gwen had torn the place apart. A top-to-bottom violation of the place we all considered home. I didn't believe for a second they expected to find the heirlooms. The destruction had been a careful shredding of everything we held dear, a reminder that he still knew our hearts and where to hit hardest. He wanted us to run. He wanted our fear, because he no longer had our love. One way or the other, it all came down to control. I closed my fist around the locket I hadn't taken off since the night Stacey gave it back to me. Soon.

The stairs to the second floor creaked as I approached the apartment with caution. The door was wide open, revealing the mess to the street below. Elton had broken the lock the night he ransacked the place, but I could've sworn we shut it when we left. My senses went on high alert as I stepped over the threshold, and I froze as Parker swung around with a yearbook in her hands. Glen River West's

1987 yearbook.

She held it up. "Explain yourself."

A spread of black-and-white photos had "In Loving Memory" scrawled across the top. Dozens of pictures of Stacey and me filled the two pages. The yearbook committee cropped all the photos where we'd accidently appeared in the background to make us look like a couple of Suzy High Schools. There were even a few pictures of a girl who most definitely wasn't me, but an effort had been made. I had no idea anyone had cared.

"That was nice of them," I said.

"That was nice of them?" Parker slammed the yearbook to the ground. "That's all you have to say? You died over thirty years ago."

She hadn't asked, but I felt compelled to answer, anyway. "Technically, yes?"

The rage and confusion in her eyes had me taking a step back. Deep down, she'd known. But deep down wasn't the same as upfront confirmation. The night Elton had told me the truth, I pushed him off the bleachers—even though I'd been having suspicions for weeks that there was something otherworldly about him. Then I spent the next two days denying it and shutting down any conversation related to vampires. Parker was handling it a lot better than I ever did.

"How?" Tears gathered at the corners of her eyes. "Tell me the truth."

"For the record, I never lied. I just omitted a few facts." When she shot me a glare, I held my hands out. "Okay. Not what you want to hear right now. The truth is . . ." I'd only ever shared the truth with people I intended to kill, and I couldn't afford to think about what that meant in regards to my feelings for Parker. "I'm a vampire."

She sucked in a sharp breath. "I know."

I rolled my eyes. "If you know, then why are you acting like it's some dark secret I was keeping from you? Which I only did out of self-preservation, by the way."

"I didn't know for sure." She took on a defensive posture. "The sun doesn't bother you."

"I don't particularly like being out during the day, but no, the sun doesn't turn us to dust." I picked up one of the overturned wicker chairs and took a seat. "I don't even know how that rumor got started. If it were true, we'd all just live in Alaska. And it's insulting. We're undead. It should take more than a little ultraviolet light to end our existence."

"Is that what you're trying to do with Elton? End his existence?" She said the last three words as a whisper, like she didn't want to voice the possibility, which annoyed me for reasons I couldn't explain.

"Yes. Does it make you sad? Because it shouldn't." I was pouting, but she had to understand by now that we were doing it for her. The risks we'd taken to keep her safe.

"I'm not sad. I'm scared, but not nearly as scared as I should be, and that probably means there's something deeply wrong with me." She took a tentative seat on the opposite wicker chair. "Is his intention to turn me as well? If that's the reason why you want to kill him, I'm going to ask you not to."

"That's only part of it." I explained the draw we had to Elton, the way we wouldn't be free from him so long as he walked the earth. Parker had no idea what she was getting into. "Rose, Ida, and I have all been exactly where you are now. We thought being immortal would be so romantic, but let me tell you, it's not."

"I don't think it's romantic." The wistful gleam in her eyes suggested otherwise. "Though it must be nice to know you'll never grow old and die."

My thoughts drifted to my mom, slowly wasting away in a nursing home while her mind sifted between the past and present, never knowing which was reality. Part of me was grateful that would never be me, but I'd never have any of the in between, either. I'd never know what it was like to build a life, accomplish goals, and have aspirations outside of merely surviving.

"It's not as nice as you'd think," I grumbled.

Being a teenager until the end of time was absolute hell. I could go from wanting to punch a hole in the wall to breaking down in a mess of tears on a dime; forget about finding decent employment—no one took me seriously. I couldn't even buy a goddamned newspaper without being given the patronizing "This must be for your dad" treatment.

I tried to join a book club when we lived in Texas. I was lonely, and Elton was going through a moody decade. They wouldn't let me in. Their reasoning had been that their club was for important literature only, and without ever asking me what I liked to read, they assumed everything I liked must've automatically been trash because I was a teenage girl. I spent the next month dining on each and every member of that book club.

"Half of my problems come from dealing with my mom, being worried about the future, or trying to figure out where and how I fit in the world." She ticked them off on her fingers. "But wouldn't becoming a vampire eliminate all that?"

"You're really not getting it. Any problems you have don't magically disappear the moment you're turned. You just get saddled with them for an eternity, and you never get to resolve them because you don't age, change, or grow at all."

She opened her mouth to counter, and I cut her off with a raised hand. Everything about this conversation exhausted me. I might as well have been arguing with my boneheaded living self before Elton turned me. The moment he told me I was special, reason and common sense took a flying leap out the window. I had wanted to be loved so badly. I truly thought being chosen by him meant I was designed for greater things. Not a lifetime of scraping by with part-time work at Taco Bell.

If I wanted to convince Parker to make better choices, I had to dig deeper into her fears and insecurities. "You will spend your immortality moving. Forget about setting down roots. You'll be at the mercy of Elton's whims, and he never stays anywhere for long."

"Where you live isn't as important as who you live with, though, right?"

The earnestness in her expression twisted the place in my heart that had only recently woken up and begun to feel again, even though it shouldn't have mattered. It's not like we could ever be together. I stared at my knotted fingers, my emotions tangling with my obligations. I still needed to protect her. "If Elton sold you on his genuine love act, I'm sorry to tell you that he's full of shit. I thought you'd seen through him already?"

"Why do you keep bringing up Elton like he has anything to do with this?"

My head snapped up. "Isn't that why you're asking me all these questions?"

"Is that what you think?" She came over to me and stood between my legs. Even with the fabric of our jeans between us, my skin warmed. "I thought you were smarter than that."

I gripped the backs of her thighs. "We shouldn't be doing this."

"You keep saying that, yet we continue to find ourselves here." She leaned down and pressed a light kiss to my lips. "Do you want to be with me?"

I nodded, unable to speak for fear my voice would crack.

She kissed me again. This one longer, just a bit more pressure. "Your skin is so cold." Another kiss. "I know you're dead." One more. "But kissing you makes me feel alive."

I cupped her face, running my thumbs over the freckles that splashed her cheeks like bits of melted chocolate. She wore an apple-scented body spray, and I wanted to bite into her to see if she tasted just as crisp. She belonged in a field of wildflowers. Or twirling under a moonlit sky. Someplace warm, beautiful, and free from the dark desires of vampires.

I had one last chance to do the right thing. "I think you should leave."

"Is that what you really want?" Her fingers skimmed the line of my shoulders, over my exposed collarbone, and dipped to my side. Every touch left a trail of fire in its wake.

The tips of my toes tingled. "What is it that *you* want?"

"You." Her breath whispered across my lips. "Only you."

Fuck doing the right thing.

I kissed her as I stood, dragging her body against mine. She sighed in my mouth, a little vibration against my tongue, and I kissed her harder. Walking her backward, I bumped her into the door frame on the way to the bedroom.

"Sorry." I ran my fingers through her hair. "Are you okay?"

"I'm fine." She stuck her index fingers into my jeans and tugged me forward, grinding her hips against mine. "Please keep kissing me."

Who was I to argue? We made our way to the bedroom, losing our sweaters in the process. I ran my fingers over the straps of her bra. When she shivered, I had a feeling it had nothing to do with the chill of my skin. "Can I take this off?"

"Yes." She swallowed, her cheeks turning pink as she worked up the courage to say the next words. "I want you to touch me everywhere. And . . ." She bit her lip. "I want to touch you everywhere too. If that's okay with you."

"You can touch me however you want." I took off her bra and let it drop to the floor.

She led me over to the bed, kissing me as we both crawled onto the mattress. Sitting up on our knees, we touched and explored and got to know each other's likes. Every few minutes, we'd stop to check in. I'd never felt safer.

I laid her down, and when my fingers played with the button on her jeans, she took them off and tossed them aside. I ran my hand up the inside of her thigh. Her smooth skin was like silk beneath my palm. She parted her legs, her hips tilting upward.

She reached for me, and I stilled her hand. "Let me first. Please."

I needed to feel her come undone beneath me. She quivered as I dipped my fingers into her cotton underwear and touched her. She let out a breathy sigh, and I moved my fingers in a circle, building her toward the peak until she cried out her release. With tears pricking her eyes, I buried my face in her neck and nipped her gently below the earlobe.

We kissed again, and when her hand moved to touch me in the same way, I closed my eyes and lost myself to the feeling.

We lay on the bed, facing each other with our fists tucked beneath our chins. Tiny remnants of her tears clung to her lashes like dew on morning grass, and I had done that. I was the one who made her happy enough to cry. There were very few moments in my existence where I could claim I'd been a part of a perfect moment, but I had this. I'd always have this.

We stared at each other for what felt like an eternity, and also no time at all, and I would've traded every single living memory all over again for this one.

"You should clean your apartment," Parker said.

"Really?" I sat up. "That's the first thing you're going to say after what we did?"

"I'm sorry." She let out a laugh. "But it's a disaster in here."

"We don't actually live here anymore. We're staying with Stacey until . . ."

I didn't need to finish that sentence. It hung in the air between us. She wanted to be turned, and I was doing everything in my power to stop it. There was no middle ground we could come to on that point. If only she could see the lengths I'd been going to to protect her, but none of that mattered to her. Just like it hadn't mattered to me.

"I should go." Parker reluctantly crawled out of bed and got dressed. "The last thing I need is for my mom to up and leave on me again."

"Doesn't it stress you out? Having to babysit her so she doesn't forget she has a daughter she needs to bring with her when she moves?"

"Yeah." She tugged her sweater over her head. "But I'm used to it."

I recognized the defensiveness in her tone. It was the same one I used to use on Elton whenever he'd put down my mom, even though I complained about her constantly. It was okay for me to be angry, but if anyone else commented, I'd defend her with my last breath. The complication of having a complicated parent. "Forget I said anything."

"No, it's fine. My mom is a mess." She leaned down and kissed me. "I get it."

"Still, it's not my place to put her down. That's your job." I got up and started throwing my clothes on, not really paying attention if they were on right.

She ducked her head, suddenly shy. "Walk me to the door?"

As she stepped into the living room, I grabbed her hand and pulled her back against my chest, trailing kisses along her neck. Once we left this room, the spell would be broken. The perfect moment would be over. I wasn't ready to let go yet.

Voices floated up from the stairwell, through the open front door. Parker hadn't heard them yet. I put a finger to my lips and motioned for her to stay in the bedroom. Creeping toward the front of the apartment, I peeked my head outside. Elton and Frankie were making their way up the stairs. Shit, shit, shit. If Elton found Parker here, everything we'd done to protect her would be useless. His rage would be uncontainable.

Elton bent down to tie his fancy leather shoe. "I don't think they'll be back here, but like I said, it doesn't hurt to take another look."

Frankie looked up, and his eyes met mine. "Go," he mouthed.

I didn't need to be told twice. I rushed back to the bedroom and shoved Parker toward the balcony. "Elton is here. This is your only way out. Get to the ground. The alley will take you out to the opposite street. Run fast."

"Wait." She spun around the moment I dropped the ladder. "What about you?"

"Don't worry about me. I'm already dead." I gave her a quick kiss and left her on the balcony to head off Elton. I could only hope she'd listen to me and run.

I stopped at Rose's overturned dresser and flipped the latch to reveal the hidden door. Grabbing all her notes, I stuffed them down the back of my pants, then went out to the living room just as Elton and Frankie came through the front door. Frankie hung back, doing an excellent impression of a nightclub bouncer, except his job was to keep me in. His enormous body took up most of the frame, like a human brick wall.

"Holly." Elton bowed his head. "Didn't expect to see you today."

"Likewise. In fact, I had hoped we could spend eternity without ever crossing paths again, but I guess that's just too much to hope for."

"Is that what you really want?" He circled me with a cocky grin etched into his sculpted face. He stopped and tilted my chin up with the tips of his fingers, and I shivered at the contact and familiar gesture. "You're a terrible liar, Holly. I think you miss me very much."

The blood in my veins was attracted to his, like an instinct void of emotion. I no longer had genuine feelings for Elton. Only a lingering sadness and the ever-present regret of my choices, but nothing close to the love I'd felt when I agreed to become this.

I patted his cheek. "I promise to miss you when you're dead."

His confident smile died on his lips as his eyes frosted over. "You ungrateful little bitch."

Such mood swings. He reached out to grab my throat, but I'd already danced away from him. "I already ripped your head off once this past week. Do you really want round two?"

As I spun away, my locket had worked its way out of my thin sweater. His eyes widened, and he was on me before I could move, pushed by adrenaline and a will to live. "You told me you lost it." His fingers closed around the locket, and my heart beat in my throat. *Fuck. Me.* "You swore it was gone for good. Where did you find it?"

"If I told you . . ." Any moment now, he'd tear it from my neck. I had only a breath of time to make a move. I ripped off his hand that still clung to the bulky part of my heirloom and tossed it aside. "I'd have to kill you."

He lunged for me, breathing hard and swinging his fist. Playtime was over. "I will tear you into so many pieces, you won't be able to reform."

"Oh, sweetie. We know that's not how it works." I dodged his punch, and his knuckles barely grazed my cheek. He fought like he moved, with a certain elegance I used to find charming. Now, I just saw a cranky boy who threw a tantrum because a girl dared not to fall at his feet. "This has been fun, but I have to go. See you on the other side of hell."

I needed to get out of here before he called Frankie in to hold me down. I couldn't fight off them both, even if Frankie was slower. And I couldn't trust our secret alliance enough to risk it. With another sidestep and a roll, I made it back into the bedroom.

I leaped over the mattress and narrowly avoided getting my foot tangled in the sheet. Elton tripped over a dresser drawer, sloppy in his rage. I gave him a wave as I ducked out the window. Parker was nowhere in sight. If she was smart, she would've already jumped onto the nearest bus. I took the ladder, disappearing through the alley before Elton had a chance to catch up. Though I could've sworn I heard him yelling my name into the night wind.

Chapter Twenty-One

Frankie had told Gwen that he planned to break into the bank and pick the lock on Rose's box at two in the morning, so we'd planned to meet at the bank at one. Just in case Gwen got any ideas about tagging along. There was always the chance Frankie could've been playing us, setting us up to walk into a trap, but we didn't have much of a choice with the box-scheduled to be drilled. Made all the more urgent now that Elton knew I had my heirloom.

We decided Stacey would stay out front and alert us if Gwen showed up. Rose, Ida, and I would accompany Frankie into the vault, since we'd likely need all three of us to take him down if he turned on us. Hurt flashed in his eyes when we stated as much, but he had to understand why we'd be nervous after the graveyard.

We'd be in and out in minutes. So we hoped.

With only a half hour left before our meet up with Frankie, we left Stacey's house. We moved like shadows in the street. Passing cars and families with open windows were oblivious to us as we avoided streetlamps and wound our way through yards and alleys on the way to the bank. We were invisible in the night. Lucky for us, Stacey had a ton of black clothes on hand.

Rose hooked her arm through mine, separating us from Stacey and Ida as we continued walking a bit farther back. "You haven't said much about when you went to the apartment."

"It was fine." I had to tell them about running into Elton because they needed to know he'd seen my locket. We all had to be on our guard now. I didn't tell them he'd only seen my locket because

I'd been toying with him. Then I would've had to explain why I'd wanted to stall him, and I really wasn't prepared to talk about Parker. "Aside from running into Elton."

"You were gone a long time."

"Mmm-hmm." I didn't tell them about going to see my mom, either. I wasn't sure how I felt about that yet, and I didn't want to have to explain what I couldn't even explain to myself.

"What's going on with you and Parker?" Rose lowered her voice and kept us even farther back from the group. "You don't have to give me details, I just want to make sure you're being careful. Getting mixed up with her right now is trouble we don't need. I'm not against it after we finish this, but we can't risk Elton finding out before then."

"I know the risks." I swallowed the guilt of Elton wrapping his hand around my locket, so close to ripping it from my neck, and put up my walls. "I'm being careful."

I couldn't help my defensive tone when Rose acted like I couldn't separate my feelings from reality. Parker was mortal. I was not. We wouldn't be going anywhere. I fully understood that. Having Rose poke at me like I was unaware of the stakes only increased my agitation. I should've made Parker leave the apartment sooner, and we definitely should've kept our clothes on, but I couldn't bring myself to regret it.

"I just wanted to make sure." Her expression went soft and hazy. "I meant what I said before, about not being mad if you turned her once Elton is gone. When this is all over, you can keep her if you want."

"She's not an animal that followed me home," I bit out. "Leave it alone."

"Message received. I won't keep pushing it." She gave me a knowing smile, like she'd been baiting me on purpose. Bad timing for it, all around.

We caught up to Stacey and Ida in the parking lot of the bank. Frankie stepped out from behind the tall hedges that framed the lot. I jumped at the sight of his large frame, my heart racing as my guard went up. Trusting someone who spent so much time with Elton would take some getting used to.

He gave me a funny look. "I brought home a college freshman for Gwen. That'll keep her busy for a little while."

"We should still hurry." Rose gave a nervous glance at the street. "If she shows up, we know you can't act like you're helping us."

Stacey took her position by the window directly across from the vault. She'd shine a flashlight at us if anyone approached. Frankie held out the keys he'd gotten from Gwen. I grabbed them and unlocked the front doors. The alarm began to blare the moment I stepped over the threshold. The number pad flashed red as Frankie punched in the numbers with shaky fingers. The building went silent, and I exhaled. One part down.

Right as we gathered behind the teller line, a beam from the flashlight bounced off the metal vault door. I ran to the front door, and a set of headlights parked in the first space shone right into my eyes. White spots danced in front of me.

"Is it Gwen?" Ida asked.

"No." I'd never seen Gwen drive a car before. I didn't think she knew how. "Maybe it's somebody who needs to use the ATM."

A man with sandy hair, gray around the temples, stepped out of the car. His round cheeks sagged with age, giving him the look of an uptight walrus, and he wore jeans and a wrinkled flannel shirt. I nearly didn't recognize the bank manger out of his suit until I caught sight of the same stern expression as he had this morning.

"It's the manager. Stay down," I said.

Rose, Ida, and Frankie all ducked, hiding behind the row of teller windows. I crouched by the door as the manager entered the vestibule. He had his phone to his ear, likely talking to security, and said he'd been on his way home when he got the call about the alarm going off. We assumed they'd alert the manager. We had no idea he'd be driving right by when it happened.

How unfortunate for the both of us.

As soon as he opened the front door, I grabbed him by the throat and slammed him into the wall. His phone clattered to the floor. I smashed it with my foot and snapped his neck. His eyes immediately dimmed. I let go of his body, and it crumbled to the ground as I took a step back. That was the first time I'd ever killed someone without giving them a chance to run.

The blood in my veins pulsed in an uneven rhythm. I couldn't call what I was feeling guilt—I'd become too numb to killing for that—but it was something similar. Like I'd lost a fundamental piece of myself I'd never get back. Like I'd just cut one of the strings that tethered me to humanity. How much worse would it be once my living memories were gone?

Leaning down, I laid my fingers over his eyelids and forced them closed.

"Are you holding a funeral over there?" Ida sneered at me from across the counter.

I stood and dusted off my hands. "Forgive me for trying to afford him a little decency."

I didn't know why I bothered. Both she and Rose didn't get my code. I didn't really care that they thought it was a joke. It mattered to me. It was the only thing that kept me from feeling like a complete monster every minute of every day.

I joined them all by the vault, where Rose spun the crank wheel. It clicked, but when she pulled, it wouldn't open. Frankie read the combo off again, same results. "What's happening?" she asked.

"The vault door is on a timer." Frankie slapped his forehead.

"I forgot Gwen said something about that." He held down two buttons on a keypad by the vault and put a new combo in. Some mechanism inside the door clicked, and Rose opened it freely.

The heavy door dragged open slowly, and Rose slipped inside. "I need another key to open my box. One that belongs to the bank."

"It should be hanging on one of the hooks." Frankie followed Rose into the vault, and Ida and I closed in behind him. He grabbed a long, thin gold key off the wall. "According to Gwen, this should open the master lock."

My gaze kept darting to the front of the building, like Elton and Gwen would show up any second. The more time we spent there, the greater our chance of being trapped inside. My nerves wouldn't settle until we made it back to Stacey's house with Rose's heirloom in hand.

Rose put both keys in the locks on her box and turned, opening the tiny door. She slid out a long gray box and flipped the top latch. Two silver combs with a dragonfly pattern lay at the bottom of the box, linked together by their teeth. A light coating of tarnish covered them, but otherwise, they were delicate and beautiful. No wonder she'd made them her heirloom.

A siren wailed in the distance, and Rose lifted her head. "What is that?"

"Police," Frankie said. "We need to go."

I'd tensed, as if I expected Frankie to make a grab for Rose's heirloom and run, but he only turned around and fled toward the back of the bank. Rose grabbed her combs, pressing them tightly to her chest. We followed Frankie to the emergency exit and flung open the door. Stacey caught up to us near the short stretch of woods behind the bank. We ran under the cover of the trees, then doubled back to hit the main road.

Red-and-blue lights flashed in the parking lot. Through the windows, I spotted four police officers standing over the body of the manager. That twinge of loss hit me again, the wrongness of that kill seeping into my bones. I didn't have time to stew in it, though. Frankie had already veered away from us, disappearing to wherever he was staying with Elton. The rest of us used their distraction to run across the street and disappear into the neighborhood on the other side.

Chapter Twenty-Two

Rose stripped down to her underwear and threw her clothes into the fireplace. "We'll burn everything we wore tonight. Not that I think anyone will look for us."

"Frankie didn't try to snag the combs," I said. "When the police showed up and everything was chaos for a minute, I thought he might."

"He might've if it was just us," Rose said. "He wouldn't betray Ida, though."

Ida rolled her eyes and tossed her clothes into the fireplace.

"I think you can trust him. He's had a million chances to ambush you with Gwen and Elton and hasn't so far." Stacey took her scarf off, her neck flap swaying as she spoke.

Ida started the fire while Rose dug out clothes from our suitcases. I pulled a navy sweater with a hole in the elbow over my head. The rough cotton chaffed against my skin. I should've thrown the sweater out decades ago, but it comforted me to have a piece of my old life. Even if it was just a bit of lifeless fabric that was ready to fall apart.

"The manager showing up was a surprise." Ida put on a long black skirt and cream button-down shirt. She let out a giggle as she chewed on her thumbnail. "Did you see the look on that stuffed suit's face when Holly slammed him into the wall? Priceless."

"So hilarious." I gave Ida a bland stare. While I didn't hold the living in high regard, I didn't give the bank manager a chance to run and wouldn't be finding any sort of amusement in his death. "We have four more nights until the full moon."

"We'll lay low until then." Rose stroked her combs with a loving finger. "There is no need to go out other than to hunt. We can't risk Elton finding out our location."

The ancient steps on Stacey's front porch creaked. Probably just the wind, but the back of my neck prickled with awareness. A knock at the door, followed by bits of rotted frame crashing to the ground, had the four of us spinning around. My heartbeat picked up speed, and Stacey grabbed my hand. We weren't expecting company.

"We fight our way out," Ida said. "Everyone on the same page?"

We nodded. A grim finality settled over us. We'd been willing to push every limit to be free of Elton, and none of the costs concerned us. But I had crossed a very important line in retrieving Rose's heirloom, killing without giving my victim a chance to run. It wasn't one I'd come back from easily. Stacey motioned for us to move to the back of the house.

"What are you doing?" I whispered.

"Go out the back. I'll hold off whoever's at the door." She took one look at my expression and let out a long-winded sigh. "Please don't get weepy about it."

"I wasn't." I sniffed.

"Come on." Ida guided me toward the patio. "Stacey can handle herself."

"Holly?" The knock sounded again, followed by more falling plaster and a chorus of barking dogs in the distance. "Are you in there?"

My heart stumbled at her voice, and I shook off Ida. "It's Parker."

I hadn't intended to see her again. We had our perfect moment already, and continuing to see her would only complicate my feelings. We couldn't be together. End of story.

So why did the sound of her voice turn me inside out?

Stacey opened the door and stepped back. "What are you doing here?"

"I came to see Holly." She ducked her head and looked up at me through her lashes. "If that's okay with all of you."

"It's fine. Ignore them." I gestured at the sliding glass door, and she followed me outside. We walked out to the old swing, with its rusted hinges, and took a seat on the sun-bleached cushions, still a bit wet from the last rain. "How did you even find this place?"

I couldn't have found it on my own, and I practically lived here for four years between eighth grade and junior year. I never told her where to find Stacey's house. For a reason.

It'd be better for both of us to walk away while we could still look back with a sense of warmth. Hanging on would only lead to angry words and hurt feelings, ruining the small amount of time we'd been able to make just ours. I didn't want to lose that.

She smirked. "I asked Alyssa where the vampire lived."

The lone girl who had escaped Stacey's house. I hoped she'd have a long and happy life.

"I'm afraid you'll have to be more specific when it comes to using that label in this house." I picked at a loose thread on my sweater. A light gust blew over the yard from the trees, carrying the scent of rot and wood. "It's dangerous for you to be here."

Her gaze darted around the open backyard. "I wasn't followed."

"I'm not worried about that." Not necessarily true, but it didn't do any good to stress her out about it now. Elton could blend into shadows and move on the wind. As a well-honed predator, he'd had a century to perfect his skills in stealth and patience.

"Okay." She gave me a twitchy half smile before looking away.

With the rush to get her out of the apartment, it looked like we were due to have our awkward after-sex moment now. It was a wonder we'd ever managed to kiss. She kept inching her hand closer to mine on the bench, and while I wanted nothing more than to put us both out of our misery and take it, we were burning our heirlooms in four days. We'd be saying goodbye to our memories and leaving this town. Parker would be moving to Tennessee with her mom.

I needed to end this now. It had already gone way too far.

I turned to her. "Listen, Parker—"

"Elton came—" She stopped, color rising on her cheeks. "You go ahead."

"No. You first." I grabbed both of her hands, and her fingers flexed beneath mine. I squeezed tighter. As if I could hold us both together. "What did Elton do?"

"He told me everything." She bit her lip. "He made a lot of promises. We'd have new lives. Sunset walks on the beach, staying in grand hotels, poetry in the park. He made it all seem so easy. If I hadn't met you, I'm not going to lie, he would've been very convincing."

"He's good at that." I tried to keep the bitterness out of my voice. The point was, he hadn't convinced her. We'd be ending this before he could. I didn't want to be angry with Elton anymore. I didn't want to feel anything other than indifference, not when he'd be finished within days and just thinking about him made me tired. "What did you tell him?"

"I said I'd think about it, to stall him." She took a silver cuff with a turquoise stone at the center off her wrist and handed it to me. "If I had gone through with it though, this would've been my heirloom."

I turned the bracelet over in my hands. "It's lovely. What's the story?"

Every heirloom had a story. It's what made object memory possible.

"There had been one year when things were really lean. My mom's latest boyfriend decided to clean out her bank account before leaving, so she had no money for my birthday. This old lady, Vera, used to babysit me while my mom worked second shift. She watched the home-shopping network all day and smelled like cat pee, but when she found out it was my birthday, she let me pick anything I wanted out of her jewelry box."

I gave the bracelet back to her. "What makes it special?"

Heirlooms couldn't just be a nice moment from childhood. They had to be attached to the kind of memory that defined you. Their histories were personal, and while pushing Parker to tell me more wasn't helping my whole plan to let her go, I had to know. I wanted everything she was willing to give me, for however long I could have it.

"It made me feel like someone was paying attention, back when I thought no one noticed." She let the bracelet dangle between her fingers, its polished surface reflecting in the moonlight. "It's the only thing I managed to hang onto through multiple moves. The first time I felt seen seemed like a nice place to store my memories."

"It would be the perfect place to store your memories." I gave her a smile, because I didn't know what else to do when everything hurt. "Your heirloom is also the place where you store all your regrets." I clasped my locket, letting the tarnished latch dig into my palm. "So you can carry them with you forever."

"You keep talking about regret, but at least you got to make your own choices." She kicked her heel against the grass. "You should trust me to make mine."

I'd hoped to have more time with her, just a few more minutes to trace the curve of her lips with my mind, to wrap a fist around the memory so it would stay with me forever. I wanted more of her laughs and smiles. Enough to sustain me when she was gone.

But time had run out.

"I can't keep doing this." I stood to give myself some distance. The next words got lodged in my throat, but I forced them out anyway. "I need you to leave now."

"Leave now?" She jumped up. "Where do you expect me to go?"

"Home. Tennessee. Wherever." I had to look away from her scrunched nose and confused expression. I didn't think it was possible for anything to be more painful than the night I turned Stacey.

Only now when I ripped away pieces of myself, they had nowhere to go. They just died on the grass between us. "We can't be together."

"But why can't we be together after Elton is gone?" Tears filled her eyes. "I'll go anywhere with you. Anywhere you ask me to."

"Don't you get it?" I raised my voice, startling a nearby owl. "I'm sixteen years old. I will always be sixteen. That's never changing. But you're eighteen, and in a few years you'll be in your twenties, then your thirties. There is no real future with us."

"You're just being stubborn." She put her hands on her hips. "You're worried this thing between us might be real, and you're scared. But you could turn me."

"Absolutely not." I wasn't clear on a lot of things at the moment, but on that I was certain. "The entire purpose of this was to keep you alive. I told you how hard immortality has been for me. Didn't you listen at all? Do you have any idea how many regrets you'll have? What makes you think I'd put you through that?"

Afraid to look at her for a second longer, I spun around. I was a gentle push away from doing what she wanted. I could already see myself grabbing her wrist and plunging my teeth into her soft skin to suck the very life out of her while giving her enough of mine to become something else. I'd shred my own soul to ruin if that was what she wanted.

I ran my hands through my hair, the crimped strands bumping along my fingers. "Why do you want me? Why do you want any of this?"

Behind me, the comfort of her body so close to mine warmed my skin. "Because I'm in love with you. And I think you love me too."

My breath caught. There was a special kind of wonder in loving and being loved. Of this one person, in all the billions of people, finding you against all odds. The rest of the world could fall away. Nothing else mattered except holding this precious, fragile thing in your hands.

Before I could lose myself to feelings I couldn't act on, I snapped myself out of it. She couldn't possibly love me. We hadn't known each other for that long. She was just caught up in the romanticism of vampires and immortality and the night sky.

"You do, right?" She probed a little more as she stepped closer. "It's not just me."

I turned around. Her eyes searched mine, silently pleading for me to say what was in my heart. My throat had gone dry. "You don't know what you're talking about. You were with Elton for months and didn't love him, but you've only known me for a fraction of that time."

"And the prince spent hours trying to force Cinderella's slipper to fit one of the stepsisters before it slid easily onto her foot. So what is time?" She cupped my face and rested her forehead against mine. "Let me stay with you. Let me be with you and love you. It could be like this, the two of us, always."

And that was the problem. She saw this as a fairy tale. She didn't see the reality. I closed my eyes, held this moment, then let her go. "It's not going to happen."

"Why are you doing this?" She shoved me. Tears choked her voice, welled up in her eyes. "What's so wrong with the two of us being together for an eternity?"

"It's not you." For the first time in my existence, I finally understood how that had become a line. "You don't understand what you'd be getting into. Not really."

"I understand perfectly fine." She crossed her arms and glared at me.

Maybe she thought she did. The same way I thought I knew what I was getting into with Elton. But she'd never truly understand, because it wasn't something she'd ever lived through. I could tell her what it was like to take a human life, but she'd never understand how numb you had to become in order to take pleasure in it. I could tell her about barely scraping together enough money to keep myself in a dumpy motel, but she'd never understand the feeling of being so alone, the sound of roaches scuttling along the walls became a comfort. She had no idea what a gift it was to keep the mortality she was so eager to throw away.

Mascara tracked her cheeks as she continued to cry while I refused to react. If she thought me cold and unfeeling, maybe she'd see that she didn't really love me after all. "You went all in on Elton, and he hurt you. So now you're, what? Just giving up on love? I never thought you'd be such a coward."

"Don't you dare." I turned away before I said something I'd regret. "It's so easy for you to call me a coward when we've been carrying you for weeks, making sure you stayed alive."

"I've been carrying myself. Don't think for a second that I'm as weak as you."

I grabbed her before she could react, pulling her against me. She let out a squeak of surprise. Her neck was so smooth, the curve so perfect. I scraped my teeth over her tender skin. "Don't make me show you how weak you really are."

Her body stiffened, readying itself for me to pierce her flesh. "Do it already."

With her breathless voice, the flutter of her lashes, a flick of her tongue over her lips, I'd eat her alive. And when she looked at me like she'd let me, I knew I'd gotten in too deep. I released her and put some much needed space between us.

"In four days, we're burning our heirlooms." I held out my palms to keep her at a distance. If she loved me like she claimed, she'd hear me and walk away. "I will lose every one of my living memories. That's what I'm giving up to keep you from turning."

"You're not going to change your mind about this, are you?"

I shook my head. "Give yourself the chance to do better than us. Please."

"Okay. If that's what you need, I'll go." My heart broke as she took my hand and placed her bracelet in it. The cool silver felt alive against my palm. "Put this in the fire, so I might have a chance of forgetting you too."

"That's not how it works. You'd have to be a vampire, and this would have to be an heirloom." I tried to push the bracelet back on her, and she refused.

"I don't care. Let it be symbolic. Do it because I asked you to." She lifted her chin, her expression set and defiant. I'd never seen anyone more beautiful in my life. "You're not the only one giving up something that matters here."

"I need you to go into hiding for the next four days." Now that Elton knew I had my heirloom, he'd force her hand, and if she refused, he'd kill her. My own careless mistake. "Don't go to school. Don't stay at your apartment."

"My mom is leaving tomorrow to see her boyfriend in Tennessee."

"Perfect. Go with her, tell her you want to meet your future stepdad, or whatever you have to say." I couldn't believe this was actually going to work. We had our heirlooms, and we'd get Parker out of harm's way, all before the full moon.

"You'll be here, right?" She laid a hand on my cheek. "When I get back?"

I kissed her palm so I wouldn't have to meet her eyes. "Sure."

By the time she came back, we'd be gone and Elton would be dead. She'd probably hate me for leaving without saying goodbye. One day, when she was old and tired, but satisfied with everything she'd accomplished in life, she'd look back and thank me.

With that, I watched her walk away, and I didn't do a thing to stop her.

Chapter Twenty-Three

I spent the next two days pacing around the house, biting my knuckles, and generally annoying everyone with my inability to sit still. Stacey got sick of it and went out hunting just to get away from me, and she hadn't been back since. Rose kept shooting furtive glances at my wrist, where I kept Parker's bracelet. I didn't explain to them what it meant. They didn't need to know. That was between me and Parker and no one else.

Since I'd be breaking every other promise I made, I had every intention of keeping this one. I'd put her bracelet in the fire with my locket. Who I had been and the symbol of who she had been would burn together. Even if I was the only one losing my memories.

At dawn, Rose and Ida went outside to watch the sun rise over the trees. They both had a thing for the way the light filtered through the remaining autumn leaves. Though there were only a handful left now, clinging to dark and crooked branches.

I didn't have Rose's knack for stress-cleaning or Ida's patience for art projects. The only thing that calmed my nerves was reading. There was something soothing about getting lost in someone else's love and life. But I hadn't been able to concentrate on any of the books I'd picked up from the library. Not when I had so many worries running through my mind.

Every minute of the day, Parker occupied my thoughts. While I trusted she had kept her word and left town with her mom, I still needed to make sure they were really gone for my own peace of mind. Getting in and out of the school would be risky. If Elton still prowled the halls, he'd take his frustration out on me. I had no doubt. He had to know Parker was gone by now. I could only imagine his fear-fueled rage.

I threw on the Glen River West sweatshirt Stacey had stolen from the girl's locker room and went out to the backyard. Rose and Ida lounged on the swing while Rose read out loud from a water-stained book of sonnets. Sneaking out the front had been an appealing idea, but Ida would probably harvest my organs if I left without telling them.

"I'm going up to the school for a minute," I said.

Rose dropped her book in the grass. "Absolutely not."

"I have to make sure Parker is really gone." Even they had to see the logic behind that. If she stayed in town, she was still susceptible to being turned. "It's for our protection."

"Do whatever you want." Ida tipped up her sunglasses. "But leave your heirloom."

Okay. That was fair, all things considered.

I lifted the chain over my head and handed my locket to her. My neck felt strange without it, as though I'd just exposed myself by taking it off. Maybe my memories clung to me the same way I clung to them.

"Don't you care?" Rose pushed her foot into the leg of the swing, sending the whole structure crashing to the ground and flipping Ida over her head. "You just tell her to leave her heirloom, like she's not about to expose herself to unnecessary danger."

Ida jumped to her feet, pushing her hair out of her face. She glared at Rose. "You need to relax. Holly knows how to take care of herself, and it's not a bad idea to check up on Parker."

"Honestly." I gave Rose a kiss on the cheek. "I'll be fine, Mother Hen."

She grumbled in response.

"We only have two days left," Ida said. "If he has Parker, I'd rather prepare for Plan B now than be left scrambling after the fire."

"Exactly." I didn't tell them that I had what would've been Parker's heirloom. Rose had her suspicions, but I didn't bother confirming. They needed to believe that if Elton did have her, he'd still be able to turn her, otherwise they'd never let me leave the house this close to the full moon just to make sure a mortal girl was still alive.

I headed over to Parker's apartment first. I didn't think she'd be home, but it was the easiest place to get in and out of quickly, and it gave me a chance to mentally prepare to enter the school. The blue-and-brick buildings came into view, and I went around the back of Parker's unit to peek in the window over the kitchen sink. Just as I suspected. Everything had been packed up in boxes that had frayed edges and multiple tape tears. No sign of Parker or her mom, and most relieving, no sign of a struggle.

Leaving the apartment behind, I walked over to the school. The three-story brick building loomed over me, casting its enormous shadow over my small frame and making me feel even more insignificant. I never mattered there. And after today, I'd never have to walk those halls again and be reminded of all the ways I had failed myself when I should've known better.

Time would be relieved. It never wanted me to come back there, either. Or maybe time would forget me once I forgot who I used to be within those walls.

I pressed my hand against the door and closed my eyes. Memories flashed in front of me. Stacey blowing cherry-flavored bubbles, her wrist covered in rubber bracelets as she reached for the door, the two of us laughing over David Fisher's less-than-smooth attempt to get a hand job. She'd punched him in the balls. Elton wrapping his arm around my waist, holding me against his chest like he'd claimed me and wanted everyone to know it. Walking through the halls with people who had tortured me in middle school and feeling like they could no longer touch me. I'd matured and moved past it, because I had a boyfriend with a secret who took me seriously.

I shook my head at past me.

A wave of nostalgia hit me as soon as I pulled open the front entrance doors. Time pressed down, churned in my gut, made its presence known. I passed through the metal detectors, scrunching my shoulders. If I'd gone to this school a generation later, would this be normal to me? Would I just expect gun violence to be a part of everyday life the way Cold War drills had been a part of Rose's?

I stood in front of a dusty trophy case filled with pictures of championship teams from days past. Faces of people I knew in distant ways, and faces of those who had come before and after me. How many of those people looked back on high school as the best days of their lives? How many wished they could go back, just to live it all one more time? There was more than one way to be a ghost, I supposed. The distance between the inability to move on and the inability to move forward wasn't all that great.

"You could've done big things, Holly Liddell." I touched a finger to the case, leaving my print behind. "And you never would've looked back."

Aside from the occasional squeak of my shoes against the floor, the halls were silent. Everyone was either in class or at lunch. I didn't know where I'd intended to go until I stood in front of Mr. Stockard's classroom, as if I'd meant to come this way all along.

He shuffled papers on his desk in front of his open briefcase. The lines around his eyes were even more pronounced under the florescent lighting. I tapped on the door, and his head snapped up. He let out an exhausted sigh at the sight of me but motioned for me to come in.

"What brings you by, Holly?" He gave me his best tired smile.

His voice was still the same, but everything else had changed.

It hurt to look at him, in this place, and understand the depth of change. I might've been in stasis, but time marched on for everyone else. They lived whole lives, became different people, made mistakes, and moved past the consequences. That's why time hung so heavy in this building. It was why Rose felt as if she were being left behind. It wasn't trying to shove me out. Time wasn't sentient or caring. It was my own discomfort with what I'd done. It was standing at the starting point of the race, unable to move, and watching everyone else celebrate at the finishing line. Mr. Stockard wasn't the same man who had taught me, and I thought I'd been angry with him for not becoming better. Maybe I'd really just been angry with myself.

But my time here was over. I had to give myself permission to let it go.

"Has Parker come to class the last few days?" I asked.

He leaned back in his chair with his arms folded over his chest. "Parker is a nice girl. A bit of a loner. She reminds me a lot of you."

"Yes. I know." That was all well and good, but I didn't come here to talk about her personality and our mutual mommy issues. "See, I'm working on something with her—"

"No." He stood, his ancient chair creaking with the release of his weight, and stood in front of the door. "You don't get to come back into my school and use it as a hunting ground. If you want at my students, you'll have to go through me first."

Wow. Okay then. Part of me was stunned he'd shown that much gumption. The larger part of me was wholly annoyed that he thought I'd hunt Parker. Did he really see me as someone who would feed on high school girls? Or use this place for a hunting ground? That would make me no better than Elton. And so unnecessary when there were plenty of assholes wandering around this earth just begging to not be alive anymore.

"I had no idea you cared so much about your students. Good for you." I gave him a playful punch on the shoulder. "I'm not looking to do her harm, though."

He narrowed his eyes. "What business do you have with her then?"

"I do other things besides hunt and kill, you know." People read a couple of vampire books, watch a few movies, and suddenly thought they knew everything about us. "Since you're insisting, I want to make sure she stays away from Elton. So she doesn't become like me."

"Is that right?" He gave me a considering look. "She's been absent the last few days."

My muscles unclenched. She must've gone, believing I'd be here when she got back, and all my worrying and sneaking around town had been for nothing. Still, better to know than not. "Thank you. Was that so hard?"

"I don't know what you've done or who you've become since you went away. Do you blame me for questioning your motives?"

"I guess not." After all these years, the teacher tone could still shame me like nothing else. "Has Elton still been coming to school?"

"Yes." He rubbed his jawline, where his facial hair had taken on the patchy quality of "broke musician meets Sunday-morning alcoholic." "Be careful. He's taken a lot less care to hide what he is recently. His agitation is alarming."

That wasn't a surprise. With Parker gone and the full moon approaching, he was bound to get a little twitchy. "Don't try to be a hero with him. Stakes don't kill vampires."

"I'll do what I have to do." Mr. Stockard stepped aside to let me pass. "For the record, I always cared about my students. I just needed someone to remind me how much."

Underneath his wry smile, I caught a glimmer of the teacher he used to be. He wasn't exactly the same, but maybe that was okay. He still kept a shelf full of contemporary books for anyone who needed them, and he stood up for Parker when he thought I'd hurt her.

Not all cool teachers had to jump on desks and throw candy. Sometimes they just had to show up.

I headed down the hall and turned the corner that would take me outside. That strange pressure on my chest—the one I thought had been time—had eased since I identified it as my own lagging regrets. It still didn't make me want to take a leisurely stroll down memory lane in the place where I had made all of my worst mistakes. At the end of the hall, Frankie leaned against the front door with his arms crossed over his broad chest. His enormous body blocked out the light filtering through the dingy windows.

I stopped in front of him and craned my neck. "Why aren't you at lunch?"

"Guard duty. In case Parker shows up for class." He scratched his dome-shaped head. "I need to meet with you, Rose, and Ida. When can I come by the house?"

Guard duty for Parker? My bullshit meter started pinging. Elton would've gone to her place by now. The week I got the flu, he showed up at my house with chicken noodle soup and sat by my side, even though I asked him to leave several times. At the time, I thought it had been sweet. In reality, he just didn't want me out of his sight. Now that he had revealed himself to Parker, he wouldn't leave her alone for two days and just trust her to show up to school whenever. That would require him to give up a fraction of control.

"We're not staying at the house anymore, and it's not my place to share where we are now." The lie rolled off my tongue easily enough. He was being entirely too cagey for my liking, and my patience was running thin. "Just tell me what you want to say. I'll pass it along."

"Can't." He shifted his stance. "The three of you can meet me at Ghost Bridge. After school tomorrow. You know where that is, right?"

I nodded. The first summer Stacey and I chased information about Edie, we filled a backpack with baloney sandwiches and orange

Tab and rode our bikes over to Ghost Bridge. The covered bridge had been built over a creek on a dirt road. It led up to a house that had burned to ash in 1921. Only the cinder-block foundation remained. According to rumor, an entire family had been killed in the fire, and they continued to haunt the bridge in hopes of stopping anyone from crossing up to their house again. At the time, we figured, who better to help us contact a spirit than a bunch of already dead people?

Meeting in such a secluded place made me nervous. I didn't like the idea of exposing ourselves at this late stage in the game. "I'll bring Rose and Ida, but we won't bring our heirlooms. If you ambush us, I'll—"

"I won't." Frankie's gaze darted down the hall. "Go before someone sees you."

I hurried out the door and crossed the street into the adjoining neighborhood. Rose and Ida wouldn't be pleased about the meeting with Frankie. Even though we trusted him to a certain degree, it would still be a risk to leave the cover of Stacey's house. I just hoped whatever Frankie had to tell us would be worth it.

And I could admit it would be nice to get out for a while on the last day with our memories. Ghost Bridge seemed a fitting place to say goodbye to our living selves.

Chapter Twenty-Four

The next day, I lay on the red-satin bed in Stacey's living room, staring up at the patterns of mold in the ceiling, like black clouds gathering in the plaster. I'd just come back from finishing off a guy in the nearby park, and his blood still stained the front of my sweater. He'd been a fighter. Not normally an issue, but my mind had been elsewhere.

Stacey had gone out hunting. She'd spent more and more time away from the house lately, as if she couldn't get away from there fast enough. I couldn't blame her. The house her mom used to keep a Rose-standard of clean was now crawling with rot and reeked of dried blood and mildew. It didn't feel like the same place anymore.

In another hour, we'd meet with Frankie and find out whatever he wanted to tell us. I still didn't know why he couldn't give me the information to pass along, but it seemed really important to him to meet with all three of us. Rose insisted it was because he wanted to see Ida. I had my doubts. Still, we needed him to keep tabs on Elton, and better him than Gwen.

"I can't believe we're spending our last night with our memories in this dump," Ida said.

"Why should we, though?" I propped myself up on my elbows. "Let's stay out after we meet with Frankie. Aren't we supposed to be creatures of the night or whatever? We can go where we want."

"She does make a good point," Rose said. "I don't want to stay here, either. It smells weird, and it's already going to bother me forever that I never did get it all the way clean."

"We'll figure it out on the way. We should get going now, though.

It takes forever to get to the bridge." I twisted Parker's bracelet on my wrist. She was already gone, but it wouldn't feel final until we left town.

Ida grabbed my notebook and pen from the bed and left a note for Stacey, letting her know we wouldn't be back until morning. She'd likely be gone that long as well.

The three of us took a bus to the edge of town. I hadn't been up there since the summer between eighth and ninth grade, but everyone knew where to find Ghost Bridge. It was an intrinsic part of growing up in Glen River.

This part of town stopped being developed after the fire. A few places that could've been banks or stores were now nothing but a few posts rising out of tall grass. A wall or two still stood back when Stacey and I had come here years ago. From the disturbed expression on Rose's face, I had a feeling that whole buildings had been intact during her time.

I swatted a fly away from my face. "We should've made him meet us at Burger King."

"Why? So you could pick up a job application?" Ida asked.

"Hilarious." At least I'd attempted to work. Productive member of society and all.

I walked ahead, picking up my pace at the sound of water splashing against muddy banks. The temperature around the bridge ran ten degrees cooler because of the creek. It wound all the way through the heavily wooded area and emptied into the Glen River. A storm had blown through the night before, taking out most of the remaining leaves. Trees pricked the skyline, their dark and empty branches like the thin and scratching fingers of nightmares.

"This is an odd place to meet." Ida jumped on the bridge, testing her weight against the time-worn planks. "Why did he pick Amelia's?"

"Elton's maker?" I shielded my eyes from the sun as I looked up the hill. "No way. This place was a legend to me growing up.

Her family is supposed to be haunting this bridge."

"I heard the same growing up." Rose gave me a soft smile. We grew up a few streets over from each other, but it never really clicked until this homegrown ghost story connected us across a generation. "Someone set fire to their house in the middle of the night, and they still wander this road, searching for their murderer."

"Her family might very well still be haunting the area." Ida grabbed the railing stained with rust and peered down to the rushing water below. "They seemed the type to hang around and annoy the living long after their welcome."

It struck me then just how many years Ida had been walking the earth. She remembered actual people I'd only heard about through rumor and speculation. She knew the truth behind the stories I always thought had been made up to scare teens away from having sex up there.

"Was her family really murdered?" I asked. All those summer nights Stacey and I had sat out here with a Ouija board, never knowing ghosts from the past didn't haunt bridges. They wandered in plain sight, attended high school, and worked at Taco Bell.

"The vampire who turned Amelia burned down her house." Ida turned her gaze up the hill. "Everyone assumed she died in the fire. At the time, I assumed she had set it."

"There was no love lost between Amelia and our Ida," Rose said.

"I'm not sorry she's dead." Ida shrugged. "She was a lot like Gwen. The type of girl who hated other girls. She once let a creek snake loose in my family's store, just to be mean. It caused a panic for weeks and nearly bankrupted us."

"That sounds like something Elton would do," I said.

"If only I'd seen that at the time." Ida let go of the rail and dusted off her hands. "This used to be part of a larger business district, but it appears nature has reclaimed the area."

"No one would build up here because of the ghosts," Rose said. "My father was a land developer. He mostly looked for places to build auto plants in the post-war boom, and the town commissioner told him they wouldn't be able to find a single man to work up there if they built the plant over what they considered a burial ground."

"It's just like Amelia to tarnish a place for an eternity," Ida said.

The crunch of heavy footfalls on gravel had us turning our heads. Frankie walked up the hill looking like a lumberjack in a Technicolor film with bad '70s hair. Lucky for him, he came alone. I'd half expected him to set us up. Even though he'd proven himself several times over, I still couldn't shake the feeling that something was off.

"Hey." He stopped at the entrance to the bridge. His shoulders were wide enough to block our view of the road. "Did you bring your heirlooms?"

"No." The cooling silver of my locket pressed against my skin beneath my sweater. We'd debated leaving them behind, but Stacey wasn't home. It was too risky. Anyone could just wander into her house, even if it was hard to see from the road. "I told you we wouldn't be bringing them with us, but don't worry. They're somewhere safe."

Ida watched Frankie with the kind of intensity she usually reserved for her art projects. As if she were debating which of his body parts she'd like to remove next. His gaze darted to hers, and he gave her a smile. She cracked her knuckles in response.

"I'm glad they're safe." Frankie scratched the back of his large head. He kept glancing at Ida, like he wanted to pull her aside and talk, but she kept her chin firmly lifted and her gaze on the open field behind him.

I took a step forward, placing myself in front of Ida and blocking Frankie's continued attempt to get her attention. Rose stood beside me, the two of us forming a wall that all but said, "Back off, she's not for you." Ida had no interest in Frankie, and the sooner he understood that, the better off he'd be.

"Why did you bring us up here?" Rose asked.

"Elton has been going out of his mind since Parker skipped town." Frankie shuffled his feet, kicking up dust from the dry road. "He wants to leave tomorrow."

My head went light as the blood in my body dropped to my stomach. Rose looked at me, her brow wrinkled. Surely, he would wait for Parker to return. There were still boxes in her mom's apartment. He had to think she was coming back.

"Why is he leaving already? What about Parker?" I asked. Elton wouldn't leave this town without a new girl to take my place. Much like my kill code, Elton had his own rituals.

"He thinks Parker is gone," Frankie said. "He knows you have all three heirlooms, and he's worried. I've never seen him like this. He won't go hunting. Makes Gwen bring kills home. She doesn't mind, but you know. It's gross."

"Tell him you heard she's coming back in two days," I said.

"Is that true?" He gave me a funny look, and I could feel his questions about Parker and me crawling across my skin like a multi-legged insect.

"Does it matter if it's true?" As far as Frankie was concerned, I didn't know where Parker had gone or when she was coming back. I didn't know anything about Parker at all. "Just tell him that so he'll stay."

"It makes very little sense for him to leave," Rose said. "We'll just follow. It's not like he can hide from us, though it would give me immense pleasure to see him try."

A vision of Elton hiding in a cold, dark cave with none of his pressed shirts or leather shoes brought a smile to my face. He treated us like a joke at every turn, constantly underestimated our capabilities, and in the end, he was the one running scared. Karma could be known to take her time, but she made one hell of an entrance.

"I'm trying my best." Frankie lifted his meaty hands in the air. "He doesn't see me as a voice of reason. What do you want me to do?"

"Bring him to the school parking lot at midnight," Ida said. "We'll light the fire at eleven. It'll be done before you arrive."

Frankie gave a curt nod. "I'll do my best."

He informed us that as soon as Elton fell, Gwen would be outmatched, and he assured us she would lose interest the moment the odds were against her. She only fought battles she was confident she could win. Ida kept her distance from Frankie as we set up the final details of our plan. She rubbed her arms whenever he looked at her, as if she could feel the chill coming from his stony gaze. While he and Rose got into a debate about what time to bring Elton to the school, I took the opportunity to sidle up next to Ida.

"Everything okay?" I asked.

"Yeah." Ida glanced at Frankie. "I just can't shake this bad feeling."

At least I wasn't the only one. Maybe we shouldn't have trusted Frankie so much, but it was too late to do anything about it now. Though we'd probably all breathe easier after tomorrow night.

After Frankie left and disappeared down the main road, Rose turned to us. "Okay, we're obviously still doing the ritual at ten, correct?"

"Yep," Ida and I said at the same time.

We planned to light the fire at the exact moment the moon was highest in the sky, allowing night to fall while we prepped the ingredients needed to poison the blood housed within our heirlooms. The ritual would be done hours before Frankie was due to bring Elton to the parking lot. We weren't taking any chances.

"What should we do now?" Rose asked. "It's the last night we'll remember being in high school. Should we do something wild, like make out with some boys in the back seat of a car?"

"No boys, please. I have a better idea." Ida opened my notebook, flipping past the pages that detailed that day at the county fair when she let a pig loose from its pen because it made her sister happy. "My best memory is in here. I think we should all have one recorded."

"I don't know if I have one." I had a lot of little things she could write down. The things I'd never fully experience again. Like summer slushies melting on my tongue, the feel of the wind in my hair as I rode my bike down a steep hill, and the scent of chlorine clinging to my skin when I was still young enough to believe in mermaids.

"Try me." Ida held the pen poised over the paper.

"The day Stacey and I found the lockets." I could still smell the mustiness of the attic, feel the sweat dripping down my back, and the grime of fifty-year-old dust beneath my fingers. A summer full of adventure, romance, and ghosts lurked around every corner, the kind you could only believe in when you were thirteen. "That's what really solidified our friendship."

Finding Edie's lockets had been a turning point in my life. It had been the moment I stopped trying to get whatever I needed from my mom and started becoming my own person. The summer of possibilities. Stacey and I had bikes and the spare change we found under the couch cushions. It was enough to conquer the world.

As Ida finished noting every detail, the sights, sounds, and smells that wouldn't mean anything to me after tomorrow, I turned to Rose. "What about yours?"

"Mine is really a small series of memories from the summer before my sophomore year, at the drug store. They had a soda fountain and a coin-operated machine, which you all call jukeboxes now. That was the last summer I had all to myself, before my parents started pressuring me to get serious with Mike, get serious with helping out around the house, get serious about becoming a wife, because that's all I was good for." Her delicate face had become pinched and angry, and she let out a breath as she smoothed over her expression. "Sorry. This is supposed to be a happy memory. Let me start over."

Ida wrote down the details of Rose's only summer of independence, when she was old enough to go around town by herself but still too young to be groomed for marriage. Her memories smelled like fresh-cut flowers and tasted like root beer. Her frustrations with her parents were completely different, yet also perfectly mirrored mine. It made me wonder if we had been given the chance to grow and change, if we would've ended up exactly like them.

When Ida finished documenting the details for Rose like she'd done for me, she closed the notebook. "There. Now we each have one moment from our lives we get to keep."

Rose took the notebook and flipped through the pages. "The thing is, I can read those memories again, but it will never feel like it used to. I'll never be carefree like that again."

"If our memories are gone, won't there be a new definition of carefree?" I asked.

"If this is the new carefree, I don't want it," Rose said.

"Only because you think things used to be better," Ida said. "Nostalgia clouds your judgment. It's hard right now, but once Elton is gone, we'll find our way. Maybe we'll actually enjoy being vampires."

There was a concept. I took my locket out of my sweater. Sunlight glinted off the tarnished silver as I raised it in a toast. "To the new carefree."

Ida and Rose took out their heirlooms and clinked them against mine. With the freedom to go where we wanted, without our pasts weighing us down, we could do anything we wanted. A new summer of possibilities. It wasn't too late to conquer the world, once we had the space to find ourselves.

Chapter Twenty-Five

Stacey slung a backpack over her shoulder and looked over the wreckage of the last place she'd been able to call home. Not even an echo of our childhood lingered there anymore. The space had become a wasteland. Her expression held no sorrow as she took in the crumbling plaster and specks of mold. Only resignation. This was the end, at last.

"I feel like I should make a speech," she said.

I stood beside her and put my arm around her shoulders, tilting my head to rest against hers. "You could say goodbye to your mom. Or say goodbye to Edie."

"I've already done both those things." She turned around. "Let's just go."

For Stacey, there would be no lengthy reminiscing. No last words. If she got caught up in sentimentality, it would be that much harder to walk away. Later, after this was all over and we were far from here, she'd find what I wish she'd been able to say now.

Rose, Ida, and I followed her out of the house. We didn't bother to shut the door. There was no point to it. In another fifty years, the house would be reclaimed by nature and crumble to dust. Maybe it would become another town legend, like Amelia's house had been for both Rose and me. Or maybe the history would die out, like so many others. At least it would live on in Stacey. If she allowed herself to look back every now and then.

The last of the fallen autumn leaves crunched beneath our feet as we trekked through various yards on our way to the school.

The air held a snap of winter chill. Snow would be coming soon. "I can't believe this is our last night in this town."

"Will you come back for your mother's funeral when she dies?" Stacey asked.

"No." I wouldn't have any memories left to mourn. "She probably won't even have a funeral. There is no one left to arrange it, no one who would even bother."

Her death would be quiet. She spent her life chasing people who never wanted her, while pushing away anyone who would've cared. Guilt threatened to make its familiar presence known, but more than anything, it just left me feeling empty. Wishing things had been different.

As soon as we set foot on the black concrete of the school's parking lot, Stacey shuddered. "I hate it here. It's like walking over my own grave."

A few weeks ago, I would've blamed time, but time had nothing to do with Stacey's discomfort. Regret was a heavy burden to carry. It made everything feel like it fit wrong, even the air we breathed.

Rose and Ida walked ahead, and I hung back with Stacey. As far as we knew, it wasn't technically necessary for us to burn our heirlooms in the place where we'd all been turned, but so many rituals were nothing more than established patterns. We figured it couldn't hurt.

"You can stay on the edge, until we're done, if you want," I said.

"Yeah." She looked over my shoulder at Rose and Ida. "I don't need to be a part of this, and I hate it here." She tossed her backpack onto the grass. "I'll just wait until Elton shows up."

"I'm sorry." I squeezed her arms. "Sorry you died here because I wouldn't listen. Sorry your mom died alone when you should've been there. I'm sorriest I won't remember you."

She nudged me. "You'll remember some of me."

If we hadn't reconnected these last few weeks, all I would've had was the memory of turning her. I grabbed her hand. "Please keep who I had been alive, remind me every so often, even if it'll mean nothing to me."

"I won't forget." She gave me a half smile. "There are worse people to be tied to for eternity. If I have to be stuck with anyone, I'm glad it's you."

I left her on the edge of the parking lot as I joined Rose and Ida for the final walk. The clouds, tinged gray by the twilight, parted to reveal the moon. Its soft glow illuminated the ground, throwing a hazy filter over the world. The days, hours, minutes we had left had run out. The time had come to say our final goodbyes.

I twisted Parker's bracelet on my wrist as we walked to the center of the blacktop. Rose set down her portable workshop and pulled out a cast-iron cauldron she'd bought from Walmart. She needed to get the fire hot enough to melt our heirlooms but weak enough to keep the cauldron intact. A balancing act. She began to stoke the fire with small sticks she'd been drying in the sun for weeks, then added a bit of thermite to make it hotter. Once she was satisfied with the results, she set out the ingredients she'd need to poison the blood.

I touched a finger to one of the plastic bags. "What are these?"

"A little hemlock and some foxglove, plus oleander, castor oil seeds, and belladonna. All the classics." She sprinkled them into the fire. "Watch the flame. It might throw sparks. The thermite can be temperamental."

"Where did you find all those murder plants?" I was pretty sure oleander didn't even grow in Michigan. Or anywhere we'd lived in the past decade.

"eBay." Rose finished emptying her ingredients into the fire and tilted her head as she studied the flame for temperature. "The plants will kill the blood; the fire will kill the object. I'm not sure what the moon does, but Frankie said we needed it, so here we are."

I kept my distance from the fire, mindful of the sparks. "It's only mildly terrifying that we'll be giving up our memories because of what Frankie said."

"We don't have another choice," Rose said. "And he's been on our side."

Just because she wanted to believe it didn't make it true. Frankie had proven himself, yes, but my gut kept warning me there was something off about him, and I'd survived best by trusting my gut. Ida felt it too. Nothing we could do about it now, though. And I had to agree with Rose on that point. If this was our best and only shot at killing Elton, we had to take it.

I wandered to the edge of the parking lot where a picnic table had been set up for those wanting outdoor lunch. Hundreds of initials had been scratched into the surface, much like the dollar-theater bench in the abandoned field. All those little moments captured in ways that went beyond individual recollection.

I'd be saying goodbye to my memories, but I was still here. I could still make new ones and let those be the ones I'd hold forever. One person in particular would be occupying a lot of my mind in the coming days, I had no doubt. I wondered if our paths crossed decades from now, how that would make me feel. Would I still think I'd done the right thing in letting her go?

But I couldn't let uncertainty cloud my judgment now. Not on this night.

It would take an enormous amount of willpower to leave after we finished this, knowing Parker was coming back. It would be so easy to tell her I'd been wrong. That even if we only had a few years together, I'd take what I could get. But it wouldn't do either of us any favors.

Rose laid a hand on my shoulder. "It's ready."

I shut out thoughts of Parker as I stood next to Rose and Ida and steeled myself for what would come next. Would losing my memories hurt? Would it feel like dying all over again? I didn't have the answer to those questions, and maybe it was better if I didn't ask. My hands trembled as I took off my locket and held it in my clenched fist.

Ida went first, as we agreed it would be best to go in order. "Tonight, I say goodbye to my sister, Bea. The sun to my clouds, the heart to my soul. She loved fully with the short amount of time she had, and I'm letting go of her to save countless other girls."

She dropped the tiny silver-and-glass horse into the fire. It glowed brighter, hissing as it spit up sparks. A light in the parking lot popped and burned out. Both Ida and Rose had warned me nature might get twitchy during the process—killing someone who was already dead messed with the delicate balance of the universe—so we paid it no mind.

Ida took a step back, clearing the way for Rose, as the second, to take her turn.

"Tonight, I say goodbye to the life I could've had outside of my parents' expectations, now that I know I would've been bold enough to live it." Rose held her combs over the open flame, which reached up to lick her hand. Her skin dripped off her like melting wax and instantly grew back. "I'm letting go to find a new life in death. One of my choosing."

She dropped her combs into the fire. Sparks flew from the cauldron as a bluish smoke billowed into the air. A raven fell from the sky and dropped dead at Rose's feet, followed by six more forming a perfect circle around her. Their glossy wings lit with the reflection of the fire.

She took a step back and gestured for me to finish it.

I held my locket, wrapping the chain around Parker's bracelet until they linked together as one. "Tonight, I say goodbye to my past. The choices I made will no longer define me. I'm letting go so the family I found in death might truly begin to live, and the girl—"

My voice cracked, and I swallowed the hurt that followed my next words. "The girl I love might have the chance I never got to change."

I dropped both my locket and Parker's bracelet into the fire at the same time. It immediately erupted, shooting a wall of flame into the air. I stumbled back, coughing on the black smoke that now poured into the sky. My eyebrows had taken a hit, but they grew back before I could reach my fingers up to feel the singed hair. The cauldron had melted down to a pool of black liquid. It filled the cracks of the concrete like spilled ink.

"Might've overdone it with the thermite," Rose said.

Dark clouds gathered overhead, moving in like floating specters and blocking out half the stars. A roll of thunder rattled the ground beneath our feet, despite the lack of moisture in the air. As quickly as the fire had burned out of our control, it died back down again, and through the murky air, we could see that our heirlooms were gone.

It started slowly at first, like the pages of a flipbook, working backward to the beginning. Things I couldn't recall but my mind had stored, anyway. My mom holding me in the hospital after I'd been born, learning how to use the potty, eating applesauce off the end of a soft spoon. Things that meant nothing to me, so I let them go easily.

The memories moved faster as moments I recalled came into focus. Crying when a mean boy with a Popsicle smile made fun of my mismatched clothes at the park, laughing when I pushed a Slinky off the top of the stairs. My first day of school. The first time a girl told me I couldn't sit next to her at lunch because she said her mom hated my mom. Every memory, good and bad, flipped by for an instant, and then it was gone.

I'd made it to the one where my mom had called in sick to take me to *The Muppet Movie* when I was eight. She'd also gotten me the Kissing Barbie doll as an extra surprise, and it never occurred to me until just now the kind of expectations she placed on me. I never got

Doctor Barbie or Astronaut Barbie. I got the one who could kiss.

In the distance, as though I peered down the end of a long tunnel, I caught a fuzzy glimpse of Rose and Ida. Their expressions twisted with anguish or lit with delight over each new memory that passed in front of them. I turned my concentration back to my own life as it curled into ash and blew away.

I'd now reached the awful middle-school years, when Megan Bear ruled my world. I always thought she'd been destined to be a pageant queen or a weathergirl, not a hard-faced diner waitress who spent too much time in the tanning bed. All of my memories associated with her peeled away like layers of tissue paper, thin and barely visible. The days of relentless teasing. Picking spitballs out of my hair at night. Blowing up an egg in the microwave when my mom told me to make myself a sandwich for dinner, because she was going out with Mr. Bear again.

I had no problem letting those memories go.

The ones with Stacey were harder. The first time she sat at my lunch table. My entire body swelled with gratitude all over again, and a memory from my present layered over the top of it: The one where Stacey took me to where the dollar-theater bench had been abandoned in an open field, and she told me it hadn't been a sacrifice to care about me. The memory from eighth grade dissolved, and with it, the feeling that I owed Stacey something. The one from my present remained, and a fondness for Stacey, free from guilt, took its place.

The last good memory I had of my mom came to the surface. It wasn't an important one. I hadn't even remembered it at all until now. She stood in our kitchen, with the cord from the wall phone wrapped around her waist, and she smiled at me. It wasn't for any reason. She didn't want anything from me. She smiled just because I was there, and she was happy to see me.

A present-day memory layered over the top of it. From the

nursing home. The old and confused version of herself slipped over the vibrant woman she'd been. They tangled together for a moment, then the past memory was gone. Wordlessly, I said goodbye to who she could've been if only she'd tried a little harder and seen her own worth.

When the memories of Elton came, I knew I only had minutes left with my living self. The girl I had been came down to a handful of moments in which I'd been so infatuated with a beautiful boy who promised me eternity, I couldn't see the dark that gathered behind him. The wondrous and heady feeling of first love filled my senses, painting the world in soft colors and cloudlike textures.

And through it all, I could see myself as I was now, standing on the other side of that love. I saw a girl who became a monster but still managed to find her humanity. I saw someone stronger than I'd ever given her credit for. I saw me. As I had been, as I could be, as I truly was.

With that final memory, I let go of the regret I'd been carrying.

And finally learned how to forgive myself.

Chapter Twenty-Six

By the time the fire had settled to shallow embers, I had no memories from my living years. Nothing left to remember the person I'd been before. The emotions lingered, like an afterthought. I could poke at those dark and empty places, and they would poke back, making me hurt in ways I couldn't name. As the minutes passed, even those began to fade. The way a bruise would hurt for a few days after impact, then eventually disappear.

A sense of relief settled over me. The heavy weight that had lived on my chest for my entire existence was no longer there. I could breathe. But at the same time, the little things that had given me joy were gone. I remembered talking about some kind of doughnut-eating contest with Stacey, but I couldn't remember participating, or even what doughnuts tasted like. I knew what cats looked like but couldn't remember ever petting one. I'd gone swimming as a vampire, but knew it felt different when I was a kid. I didn't know how or why, just that it was. I had a large expanse in my mind where things used to be, and without them, there was just nothing.

Stacey approached us. Her scarf had gotten twisted around in the uproar of wind. "That got wild for a minute. Do you remember anything?"

I looked at her and blinked. Pale skin, frizzy black hair, amber protruding eyes. I shuffled through the memories I had left. On the surface, I knew she'd been my best friend, but I had nothing specific to solidify it. As if someone held up an apple for me and told me it was blue. It was a reality I didn't recognize but had to accept. I had the memory of turning her so many years ago, then the last few weeks. That was it.

"I remember my time as a vampire," I said. "I know from a factual standpoint you were my best friend, but I'm sorry, I've got nothing beyond that."

The devastation on Stacey's face had me turning away in shame, like I'd done something wrong. We had no other options, though. I couldn't allow myself to feel guilt for losing something I no longer knew how to miss, but I cared about Stacey. Not, I suspected, on the level I'd cared for her before the fire, but we'd become friendly over these last few weeks.

"It's fine," Stacey said. "I told you I'd remember for you."

"Okay." I probably should've felt gratitude for that, but I didn't care. My life before I'd been turned was gone, and knowledge of those days wouldn't bring them back. Part of me didn't want to hear about the old days. I couldn't miss what I didn't know.

"I remember that I had a sister." Ida touched her temple, like she could still feel the ghost of her memories wiggling around in there. "I remember going to the funeral home, and feeling sad, but I don't remember anything about when she'd been alive."

The hollow way she spoke about Bea made my heart ache. The cadence of her words held none of the feeling, the joy and despair, of having known her sister. Like she'd become a character in a book Ida had read about once but had no significant emotional attachment. She frowned, as if she knew she should've felt something for Bea, but couldn't quite touch on how or why she'd been so undone by her death.

"It's so strange." Rose stared up at the school in wonder. "Logically, I know I went to this school, but I don't have a single memory of walking those halls while alive. I know the names of the people in my photo album, but I couldn't tell you a single thing about them or even recall what they looked like outside pictures."

"Does it make you sad?" I asked. I wanted to understand what Rose and Ida were feeling, so maybe I could begin to understand what I was feeling. "Because it doesn't make me sad, or happy, or anything. It just is."

Ida nodded. "That's how it is for me too. It's an absence of the past."

We let our new sense of reality settle over us, adjusting to the idea of having always been like this as far as our memories were concerned. Eventually, those empty spaces would fill with new memories. The shadowy clouds had cleared, revealing a glorious expanse of stars. Moonlight bathed the parking lot in a peaceful glow.

"It'll take some getting used to." I probed at my mind again, and it was like reaching into a pitch-black room and watching my hand disappear. It made me feel fuzzy and disconnected, so I let it go. The memories were gone. I had no way to recall them.

"You all still want to kill Elton though, right?" Stacey shot a worried glance over her shoulder. "Because now would be a really bad time to change your mind about that."

From this distance we could only make out his outline, standing atop the hill beyond the school grounds with his long coat billowing around him like a windswept hero in a regency romance. My heart gave a little lurch at the sight of him. I couldn't wait to sever this miserable connection, though it didn't hit me quite the same way. My draw to him wasn't nearly as powerful. With all the memories of falling in love with him gone, it eased the tension that squeezed at me every time he was near. The possible silver lining.

On his right, Gwen walked like a willow in the wind. Her delicate frame and stunning face disguised her cruelty well. Frankie lumbered along on Elton's left. Rose and Ida still thought he was our spy and confidant, even if I had my doubts. Though he did make good on his word to bring Elton to the parking lot. Unless . . .

I grabbed Ida's wrist. "What time is it?"

She checked her watch. "Ten-thirty."

"I thought the plan had been for him to come at midnight," I said.

Ida's face twisted into a snarl. "He was going to let Elton ambush us."

"I knew it." I'd been so right not to trust Frankie completely. If we hadn't come here before our intended time, there was no telling what Elton would've been able to do to us while we'd been lost in the past. "We never should've listened to him."

"At least he hadn't been wrong about the moon," Rose said. "It worked. Our memories are gone. It doesn't matter that he sold us out. We did our part, and we can still end this."

She made a good point. Frankie's loyalties were irrelevant. Elton constantly underestimated us, sent out his coven to confuse and distract us, but we'd come out on top in the end. With the heirlooms destroyed, the final stand was upon us.

Elton turned his head to look behind him as he drew nearer. His marble-white face could've been carved by the masters, and he gave me a cocky grin as he approached. I couldn't wait to wipe that expression off his face. There was nothing worse than a boy who held the world in his hands and knew it.

"Ladies. I heard you sent me an invitation to your little party." He looked at the puddle that had once been our cauldron, where our fire burned on, cracking over the ruin of our living memories. "It's such a shame you wasted your time on all this ceremony."

"What are you talking about?" Dread curled in my stomach, like a sleeping snake, ready to wake up and strike at any moment. "We beat you here. The ritual is done."

"He's just trying to buy time," Ida said. "He knows he doesn't have much left."

"We tried to negotiate with you." Rose stepped up beside me. She glared at Elton with seventy years worth of built-up resentment. "This all could've been avoided if you hadn't been so selfish. If only you'd given us the same choices you got to make without consequence."

"Funny how you insist on calling me selfish, when you only have the life you're enjoying now thanks to me." He examined his nails. Ever groomed, presenting as a flawless prince of the dead. "It's no matter. You didn't accomplish your end goal."

Gwen rested her elbow on Elton's shoulder and blew me a kiss, as if to say she'd already gotten a chance to play with Rose and Ida and she wanted a turn with me. Her catlike eyes lit with pleasure when I scratched the side of my cheek with my middle finger. If she wanted to play, I'd be more than happy to play. I couldn't wait to crush her skull to dust.

"You didn't really think we'd trust the word of your coven, did you?" Ida glared at Frankie, who shuffled his feet as he stared at the ground. "We burned the heirlooms already. We can't remember anything from before. You're too late."

"But did you burn them all? That is the question of the hour." Elton gave her a razor-edged smile and the snake in my stomach peeled open an eyelid. "Because I was under the impression that everyone who I turned had to destroy their heirlooms," He moved to the left, while Frankie moved to the right. "Hey, Parker. You can come out now."

Parker stepped out from behind a large tree trunk, and approached us. There was no telling how long they had left her there to wait. Her skin had turned the color of the plaster rotting off the walls of Stacey's old house. Her sun-kissed cheeks were now pale as the moon, making her freckles stand out even more. She had a stillness about her that hadn't been present before. The kind of poise that could only come from eternal death.

She'd become one of us.

I dropped to my knees, my heart pounding in my throat. It beat so hard, it felt as though it were trying to claw its way through my skin. Everything we'd done had been to prevent this. All of it wasted. I'd given away my memories for nothing.

"What did you do to yourself?" I wanted to scream and pound my fists into the pavement until I broke the earth in half, but I couldn't bring my voice above a whisper as I stared at the girl I loved. The one I'd gone to every extreme to protect. I spread my hands on the concrete, begging the earth and sky and anything that would listen to make this go away, to give Parker back the life she was supposed to live. I'd never felt more lost. "How could you?"

Her blank eyes roamed over my face. None of the tenderness we shared in the ruined apartment was present. "You don't know me."

Nothing she said could've cut deeper.

"It's a funny story, really." Elton stood before me, bringing his polished leather shoe down on my splayed fingers. I didn't feel the pain as my bones were crushed into the concrete. I couldn't feel anything at all. "Frankie told you all the ritual had to be done under a full moon, buying me just enough time to convince the lovely Parker here to embrace immortality."

"You bastard," Ida spat at Frankie, and he recoiled from the venom in her voice. "We could've done the ritual the night we broke into the vault? Is that what you're saying?"

"I'm afraid so." Elton turned on his heel and kicked me in the face. My cheekbone cracked, the skin around it swelling for an instant, before it corrected itself and smoothed over, the pain nothing more than the echo of a dull throb. "It's such a shame you put your trust in someone who has been a dear and loyal friend of mine for years."

Rose and Ida crouched beside me and grabbed me under my arms, hauling me to my feet. I hung limp between them. My mind refused to accept what had happened. I couldn't believe after everything we shared, Parker would make this choice.

"Tell me you didn't choose this." I begged, pleading with her to give me an explanation that would make sense. Her expression held no emotion. "Tell me he made you do it."

"Stop talking to me." She turned her gaze from mine.

"I didn't make her do anything." Elton ran a finger along her cheek and tilted her chin. I could've sworn she flinched, just an imperceptible amount. Or maybe that's just what I wanted to see. He pressed a kiss to the side of her mouth and released her. "It took some convincing on my part, no doubt thanks to the poison you've been whispering in her ear these last few weeks, but she eventually came around. She finally understood that an immortal life is better than no life at all. We completed the transformation just this morning."

"Without an heirloom?" I'd burned the bracelet. There wasn't anything else.

"The silver hoops her mother gave her are tucked away." Elton smirked. "You didn't really think I'd bring her heirloom to your bonfire, did you?"

Eyebrows raised, I shot a questioning look at Parker. She turned away from me.

Gwen clasped her hands together, holding them under her chin. I imagined she had the same look on her face the day her maker found her plucking the heads off of barnyard cats. "Tell them the best part. They're going to love it."

"Ah, yes." Elton tapped a finger to his lips, with a tight smile cutting into his cheeks. "Just beyond the field we set up four boxes. They're very nice. Lined with satin."

Frankie took a roll of rope out from behind his back and began to unwind it. Cold fear zipped down my spine and curdled in my stomach. The shadowy clouds passed over the moon, throwing the world into even deeper darkness as Gwen let out a terrifying giggle.

"We spent all day digging the holes," Gwen said. "Frankie has a soft spot for you girls, for whatever reason, and he wasn't too thrilled with this idea. But he eventually came around."

"Sorry, Frankie." Elton tipped his head to him in a short bow.

"If the three of you had left the heirlooms alone, we could've gone our separate ways at the end of this. But you insisted on trying to kill me, so what choice do I have?"

"Can you just spit it out already?" Ida rolled her eyes. "God. Were you always this long-winded when we dated? I should've dumped your sorry ass the moment Amelia turned you."

"Since you have no patience for a good story"—he flashed his fangs—"The boxes are for you, ladies. I'm afraid it's become too much trouble to leave the three of you to wander."

No. Even at his absolute worst, I couldn't imagine Elton to be so cruel.

"The satin is soft," Gwen said. As if that were a consolation and more than she would've done if given a say in it. "At least you'll be comfortable when you go mad."

They intended to bury us alive and starve us out. Except we wouldn't die. We'd just wither to paper husks made of tissue-thin skin and brittle bones. We'd go out of our minds, for all of eternity, buried beneath the earth's surface. Where no one would ever dig.

"You're making a pretty big assumption," Rose said.

"Oh?" Elton plucked a loose thread from his button-down shirt. "Do tell. What assumption is it that you think I'm making?"

Ida tightened her stance beside me, and I spread my feet. It wouldn't end this way. We didn't come this far to back away now. If we had to go down, we'd go down fighting.

"You assume we'll go quietly." Rose launched herself at Elton, claws flying, a tiny tornado of death he never saw coming.

Chapter Twenty-Seven

This was the moment Gwen had been waiting for. She'd set her sights on me the moment they showed up to the parking lot. Ida and Stacey had already launched themselves at Frankie, who moved slowly but had enough muscle behind him to make up for it.

Gwen spun toward me, her feathered hair flying around her face, with one leg kicked outward. A spinning top of horrors. Her pointed grin flashed before me like a stop-motion movie. I couldn't show fear. It would only delight her.

I jumped out of the way, but she pivoted and caught my side with her powerful leg. A splitting pain burned through my side, and a crack split the air as one of my ribs broke in half. With another sweep of her leg, I went sprawling across the concrete. Asphalt seared my face, peeling away my skin like a cheese grater. I lifted my head from the ground. Rocks and dirt plinked against the concrete as my face healed and pushed out the debris.

Gwen stood over me with her foot on my throat, laughing. She had the kind of laugh built for faceless dolls and midnight funhouses. She grabbed my hair and lifted me from the ground. "I've been wanting to spend a little time with you ever since the graveyard. Such a spunky fighter. You and I are going to have so much fun together."

"Define fun." I kicked my useless legs against her shins. She didn't even flinch; she just spun me around and snagged my hair into a tighter rope.

Gwen was too tall and quick, and she dodged my feet with ease. She wrapped her hand around my elbow and pulled until it started to give. Her eyes turned a brilliant shade of emerald green as my bone popped out of my socket. The skin around my shoulder sounded like Velcro as it began to tear. A burning sensation coursed through my body as Gwen finally wrenched my arm clean off. I'd never felt worse pain, including the time Elton ditched me in the Tulsa Quick Stop, but I ground my teeth to dust to keep from crying out. I wouldn't give her the satisfaction of an outward reaction.

"Aren't you going to scream for me?" Gwen pouted, as if my vocal terror was her reward for a mutilation well done. "Maybe I'm going too easy on you?"

My arm had grown back, but it would only be a matter of seconds before she ripped it off again. Panic had me flailing about. My hair twisted and tangled in her fingers. Using my body for momentum, I dropped to my knees and caught her square in the gut with my shoulder. She bent forward, and with the wind knocked out of her, she loosened her grip on my hair. I yanked it free, losing half of it in the process. Sadly, it all grew back right away.

Frankie had Stacey and Ida by the throats, one in each fist. Stacey's eyes bulged more than usual and her tongue had swollen to twice its normal size. He'd pop her head right off as if she were one of Gwen's kittens. I jammed my foot into his kneecap and he crashed to the ground like a towering pile of bricks.

Gwen caught up to us. She reached for me, but Stacey cut her off. The two of them began taking swings at each other, Stacey landing just as many blows as Gwen, with as much force. Gwen's neck snapped, her head tilting limply to the side, and I cheered out loud, forgetting for a moment that we were fighting for our lives. I had no memories of Stacey from high school, but I would've bet everything I owned she hadn't been a brawler. Whatever skills she possessed now, she'd picked up from hunting and living in the streets. An odd sense of pride welled up in me as I watched her take on Gwen with matched skill.

I looked around for Elton and Rose, but they had disappeared. So had Parker. Across the other side of the field, toward the boxes that had been set up for our burial, I could just make out two figures struggling to hold a tiny one between them. My heart shattered. How could I have been so wrong about Parker? Everything that we shared, everything that had felt so fragile and wonderful and real, how could any of that have been one sided?

I got so distracted by my feelings, I didn't hear Frankie approach from behind, and he had all the subtlety of a bear at a campsite. He knocked me off my feet from behind. Both of Ida's legs were missing, and he had one giant foot on her torso, pinning her to the ground. My nails bent backward and snapped off as I dug them into the concrete, scrambling to get away. He hauled me off the ground by my throat.

"Why?" The word came out as a choked gasp, but he must've understood what I was asking. Why had he bothered to help us at the bank at all if he never planned to let us see this through? Why lead us on this wild goose chase when he could've left us to flounder without him? If he hadn't assisted us in getting Rose's heirloom, we never would've gotten this far.

Frankie's muddy eyes held a note of regret, but he shook his head. "I thought if things had worked out with Ida, I could've gone with you . . ." He trailed off, and while he couldn't technically blush, I could've sworn the ghost of a rosy tint touched his cheeks. "But you all made it clear you're a unit, and you weren't willing to make room for me."

"I told you it was never going to happen with us," Ida spat from the ground. One of her legs had already healed, and she scrambled to get out from under his foot.

"It's not just about you." Frankie refused to look down at her, like he couldn't stand the sight of what he'd done to her before she'd fully healed. "You all made me choose, and none of you were very nice to me, so what did you expect?"

"Is that what you wanted?" I clawed at his beefy hand, but no amount of scraping and tearing would get him to release me. "We had to be nice for you to do the right thing?"

"You think you're right. Elton thinks he's right. It's not the right side just because it's your side." He caught one of my flailing legs and pulled it off in one quick motion. That time, I did scream. It echoed back at me, pounding into my ears. Pain like I'd never known stabbed through every nerve. "You should've compromised."

"We tried compromising." I bit down on my tongue as the pain numbed and my leg grew back. "Elton wants to keep making vampires. He wants to overrun whole cities with teenage girls that he's made for his amusement. Because he's a bored little boy with a death fetish. How can you stand there and act like that's at all the same as what we want to do?"

"It's just hard, okay? I've been with him ever since Gwen turned me. I didn't want to be alone." He averted his gaze, knowing full well he'd had a part in Elton leaving me by myself in the not-so-distant past. I took the opportunity to tear his hand off at the wrist and free myself.

The moment I dropped to the ground, I slammed my foot into his ankle. The bone cracked, and he fell over. Good to know his weak spot. Ida rolled out from under him, both of her legs intact, and launched herself at his face. He swung his fists, catching her in the side of the face. Her head whipped to the side, healed, and she kept going. Rage lit her eyes, and she dug her nails into his face and punctured holes in his cheeks.

I spun around, frantically scanning the parking lot for Gwen and Stacey, but they had disappeared. Across the field, a tall, willowy figure carried what looked like a sack of potatoes. One of Stacey's arms grew back, and Gwen ripped it off again.

Parker stood to the side of the parking lot with a horrified expression on her face. Just looking at her made everything inside me hurt worse than having my leg torn from my body. There had to be an explanation for why she'd gone back to Elton. She'd seen through him. That couldn't have been fake, none of it could've been fake. I took a step toward her, not having a clue what I would say, only that I needed to hear why she'd done this. I would've accepted any explanation. If she wanted to lie to me, I would've accepted that too.

"Going somewhere?" Elton blocked my path. A cruel grin twisted his handsome features until I barely recognized the boy I used to love. "Did you like my little surprise?"

"You know I didn't." We began circling each other. "How did you convince her?"

"The same way I convinced all of you." He was so arrogant. So in love with himself that he truly believed he had Parker's heart just by floating a few compliments her way. And maybe that was how he'd gotten the rest of us, but Parker didn't buy his bullshit. She was supposed to end up better than us all. "You almost convinced her not to go through with it though, so maybe I should be giving you kudos. Close, but not quite close enough."

"It's not necessary." I swung for him, and he dodged. "This isn't fully over, you know. We can burn Parker's heirloom next and still finish you."

"Good luck finding it once I tire of her." He wore a bored expression. As if he'd been toying with me, but now had worthier things to do.

An anger like I'd never known rolled through my veins. Whatever lingering draw I had to him while I still had my memories was gone. I no longer saw the ethereal beauty who had captured my heart at sixteen. Eyes that had once been soft had turned hard. The crooked smile that used to humor me now insulted. He took the love I felt for him and distorted it in his obsession to control.

I swung for him and missed. "I don't know what you did to convince Parker to turn, but she deserves so much more than you."

"Like who? You?" His eyes lit with malice, and something much darker that turned my stomach. "Holly. Sweetheart. Are you in love with my girlfriend?" He let out a laugh at whatever I hadn't been able to hide in my expression. "You are! How sad. Are you hoping she'll call out your name while I fuck her?"

I was on him in a flash. He didn't have time to block me as I raked my nails across his face. I wanted to rip out his eyes and chew on them. I wanted the symphony of his screams while I tore into his flesh. The blood dripped down in a steady stream from his open wounds, leaving droplets on the dark concrete.

But his skin wasn't knitting together.

He held his face as the gashes continued to bleed. "What did you do to me?"

My eyes widened. He wasn't healing. I spun around to where Parker still stood at the edge of the parking lot, staring intently at Elton as if she were waiting for something.

The bracelet.

She'd made her bracelet into an heirloom on her own.

And gave it to me to burn.

My mind reeled as I put all the pieces together. She must've planned everything. She'd wanted me to turn her, and that night she came to see me, she asked me again. I should've known. She gave up way too easily. I didn't even question it. I should've questioned it. I should've been able to save her from what she'd become. Now, not only was she stuck in this form forever, but she didn't have a single memory beyond today. Her gaze met mine across the parking lot. No recognition. No love. Nothing.

"What the fuck is happening?" Elton clutched his bleeding cheek.

I punched a hole through his chest and pulled out his still-beating heart. It pulsed in my hand, cold and black as his soul. "Correct me if I'm wrong, but I'm pretty sure you're dying."

I threw his heart into the fire. Though it had burned down to mere embers, new flames rose up. They licked the edges of his heart before embracing it completely. Elton let out a scream that split the earth. I'd never heard a sweeter sound in my life. He dropped to his knees, clutching his chest as old blood flowed through his fingers like mud, as if it had congealed in his veins.

"What's the problem, sweetheart?" I toed his spine with the tip of my shoe. "You've managed to go the last hundred years without a heart. This shouldn't be anything new."

He reached a hand out, his fingers stretching toward the fire as his heart burned to ash before his eyes. He let out a low moan and slumped to the side. Still alive, but barely. I felt like I should've had more profound words for him in this moment, but when I reached into my mind, all I felt were those empty spaces.

Parker watched Elton bleed out with a blank sense of morbid fascination. She caught me staring and gave me a tentative smile. I held my breath. Did she . . . ?

I took a careful step forward. "Do you remember me?"

"I . . ." She rubbed her temples, as if trying to shake out the memories. The ones we'd burned away. "I remember nothing before today."

"Parker," Elton choked out. Blood dribbled from the corner of his mouth now, in a slow crawl, as if it began to dry the moment it exited his body. "I thought you loved me. You told me you loved me." I wanted to wipe away the guilt clouding her expression. It was just like him to use his last breaths to manipulate. "How could you do this? What about our plans?"

"Don't listen to him," I said. His heart crackled behind me, beyond repair. It would only be a matter of minutes now. "This is what he does.

He lives to make you feel bad about yourself, so he can swoop in as the savior and make himself the center of your world."

"Fuck you." He spat a mouthful of blood at my feet.

I crouched down and took a fistful of hair as I grabbed the back of his head. "No, I'm afraid you're the one who's fucked."

Fear filled his expression as death crept around the corner of his dwindling existence. The light in his eyes began to dim. "I hope this moment haunts you."

"Ending you has put my life back in my hands. I regret nothing."

Night fell darker as even the stars looked away. Elton had no one to stand by him while he died, and I couldn't bring myself to feel bad about that. It was a choice he made the moment he took the mortality of four girls to feed his ego. He underestimated us at every turn, treated us as if we were disposable and replaceable, and never once considered us worthy of care. He never would've stopped.

While I'd probably always consider his end bittersweet—I *had* loved him once—I could only feel a sense of peace as he took his last breath, still staring at me like he couldn't believe we'd gotten the best of him.

Chapter Twenty-Eight

Standing over Elton's dead body turned out to be pretty anticlimactic. Not that I had expected balloons and confetti to drop like I was the millionth shopper at the Piggly Wiggly, but I thought I'd feel . . . something. Anything. A fleeting bit of emotion for the boy who had taught me how to dream in centuries. But I had nothing left for the corpse at my feet.

"Did I really kill him?" Parker stood beside me, her voice barely above a whisper.

"No." Not in a direct way. I tried not to take it personally that she sounded so horrified by the prospect. She didn't remember me. "Did you miss the part where I pulled out his heart?"

She shook her head, and an uncomfortable silence settled between us.

I had so many questions about her heirloom. When had she planned everything? Did she always intend to let Elton turn her? Did she ever leave town at all, or did she go straight to Elton? She played a dangerous game, assuming I'd burn it. If I'd left it behind at Stacey's house, or hurled it into the woods, tonight would've gone a lot different. I wanted to know every detail, but I'd never get them. Her memories were gone. Which included all the feelings she had for me.

Parker pulled a piece of paper out of her back pocket. "You're Holly, aren't you?"

"I am." Hearing her say my name squeezed the air from my lungs.

"I wrote myself this letter. I think maybe you should read it."

I took the paper from her and scanned over the words in her handwriting, written before she'd been turned. She told herself not to trust Elton. That if she was reading that letter, then her memories were gone. She explained what it meant to be a vampire and warned herself that she'd probably believe Elton at first. She broke down all of his history. What he'd done to Ida and Rose and me. My throat tightened when I got to the part where she talked about us, the time we spent together. Her last words to herself: *Trust Holly. You're doing this all for her.*

"You did this for me?" My voice cracked as I handed her back the letter. "Seems like you lied to yourself, then, because I tried very hard to keep you alive."

"I know." She folded the paper back up and tucked it into her pocket. "I must've loved you very much if I was willing to give up my entire life of memories for you."

"I think you did." I pulled on the neck of my sweater, finding the air to be a little too tight. "But you probably don't now."

She stared at her knotted finger. "I don't. I'm sorry."

I'd been prepared for the words. Without her memories, she had no feelings attached to me, but it hurt nonetheless. I should've been happy I had this final moment to say goodbye to her. I couldn't find the silver lining, though. Everything had gone wrong. We killed Elton, but we failed to save the girl. As far as I was concerned, we didn't end with a win today.

I had started to turn away when she caught my hand. Just like she did that day at her apartment. Like she couldn't let me go. "Are you leaving?"

"I have to dig up my friends." A sentence I never thought I'd say out loud. "I promised Stacey we would leave town as soon as it was over."

"Oh." She shuffled her feet. "It's just . . ."

She stopped talking as Frankie and Gwen drew nearer. Her gaze passed over Gwen and her shoulders hunched, as if she wanted to disappear. Gwen had that effect on people. Frankie increased his stride across the field, his footsteps gaining speed. He must've seen Elton lying on the concrete. That was going to be a fun surprise.

Gwen let out a terrifying scream as she fell over Elton's body. "What did you do to him?"

"What does it look like I did to him?" I had no love lost for either of them.

"How?" Frankie scratched his head. "You don't have Parker's heirloom."

If they believed Parker's heirloom to be hidden, who was I to correct them? "I found a way to kill vampires without destroying the heirloom."

"No, you didn't." Gwen leaped to her feet. "It's impossible."

She was on me in a flash, wrapping her hand around my throat and dangling me off the ground. I didn't feel pain though. Not this time. The adrenaline of having the upper hand ran through my veins. I glanced at Frankie. A worry line creased his brow as he looked between Gwen and me. He knew more about heirlooms than Rose and Ida. He must've known I was bluffing. Maybe he thought he owed us, or maybe he couldn't stomach what he'd just done to Ida, but he gave me a slight nod. A sign he was willing to play along.

"Put her down," he said to Gwen.

"But she's lying." Gwen shook me like a rag doll. "I know she's lying."

I bared my fangs. "I'd be happy to give you a demonstration."

"I don't think she's lying." Frankie grabbed Gwen by the arm, forcing her to drop me. He backed them both away. "I watched Elton bury Parker's heirloom. We should go."

I held my breath as I waited for Gwen to decide if I had some kind of powers she never knew about. Other than being magnificent at bullshit, I didn't have any special skills. Something she'd realize if it dawned on her to ask Parker what she had for breakfast yesterday.

Frankie laid a hand on her shoulder, and a meaningful look passed between them. The kind of look I often saw pass between Rose and Ida in their silent communication. She took a step back.

"Fine. Let's go." With a last lingering look at me, as if she could sniff out the truth beneath my lies, Gwen spun around. "I'm over this town, anyway."

I blew out a breath as they walked away. They had no more ties to Elton, and neither did we. If we were lucky, we'd never cross paths with them again. Though I did hope Frankie would get good and fed up one day and end Gwen. She was too dangerous to keep alive.

I turned to Parker, still careful in my interactions with her. She had lost so much more than any of us today. All she had were the clothes on her back and a single day of memories. Could that feeling we had in the apartment even be recaptured? All the circumstances that had drawn us to each other were gone. It had been such a small, fleeting moment in my existence, but one that had been everything.

I lifted a hand, as if to touch her, and dropped it again. I clenched my fingers against my palm. "I'm sorry, what were you saying before those two showed up?"

"I was saying . . ." She twisted her fingers together. "If it's okay with you all, can I go with you? I don't have anywhere else to go."

"That all depends." I gave her a playful smile as relief rushed through me. I couldn't make her come with us if that wasn't what she wanted, but I didn't know how I would've been able to leave this place without her. "Can you help me dig up a few boxes?"

"About that . . ." Parker gave a nervous glance across the field. "I might've helped Elton put one of your friends in a box. The small one. I thought it would be a good idea to play along until I could figure out what was going on."

I had a feeling Rose would find a way to forgive her.

Stacey pulled up in front of the school with a van. It was a dull blue and smelled like paint and gym socks, but beggars couldn't be choosers. None of us asked how she'd gotten it. The blood on the driver's side door didn't leave us with many questions. She didn't want to hang around this town any longer than necessary, and with nothing left to tie us to this place, we threw all of our stuff in the back and piled in though the side door. There were two seats in the back that could seat three each. Plenty of room to spread out.

Parker ended up bringing a small backpack with a few possessions that didn't have meaning to her anymore. She rifled through the backpack with a blank expression on her face, growing increasingly frustrated when she couldn't make sense of the objects that had once mattered enough to carry into death.

"You can leave that here." I gestured to the parking lot. "If it bothers you to have attachments to the things you can't remember, you can dump it and make a fresh start elsewhere."

"I can't." She closed the backpack and held it to her chest. "It's all I have left."

In a way, I understood what she meant. For years, I carried around a ratty old sweater with more holes than Swiss cheese because it was all I had left from my time before. When you had nothing, even the most worthless things felt like an anchor.

My heart sped up when she took the seat beside me, but I really tried not to read too much into it. She didn't remember me. Those feelings she had might never come back. I had to settle into accepting that.

Ida brushed dirt off her arm as she climbed into the front seat next to Stacey. "You could've at least let us take a shower."

"You can shower in Indiana." Stacey slammed her foot on the gas, leaving rubber tracks in the asphalt as she peeled out of the parking lot.

Unburying them had taken all my remaining strength, and I'd collapsed in the first seat I'd crawled into. I rested my head against the window. The city where I'd been born, lived, fell in love, and ultimately died held nothing for me anymore. No memories, no obligations.

It could've been worse. At least I had thirty-plus years of memories to fill my mind and smooth over the empty void. Parker had today. That was all. As we left behind the places that should've been familiar, she stared out the window with a sense of wonder.

Rose leaned forward and squeezed my shoulder from behind. "You doing okay?"

"I'll be fine." I patted her hand. "We're all going to be just fine."

It scared me how close I'd come to losing them. I thought of them like family now, and I couldn't imagine eternity without them. For three girls who had fallen so hard for the same guy, we didn't have a whole lot in common. Necessity brought us together, but the bond we had formed would keep us with one another. I didn't have to be alone anymore.

They gave me a recap of everything I'd missed while I'd been occupied killing Elton. Rose had gone into the box first, assisted by Parker, which caught her off guard. Parker apologized profusely, but Rose was too much of a softie to make it an issue. Frankie and Gwen had overpowered Stacey and Ida, dragging their remaining pieces across the field and ripping away whatever grew back before they could gain any kind of upper ground. The three boxes had been tied shut and buried under three feet of dirt. Just deep enough to muffle their screams.

I had unburied Ida first, and she clawed at me, her eyes frantic as I lifted the lid. She didn't speak for a solid hour while I dug into the earth to pull out Stacey, then Rose. None of them wanted to talk about the limited time they had spent below ground, and I had no idea the thoughts that had crossed their minds when that first shovel of dirt covered their boxes.

Some things were better left unsaid.

As soon as Stacey drove past the NOW LEAVING GLEN RIVER sign, I tapped Parker on the shoulder. "How are you feeling about leaving here? You didn't live here very long, but I think you started to view this place as home."

"I don't feel any kind of way about it." She bit her lip. "It's a little disorienting."

"I can imagine." I wanted to run my finger over her bottom lip and wipe the worry from her eyes, but what she needed most was space and time to process. "Regrets?"

"None." She gave me one of her brilliant, brighter-than-the-sun smiles. "I guess that's the one good thing about giving up my memories. I have nothing left to regret."

That was how I chose to view it. Thirty-four years was long enough to pay for whatever mistakes I'd made. Without memories, without Elton, we all were blank slates. We could finally write our own stories and test who we'd be without him.

I looked forward to seeing what we discovered.

At a rest stop on the Michigan-Indiana line, Ida took over driving from Stacey. Rose moved up to the front seat, and we put in a DVD of *30 Days of Night* on the portable player in the back. Stacey had found it tucked in the center console, and we couldn't resist.

As soon as the movie started, Stacey put her feet up on the seat behind me. In the dark, Parker placed her hand on the seat between us. Halfway through the movie, her pinky overlapped mine. We stayed like that for an hour, until I worked up the nerve to turn my hand over. Our palms connected, and her pulse beat against mine.

In that moment, I knew we'd figure it out.

It wouldn't be exactly the same as it had been before, but maybe that was okay. Without the intensity of trying to keep her alive, we could take some time to learn each other again. As we were now.

Lucky for us, we had all the time in the world.

We made our way toward a little-used highway headed south, and Rose turned to face us, sitting on her knees on the passenger seat. "Where are we going?"

I looked out the window to the open stretch of road before us. "Anywhere we want."

Acknowledgments

First, I'd like to give a huge thank-you to my readers. I hope you enjoyed going on a little revenge adventure with Holly.

To my agent, Rebecca Podos, thank you for reminding me that I am, in fact, a writer when I first posted this idea on Twitter as a book I'd like to read. You remain my greatest advocate and I couldn't imagine a better partner in this wild business.

To my editor, Tamara Grasty, it has been an absolute pleasure working with you. You have incredible insight and were so helpful during the editing process. Thank you for all your wonderful suggestions that allowed me to smooth all the rough edges of this story.

To my copy editor, Rebecca Behrens, thank you so much for catching all my repeats and off-key wordings, and a huge thank-you to Lauren Knowles and Laura Benton, my designer Kylie Alexander for another amazing cover, publisher Will Kiester, and the wonderful sales team at Macmillan.

Jen Hawkins, my literary soulmate, when I come to Texas again, we're absolutely going to have a water . . . or four.

Kellye Garrett and Roselle Lim, we're still dancing.

To my coven: Kelsey Rodkey, Annette Christie, Andrea Contos, Auriane Desombre, Rachel Lynn Solomon, and Susan Lee, I love you all forever. Thank you for everything.

To my husband and my girls, your endless support means the world to me.

About the Author

Sonia Hartl is the author of *Not Your #Lovestory* and *Have a Little Faith in Me*, which received a starred review in *BookPage* and earned nominations for the Georgia Peach Book Award, YALSA's Quick Picks for Reluctant Readers, Bank Street College of Education's Best Children's Books of the Year, and ALA's Rise: A Feminist Book Project List. She is also the author of an adult rom-com, *Heartbreak for Hire*. When she's not writing or reading, she enjoys playing board games with her family, attempting to keep her garden alive, or looking up craft projects on Pinterest she'll never get around to completing. She's a member of SCBWI and was the Managing Director for Pitch Wars 2020. She lives in Grand Rapids with her husband and two daughters. Follow her on Twitter @SoniaHartl1.